THE
SUPREME
LIE

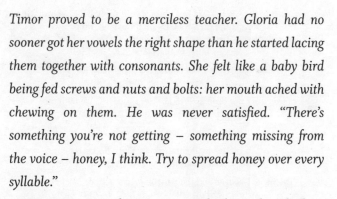

Timor proved to be a merciless teacher. Gloria had no sooner got her vowels the right shape than he started lacing them together with consonants. She felt like a baby bird being fed screws and nuts and bolts: her mouth ached with chewing on them. He was never satisfied. "There's something you're not getting – something missing from the voice – honey, I think. Try to spread honey over every syllable."

It was a sweet thing to say, and Gloria thought how terrible it must be for him to be sitting here with his maid rather than his honey-tongued wife – missing her, wishing he, too, had caught that train…

"Now add the armour-plating," said Timor. "Studded with rivets. Think barbed wire in a party dress."

For my marvellous brother NEIL, who started me writing.
(And IWONA, of course, who entered the family
like a beam of sunshine.)

First published in the UK in 2021 by Usborne Publishing Ltd., Usborne House,
83-85 Saffron Hill, London EC1N 8RT, England, usborne.com
Usborne Verlag, Usborne Publishing Ltd., Prüfeninger Str. 20,
93049 Regensburg, Deutschland, VK Nr. 17560

Text copyright © Geraldine McCaughrean, 2021

The right of Geraldine McCaughrean to be identified as the author
of this work has been asserted by her in accordance with the
Copyright, Designs and Patents Act, 1988.

Cover illustration by Leo Nickolls

Map and inside illustrations by Keith Robinson
Illustrations © Usborne Publishing Ltd, 2021

The name Usborne and the Balloon logo are Trade Marks of
Usborne Publishing Ltd.

All rights reserved. No part of this publication may be reproduced, stored in
a retrieval system or transmitted in any form or by any means, electronic,
mechanical, photocopying, recording or otherwise without the prior permission
of the publisher.

This is a work of fiction. The characters, incidents, and dialogues are products
of the author's imagination and are not to be construed as real. Any resemblance to
actual events or persons, living or dead, is entirely coincidental.

A CIP catalogue record for this book is available from the British Library.

ISBN 9781474970686 05604/1 J MAMJJASOND/21

MIX
Paper from
responsible sources
FSC® C020471

GERALDINE McCAUGHREAN

THE
SUPREME
LIE

ILLUSTRATIONS BY
KEITH ROBINSON

USBORNE

LACHA MOUNTAINS

THE ROSE PLAIN

Big Rock Dam

ROSE CITY

Old Course of the Rose River

Ossian Hills

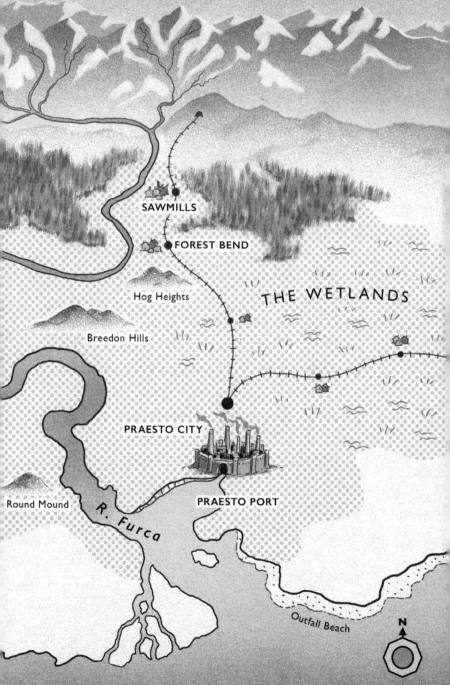

Map showing the extent of flooding
in the 'GREAT FLOOD OF AFALIA' 1928

SAWMILLS

FOREST BEND

Hog Heights

THE WETLANDS

Breedon Hills

PRAESTO CITY

Round Mound

R. Furca

PRAESTO PORT

Outfall Beach

N

The Voice

IN ATRAMENTO EST VERITAS

SENATE IN CRISIS FLOOD TALKS
WILL THE GATES BE SHUT?

As readers are all too aware, two months of rain have swollen the Furca River into a raging torrent. Its waters will soon reach our city's walls and could even flood in through the four Great Gates.

Already, the low-lying centre of the city is sodden with groundwater and rainfall. It is rumoured that the basements there are flooding.

The Senate will meet today with Madame Suprema to discuss what can be done. Many are hoping she will command the gates be closed – something that has not happened within living memory.

The Department of Public Safety has warned against panic. "Ultimately, Praesto's walls and the Great Gates will protect us all from harm," said a spokesperson yesterday.

Worries grow for those outside the walls

Of greater concern, however, to readers of *The Voice*, is the welfare of people living outside the safety of Praesto City, in the farms, riverside settlements and timberlands. Could Rose City, being further north, let us know what they are seeing? Have they been contacted?

TODAY'S ANAGRAM:
BELL NOW TOOTING

Afalia RAILWAYS

IMPORTANT NOTICE
Afalia Railways regret that, in the event of more rain, no trains will run from North Gate Terminus after Monday noon. Easterly services, suspended last week, will not restart. Passengers' safety must come first.

CHAPTER ONE

Whether the Weather
Will or Won't

PRAESTO CITY

In a mansion at the top of Praesto's highest hill, the maid Gloria sat on the stairs, reading the newspaper while she waited for the visitors to arrive. She was nervous about serving teas and coffees to so many people, and not spilling anything on anyone important. And the newspaper worried her with its talk of flooding up north. She tried to picture her home in Sawmills, water lapping at the door and the chickens all sitting on their coops to keep from drowning; the shirts on the wash-line dipping their cuffs in the muddy flood. She dared not even picture water *inside* the shack: Ma was so house-proud, so particular about keeping the rag-rugs clean...

When Gloria looked at her hands, she realized she had gripped the newspaper so tightly that her fingers were black with newsprint. She ought to wash. There was a white dog, asleep on the crimson hall carpet, too, who really shouldn't be there, what with the Senators coming. Gloria would have to sweep up the white hairs before they arrived.

But Daisy was such a soothing sight, breathing out sighs of contentment, dreaming with her paws. All over the city, dogs had been howling and carrying on, sensing something was wrong with the weather, trying to warn their people… Gloria had heard them. Not Daisy. If there really were bad things coming, no scent of it had reached her leathery nose or made her hackles rise. Gloria went and sat beside her, so that the two of them could feel safe and carefree together. The dog rolled onto her back without waking, and stretched out luxuriously. "*Wish you were mine,*" Gloria whispered, and the dog's tail thump-thumped on the carpet.

The doorbell startled them both. Gloria leaped up in panic. Daisy merely lifted her head to see if food had come to call.

It was only Madame's husband, his hat-brim full of rain and his trouser cuffs sodden.

"Have they arrived?" he asked.

"No, sir. Not yet."

While he was still trying to close his umbrella, the dog seized her chance to escape into the garden and stand in the rain. She squeezed between his long legs, leaving white hairs in the arch of his trousers.

A voice called from the Grand Salon: "Is that you, Timmy?"

Gloria peeled him out of his wet coat, opened the double

doors to the Salon, and announced him, as if he were a visitor. "Mr Timor is home, Madame."

Madame, a doll-sized woman of regal majesty, with tiny feet, sharp fingers and an even sharper voice, lay along her sofa, cradling a second, smaller dog in her shawl. She wore net gloves and, when she was expecting visitors (as she was now), a wide-brimmed hat with a veil. Her face had not been seen by the world-at-large for several years, though her bright red lipstick glowed through the veil. The pug was new to the household. With his flat, snuffling face and bulging eyes, he had quite stolen Madame's heart away from Daisy.

"Did you go to the railway station as I told you?" she asked, recoiling from her husband's cold, rain-wet hands.

"They're planning to run a train at two o'clock," he said, "and then no more until the rain lets up. They're worried about the track flooding or embankments collapsing. But the rails are still above water as far as anyone can tell. The train's there already and a lot of people are aboard it. Apparently, this morning's paper said folk up north are getting flooded out of their houses. I suppose the crowds at the station have got relations up there and want to help out. If this weather forecast of yours turns out to be bad, they'll be going nowhere. Has it arrived yet?"

"The weather people are due at ten, along with half the Senate. And look at your trousers, Timmy. Do something about them."

11

On his way to change, Mr Timor passed the hall cupboard where the maid was rummaging about for umbrellas.

As soon as Gloria heard the cars arriving, she knew to carry umbrellas out to the Senators to shelter them on their walk up the drive. The umbrellas had seen a lot of outings over the last few weeks. For Gloria, it was a chance to see powerful people up close and hear what kind of things they talked about. Disappointingly, they were only complaining about the rain, which the wind was blowing in all directions at once.

The Senators cast glum looks at the sodden dog in the garden. Then they put on hopeful smiles and entered into the presence of Madame Suprema, ruling head of Afalia.

Madame held sway over the great walled city of Praesto, with its forest of factory chimneys and its swarming, soot-stained streets. But her realm was far larger than that. Beyond the city's ancient, encircling walls lay the whole of the Furca river basin, the cliffs and forests and wetlands and farms of all Afalia. These, too, were the Suprema's domain.

The visiting Senators did not bow, but their shoulders stooped in deference to the tiny lady on the vast sofa. Despite her size, the Suprema commanded a respect bordering on fear. But they, too, were eager to know if the weather people had arrived yet. One dared to voice his anxiety.

"Is it time to declare a State of Emergency, Madame?"

"And just what would that achieve, Mr Kovet, beyond panic in the streets?" said Madame scornfully. "There is really nothing to worry about. I'm sure the meteorologists will put our minds at rest. This filthy rain will stop and the sun will shine."

"But, Madame! Have you not seen today's newspaper? About the telegrams from the north? The river near to bursting? Houses flooded? It's raining like this the whole length of the river! And now it's in the newspaper, everyone is getting anxious. We could at least close the city gates. Have *you* heard anything about the towns in the north, Madame?"

"Not a word," said Madame Suprema. "And who believes every rumour they read in the newspaper?"

"Quite a number of people, I'm afraid, ma'am," said the Senator for Home Affairs. "It has, after all, been raining for *two months!*"

"And? Do they suppose Praesto City – bound round by high walls that have defended it from wind, war and water for centuries – will suddenly be swept away by a spell of rain?" Madame gave a bell-like laugh, which was a cue for everyone else to smile and shake their heads.

"No, but *outside* the walls..." began the Senator for Agriculture. "The farmers and foresters and smallholders and—"

"That is precisely why I have asked the best meteorologists

in the country to give us the true facts – here – today. One cannot base policy on half a dozen telegrams from a few backwoodsmen."

"But since yesterday the telegrams have stopped coming…"

"Well, there you are then," purred the Suprema.

"I mean, the telegraph poles must be down – washed away – struck by lightning – who knows? You've only got to look over the walls, ma'am, to see how the river levels are rising! These people wanting to travel north – should we let them go? I mean, is it safe for them to go?"

The Suprema made a noise, something between a sneeze and a snort. "It's their money to waste, but if they have any wits, they'll stay here where they're safe."

"We should stop them going anyway," growled the Senator for Labour. "Can't have the workforce gallivanting off to visit family."

"Perfectly right," said Madame Suprema. "I'm glad *someone* is keeping a sense of proportion."

Out of sight, Gloria had lingered to listen by the parlour door, her arms full of wet umbrellas that were dripping onto her shoes. "Why don't they just send up a plane to take a look?" she murmured under her breath.

"Quite," said a voice, and she was dismayed to find the Suprema's husband standing right behind her. He, too, had been listening. He stepped round her now and into the room.

"Why not send up a plane to take a look?" he asked. "We do have an Air Force."

The Senators turned towards him as one.

"Leave us, Timmy," said his wife sharply. "You should not be here. You know you are not entitled to attend Senate meetings."

"Even so…"

"The weather has hardly been suitable for flying, Timmy. Now go."

Everyone in the room waited in embarrassed silence until Timor shrugged and left again, blushing a little.

The meteorologists – a man and a woman – arrived, having travelled to Foremost Mansion by bus. Their long grey raincoats dripped on the hall carpet. Their faces were as grey as their coats. Bowing awkwardly to Madame Suprema, they brought out a damp envelope and, unsure which of them should hand it over, presented it jointly into her net-gloved hands.

"I'm sorry…" murmured the woman.

Madame Suprema cut her off with, "Don't apologize. You are not *very* late. But we are eager to read your findings." Then the veiled face tilted quizzically, as if surprised they were still there. "I have instructed my chauffeur to drive you home in the limousine. Wait for him by the gate. We mustn't keep you from your work."

Not until they had gone did Madame Suprema open the

envelope and read the paragraphs typed below the crest of the Society of Meteorology. There was a long and agonizing silence; perhaps the veil made reading difficult. Then the red lips parted in a broad smile.

"Good news, gentlemen, ladies! The weather forecast is for the rain to die out very soon and be replaced by hot, dry weather. It is already sunnier upriver. We have the full assurance of the Meteorological Society. Close the city gates? Ha! Close the railway station? Storm in a teacup."

The room breathed out a single sigh. The Senators congratulated each other and heaped admiration on Madame Suprema, as if she personally had arranged a change in the weather. Then they left, telling each other that they had known all along there was no danger.

Their leaving allowed the dog Daisy to dash back through the open front door and into the parlour, where she shook herself dry. Astoundingly, the Suprema did not curse her or banish the dog to the scullery. She simply screwed up the letter and batted it playfully at Daisy, who caught it in her mouth.

"You there! Girl!" called the Suprema. "Pack for me, will you? I have laid the things that I wish to take out on my bed. And be quick. I am leaving on the afternoon train. You may come with me – the dogs will need someone to mind them."

Gloria gasped. "Oh! Thank you, Madame!"

Timor walked in on the remark. "*Leaving?* Why? Where?"

His wife patted his sleeve playfully. "I think we should see for ourselves if there's any truth in the newspaper's gloomy rumours. If a few poor souls *have* been flooded out, I can spread comfort and joy. Anything less might lose me popularity with the public, don't you think?" And she slid Boz off her lap in a thudding heap and went to speak to the cook.

Daisy appealed to Gloria for help. The ball of paper had wedged behind her top teeth and she could neither spit it out nor chew it. Gloria tugged the paper free, then hugged Daisy fiercely (despite her being wet as a sponge).

"Herself's going north, and she says we can go too!" Gloria told her. "We're going north, Daze! On the train! I haven't been on a train since I come down here from home. It'll maybe stop at Sawmills and you could meet my folks! D'you think she'd let us? While she's busy being kind to people? And think! The sun'll be shining, and nobody will be drowning, 'cos the weather's going to get fine again! So Grandpa *won't* have to climb on the roof with his bad leg, and the chickens *won't* drown – 'cos you know how close-to-the-ground chickens are and they might've drowned, mightn't they? I want you to meet *everybody*…"

And then Gloria was gone, upstairs, to bang suitcases about with a noise like the thunder banging outside. Daisy looked around for the screw of paper, in case it was worth another chew. But that was gone too. Boz had probably eaten it. So, she lay on her side and thought about her hackles and why exactly they were bristling. Boz the pug couldn't be the reason. Somehow Daisy was not heartbroken to lose the love of the woman with sharp fingers. For a long time now, Daisy's heart had been given wholly to Gloria, with a bit held back for The Husband. And the cook, of course.

The good news would not reach the people in the streets until tomorrow. Tomorrow they would be laughing again, fearless of the puddles and overflowing gutters, knowing sunshine was on its way! Tomorrow Gloria would be happy, too. Right now, she was struggling to push a wheelbarrow with three suitcases in it...as well as a parcel of unspoken questions. Why had they not waited for Appis the chauffeur to come back from taking the weather people home? She had never known Madame go *anywhere* on foot and in the rain.

And why the big opera cloak with the deep hood? Madame generally enjoyed jolting gasps from people who caught a glimpse of her as she passed by.

And why on earth had Madame sacked Cook? Cook made the best cheese soufflé in all of anywhere! What would happen the next time a foreign bigwig visited and there was no Cook to make a soufflé?

Where were the Civil Guards to clear a path for her along the crowded platform? Why was Madame having to share an umbrella with her husband, when she generally had some security guard holding it over her at arm's length?

The crowds at the station had *clearly* not heard the good news about the weather. The train building up steam in Praesto Station North was full to bursting with passengers, and the platform was swarming with people still trying to board it. Guards, porters, footplate-men and hired-muscle had formed a cordon to stop them, but men and women were crawling under the carriages to try and force the windows open on the far side. There was no disguising their desperation to go north. Gloria instantly pictured her family wading waist-deep through water, penniless, homeless, nibbled by water rats – or worse! – and resolved to ask Madame's permission to visit home.

As soon as the Suprema was in the shelter of the station, Timor closed the umbrella and took over pushing the wheelbarrow, carving a path through the crowds. A porter with a rounders bat blocked their path to the first-class coaches at the front. He jerked his head to indicate the tightly-packed carriages.

Gloria fully expected Madame to snap her fingers and commandeer the whole train for her own use. But no!

"Timmy, pay the man," she hissed, and Timor dutifully took out his wallet. Ten, forty, sixty afal changed hands, and the boy with the bat set about emptying one carriage of passengers.

"No luggage," said the porter, pushing the wheelbarrow away with one foot.

Astonishingly, Madame did not throw back her hood and render the man speechless with awe at finding himself in the presence of the Suprema herself. She simply snapped her fingers in her husband's direction.

Timor pulled out his wallet again, but the porter held his ground. "We'll store it for you."

The luggage was not the only casualty.

"No dogs," said a guard, pointing his rolled-up green flag at Daisy.

"My good man," snapped Madame, "her grandmother was the very first golden retriever to set foot on Afalian soil!"

"No dogs, no luggage," said the guard.

Gloria feared for the man's job. Surely at any moment Madame would say, *Out of my way, you fool! Am I not Madame Suprema, ruler of all Afalia?* But no. She simply pulled her hood further forward and said, "In that case, Gloria, I'm afraid you must stay behind and Daisy can sit in your seat."

"No dogs, no luggage, no maids," said the guard, relishing his power.

"For the love of… Just get in," said Timor with uncharacteristic heat, and bundled his wife aboard. He thrust a key into Gloria's hand and told her, "Mind the house till we get back." His eyes did not once meet hers as he added, "Back soon, I'm sure. Put Daisy in the luggage van, there's a good girl." He put the leash into her other hand, then stepped aboard and slammed the carriage door.

Bewildered, Gloria continued to stare into the compartment with its fancy drapes, plush seats and chance of seeing home, until Madame scowled at her and waved her away.

People were climbing onto the train roof now. The driver loosed off an ear-splitting jet of steam.

The luggage van in the middle of the train was (of course) already full of people, and the door had been locked to keep out more. Gloria tried to tell them that the rain would stop soon, but they would not open up. Gloria tried to lift Daisy onto the train roof, but no one up-top was ready to lend a hand, and it was beyond her strength to raise a full-grown retriever high over her head. Daisy subsided on top of her, and they both sank to the ground.

Back in the first-class carriage, Boz wriggled out from under Madame Suprema's cloak and she sat him on her lap, laughing softly at the victory she had won over the officious guard. Her husband did not sit down, but stood with his forehead against the window, his breath fogging the glass.

"So. We are going upcountry to spread comfort and joy, are we?" he said. "To see how we can help the folk who've been flooded out. Then we'll be back. Right?"

Madame crooned softly to the pug.

"*Right*, Suprema?"

His wife did not look at him. She was holding up Boz in two hands and staring him full in his round, flat face. Her reflection was bent out of shape by his bulging eyes and it annoyed her. "I do hope Daisy's alright in the luggage van. That maid is such a useless object. I hope there are no other dogs in there with fleas or dirty minds."

Timor opened the window, the better to breathe. "Gloria's a good girl," he said.

Madame gave a snort. "A maid is a maid, Timmy. A golden retriever is a rarity."

And then she said, quite suddenly, out of the blue:

"You're wrong. They never forgive a disaster."

"Wrong? What did I say?" Timor asked, but she ignored him and carried on as if she was talking in her sleep, and certainly not to him.

"'Our golden opportunity,' you said. But the people – all those wretched little people… They have to find someone to blame. You'll see. And it was always going to be me. 'Why did she let it happen?' they'll say. 'Why didn't she DO something? Make it right. Make everything the way it was.' How absolutely I despise them…"

Timor leaned out of the carriage window (despite the notice saying it was forbidden) and looked back along the platform. He caught sight of Gloria and Daisy standing helpless beside the luggage-van door. And he felt a sudden need to get off and help. For once, he did not ask the permission of his wife.

"I might be able to get her onto the roof," he told Gloria. "If I kneel down, do you think you can get her over my shoulders?" And he went down on all fours beside Daisy. Despite his beautiful woollen coat with its fancy collar, he looked somehow frayed and worn out. Wearing Daisy like a shawl, he walked his hands up the side of the train in order to get to his feet. As he did so, they all three flinched at the shrill blast of the train's whistle, and the luggage van gave a jerk. The train had started to move.

"Run, sir!" squealed Gloria. "You'll miss it! Never mind us! Run!"

But Timor did not run. He stood there, still bowed down by the golden retriever. Their eyes – girl, man and dog – flickered left-to-right, left-to-right, faster and faster as the train gathered speed in front of their very noses. It left a silent station in its wake.

"Will Madame be gone long, sir?" asked Gloria.

"God knows… I mean… There's no telling. She wants to see for herself how bad things are for folk upstream."

"I got folk upstream," said Gloria.

"Oh. I'm sorry… I mean, I'm sure they're alright."

On the walk back to the house, Timor wheeled the wheelbarrow full of luggage.

"I hope the rain stops really soon. How would Madame get back here, sir, if the train tracks got flooded?"

"No idea," he said, and then, "*Catapult*, perhaps!" with such unexpected venom that Gloria knew she had asked one question too many and dropped back to walk behind him where she belonged.

She talked to the dog instead. "Funny she laid out all her best dresses to go where it's muddy. And sacked Cook! Who's gonna cook her dinner when she comes home?"

Daisy wagged her tail, not having understood anything that had been said all morning, but relieved to be away from the whistling and hot hiss of the railway station, and happy to be with the two people she loved best.

CHAPTER TWO

Washout

FOREST BEND, NORTHERN AFALIA

Much earlier that day, far away to the north, Clem Wollen and his parents had sat on the floor of their shack, and listened to a storm that threatened everything they held dear. Their dog Heinz moved uneasily from lap to lap, wishing they had believed him sooner.

Danger has a smell. It prickles at the back of the nose. *Smell that?* it says. *Something is wrong.* All over the village, dogs had been smelling the danger and barking. Week upon week, the raindrops had been blasting smells out of the soft ground, swirling them into a rich stew of scents. But strongest of all was the smell of danger. *Look to your loved ones*, it said. *Tell them. Warn them.* And Heinz had tried with all his might.

They believed him now.

The everlasting rain hammered on the roof and rattled

like pebbles against the window. The cabin was cold, and a fire could not be lit in the grate because of the rain driving down the chimney. The lamp could not be lit either: it had already been carried up to the roof-space, along with anything useful or treasured. The family had built a makeshift tower by lashing together furniture and a ladder. If things came to the worst, the tower would also be their escape route into the roof. They had tied to it other possessions they hoped to save.

"Forty trees we took down this last week," said Clem's father. "Forty! Laid 'em along the bank as a barrier. And I'm telling you, they won't be enough to keep the river from bustin' out. Oak trees look like twigs 'longside that torrent! I seen the river angry, but I never seen her this way. Boiling and churning. Like a mad thing."

"Hush, sunshine," murmured his wife gently, and threw a warning glance in the direction of Clem. "You'll be scaring people."

"I'd best get back down there and fell another tree," he said, looking at the door as if his worst nightmares lay beyond it. "You never know: might be the one tree that makes the difference. Anyways, I want to see how high the water's come up."

After he had gone, bugs and mice crept in under the door, under the walls, looking for shelter. Groundwater oozed up through the floor. Heinz stood up, his belly-fur wet, and yapped at the water. His territory had been invaded and his warrior powers had dissolved in the damp. The rain on the roof drowned out his barks. A chill wind came threading through the trees to rattle the cabin. A precious book dropped out of the roof and disintegrated, pages moving mysteriously across the floor on a film of water. Everything was out-of-place and wrong – very wrong – and Heinz knew it.

Clem curled up on the tabletop, wrapped in bedding, just to stay warm. When Heinz joined him – contrary to all the rules – his mother did not object.

For Heinz, the warm bliss of Clem's scent and the soft nest of blanket and arms held every worry at bay for a time. But, like those bugs creeping indoors, the wrongness persisted. Clem was dressed for outdoors, in layers and layers of clothes. His mother was sitting up on a stool – just sitting – holding the empty binding of the broken book. That was when the certain promise of Danger choked off all the bliss, and Heinz gave a long low whine like an unoiled door swinging in the wind.

An hour later, the cabin door burst open and Clem's father stumbled in head-first. He was soaked to the skin and shuddering with cold, the air outside so bitter that when he shouted, his words came out smoky.

"It's coming! Climb!" They could hear distant whistles, bells and men yelling. "Get up! Get up high! Now!"

Wearing his bedding, Clem started to climb the scaffold.

The blanket snagged on everything. He swagged up one corner and wrapped Heinz in it, then slung it over his shoulder. Heinz smelled his toy – his piece of knotted rope – as they passed by it on the way to the attic.

"You got water up there, Maisy?" yelled the man, shunting his wife upwards with a shoulder under her rump.

"Six or seven bottles. And 'nuff beans to last till Doomsday... God spare our little home."

And so they reached the roof-space. Beneath the falling rain, it was like being inside a drum during a drum roll.

And then the rain paused, as if someone had turned it off at a tap. Mama began to sing, but her voice broke, and they sat in silence, their eyes all resting on Heinz. Unease worked the dog like a squeeze box, expelling wheezy whimpers from his narrow chest, but he did his best to comfort the family, licking whatever parts he could reach. The man's skin was so cold it tasted of nothing.

"You left the door open, Pa!" said Clem.

"Back window too," said Mama. "You don't keep the river out, Clem – you let it come right on through, or it knocks your place—"

Her husband interrupted. "You fetch up an axe, Maisy?"

"I thought you..."

Without another word, he started down the scaffold of furniture. But halfway to the floor, he froze, and started back up again. The sound of whistles had stopped. The whole world caught its breath. Husband and wife were looking at each other like their eyeballs were birds on the same wire. Clem, rocking to and fro on his knees, picked up Heinz and held him so close that the dog's ribs bowed.

"God and Love are going to keep us together, right?" said Mama.

The river below Clem's village did not simply lap over the bank. It rammed its shoulder through the barricade of tree trunks and came looking for conquest. It came in waves twice the height of a man, snapping sapling trees at the roots and devouring the cotton fields so ravenously that it foamed at the mouth like a rabid dog. It picked up small tin shacks and privies as if they were bean cans, and ripped them apart. Small boats were swept off the river and over the land, rolling and tumbling until they smashed against trees or the walls of cabins, houses, barns. The river armed itself as it came, with stones torn up out of the ground, with branches and fences, carts and barbed wire. Knotty sinews of water wrestled with every obstacle in their path.

But still the house was standing. Though every nail bent in its timber, every screw tried to twist free, the house still stood, and the surface of the water seemed to level off at the height of the door-lintel.

"Will it come any deeper?" asked Mama.

"Yep," said Pa.

"No!" Clem protested.

"Yip," said Heinz, watching a dead catfish float through his home on a tide of muddy water.

Pa prised his hands free from theirs – "We need that axe" – and climbed back down the scaffold of furniture, shutting his eyes against the cold clasp of water… Pausing to draw a deep breath, he sank under the brown swill, and his wife gave a banshee wail:

"I forgot the axe, and now I killed your daddy!"

He seemed to be gone for ever. Then the scaffold shook as he heaved himself up the tower, one-handed, lugging the axe they used to cut firewood. The water was rising almost as fast as he was climbing.

"Quit crying, woman," he told his wife, and heaved the axe at the roof.

Crash, crash, crash. Each axe blow showered them with wood-splinters and tar.

Then moss.

Dirty daylight flooded the loft from above and, one by one, Clem's father lifted his family through the hole and onto the roof. They were up as far as they could go. If the river rose higher, they were done for.

Five souls sat on that island of roof tiles: Heinz, Clem, his mother and father and Hound Death – though only Heinz could smell the Hound's wicked breath.

Late that evening, halfway to the sea and moving at breakneck speed – the flood surge met another fast-moving beast: the last train out of Praesto City.

The train was cast from tonnes of foundry metal and planted on rails of shining steel, so no, the flood surge did not sweep it off the rails.

It simply gouged the soil from under the tracks, until the rails sagged and the carriages, one by one, rolled over onto their sides. The guard's van uncoupled itself and was swept away. The locomotive and the wreckage behind it were scoured through and through by tonnes of rushing water, which carried off luggage, coats, hats, children, curtains, pets, the powerful, the famous, the nameless and the coal from the tender. There was no one there to see it – no one to spread the news – no one who lived. When the Furca burst its banks, it washed out every railway line and road as easily as the silver trails left by snails.

In atramento est veritas

FINE WEATHER ON ITS WAY
GATES TO REMAIN OPEN

A timely change in weather is due, according to the Meteorological Centre. It cannot come a moment too soon, as water levels rise. Four of the Five Factories are now experiencing flooding.

Praesto's best scientific minds delivered their findings yesterday to Madame Suprema and members of the Senate, at Foremost Mansion, forecasting an end to rain, and sunny days ahead.

Your Editor writes:

MORE NEEDS TO BE KNOWN

Celebrations are indeed in order. However, the loss of communications with Northern Afalia is still cause for concern. The telegraph wires are thought to have been felled by floods, and no information is reaching Praesto from the forests, farms, wetlands or Rose City.

Our country cousins may have fared far worse than us. It is hoped efforts will be made by the Senate to discover if our help is needed, and to put our minds at rest.

> *"No man is an island*
> *entire of itself."*
> John Donne

SOON BE BACK ON LINE

The Senate has said that it hopes to restore telegraphic communications with the north "very soon" and calls for patience from those asking for news of their relations in the timberlands. "We are doing our best in very difficult circumstances and do not wish to endanger the lives of our telegraph engineers."

Supreme Quality Rainwear

"DON'T LET THE RAIN DAMPEN YOUR STYLE"

UMBRELLAS   MACKINTOSHES   GALOSHES

TODAY'S ANAGRAM: LION SHUNS HEEL

CHAPTER THREE

Clearly a Good Day

Daisy was having a wonderful day.

"Look what a fool I am, Daze," said Gloria in the kitchen of Foremost Mansion. "I done it again! Laid two breakfast trays 'stead of one. That's habit, that is."

Daisy knew about habit. Each day, out of habit, she watched Gloria prepare breakfast, hopeful that one day a treacle bun would accidentally roll from the tray into her mouth. Today it did. Today, Gloria gave Daisy scrambled egg, toast and half a banana. Today there was no Boz in the house to shoulder Daisy out of the way and eat it all, no Cook to shoo her out of the kitchen.

In the dining room, The Husband smelled of sadness and fret and, when Gloria set down the breakfast tray, only sat looking at it without picking up knife and fork. Daisy nudged his knee in case he needed help to eat it and had forgotten help was at hand. The Husband gave her his treacle bun. Clearly this was going to be a very good day.

Gloria curtseyed and turned to go.

"The river's burst its banks. The docks are underwater. And still it rains," said Timor.

"It would, sir."

"Why would it? How could those weather people have got it so wrong? Sunshine. Hot sunshine, they said."

Gloria bit her lip. She could not...she must not. It was more than her job was worth to say it. But when she fetched coffee, her fingers strayed to her pocket and she took out the crumpled ball of paper she had pulled from Daisy's mouth. She somehow accidentally-on-purpose left the scrunched paper beside Timor's elbow. Watching from the door, she saw him flatten it with one hand.

SOCIETY OF METEOROLOGY
Weather House, Academy Hill

Praesto City, Afalia

```
With the barometer still falling, we see
no end to the wet weather for many weeks
more. However, far more serious is the
```

catastrophic volcanic activity taking place below the Lacha Mountains, which will cause unprecedented quantities of snowmelt, drastically swelling the Furca River still further, long after the rains abate. Therefore, we cannot but predict long-term serious flooding throughout and beyond Afalia, with considerable danger to life and terrible consequences for every aspect of day-to-day living.

Fuller estimates of the impact will follow as soon as data has been gathered.

Saul C

Professor in Chief
Society of Meteorology

M Linley

Head of Forecasting
Institute of Weather Sciences

"I suppose Madame wanted you and her and the dogs to get out before the trains stopped running," said Gloria when she brought the coffee.

"And abandon her post? Never!"

But Gloria had put a lot of thought into the matter and couldn't quite help saying: "She must've been planning it, sir, or why did she sack Cook, sir? And lie about the weather forecast?"

Timor thumped the table, his fist catching the saucer rim and sending his coffee cup spiralling across the pale carpet.

"She is Head of State! The Suprema does *not lie!* I think, girl, you had better consider your position!"

Gloria bobbed a curtsey. Finding she was too scared to run, she bobbed another. She continued to stare at him, not understanding what it meant – to "consider her position" – and too frightened to ask. "No, sir. I mean, yes, sir. Sorry, sir."

"I expect…"

They were both left "expecting" for a long time before Timor finished the sentence: "I expect Madame was not wearing her reading spectacles and mistook the message."

His breakfast was never eaten. At that moment the telephone rang in the hall: a feeble, croaking ring, as if it had caught a cold. Unlike the telegraph wires, the city's small network of telephones had not yet failed.

It was normally the Private Secretary's job to answer it, but the Private Secretary seemed to have suffered the same fate as Cook, because she had not come to work since Madame's departure. Gloria never answered calls – she had heard telephones could electrocute you if you had wet hands. Her hands were wet now, with sweat. Besides, she was fairly sure she had just been sacked, and was in the middle of crying. She stood staring at the jiggling phone on the hall table, then fled upstairs and sat on the top step, hugging her knees.

Luckily, Timor picked it up. It was Professor Lightfoot, Editor of *The Voice*:

"*…rumours…Suprema…station…disguise…true?*"

Timor leaned his fingertips on the hall table and asked, "I'm sorry, Professor. Would you say that again?"

Apparently, rumours were going about that Madame Suprema had been seen boarding the last train out of Praesto Station North five days before. Where was she going? Had she fled the city? The newspaper had reported, in good faith, that hot weather was forecast for weeks to come. The paper's reputation would be at risk if that was not true…

Gloria waited for Timor to say the Suprema had gone north to spread comfort and joy – but he said nothing. He even made to put the phone back on its hook. His eyes rested on Daisy clambering clumsily upstairs, past all the portraits of bygone Supremos and Supremas. The dog drew Timor's eye to Gloria sitting on the top stair. And there his gaze stuck, as if with gum arabic.

"*Hello? Hello?*" said the telephone, loud and strident.

"Fled the city? Absolutely not," said Timor, his voice unnaturally high. "Madame Suprema has gone nowhere. She is right here. I can't speak for the accuracy of the weather forecast, but my wife would *never* desert her post during a crisis…or even a non-crisis."

"*Excellent. Look, Timor, would she favour* The Voice *with an interview this morning – answer a few civil questions?*"

"Questions?" said Timor's mouth, though no sound came out.

Gloria, too, silently parroted the word. *Questions?* Suddenly questions seemed to infest Foremost Mansion like woodlice.

"*Since the rain shows no sign of stopping, for instance, shall the city gates be shut?*" asked the Editor.

"Oh golly, yes!" Timor laughed confidently. "It's written in the City Statutes: if the floodwater reaches the War Memorial, all four gates will be shut."

"*Not without your wife's signature on the decree,*" said the Editor irritably. "*Look, perhaps I should speak to her in person.*"

Timor shook his head at the telephone, but could not speak, so hung up. The dog lolloped back down the staircase and thrust her muzzle into his hand, sensing a strong need for comfort.

The telephone immediately rang again. It was Kovet, Senator for Home Affairs.

"*Heard some nasty rumours…*" he began, his worry tinged with gloat.

Timor interrupted him: "Madame Suprema wishes the city gates to be shut tomorrow. Fetch over the necessary paperwork, will you? This afternoon? And anyone else who has to be there to see it handed over. There's a good chap."

There was a pause. "*Oh. Yes. Of course. Straight away. Yes. To whom am I speaking?*"

"The Husband. Over and out."

All this while, Timor's eyes had not once left Gloria's. She felt as if he was pinning her in place with his pale blue gaze. And she could almost *hear* what he was thinking.

"With the veil, *you* could stand in for—"

"No! No, I couldn't!" she said. "I'm fifteen."

"And small. Like her."

"I look nothing like her! My hair's too big!"

"It won't be for long!"

"My hair?"

"The…subterfuge."

"The what?"

"The *passing off*. The impersonation. The pretending to be… We can work on the voice."

Daisy whimpered. The Husband was holding her nose so tightly that she was having trouble breathing. She could have pulled away, but supplying comfort was her one and only skill.

40

"I'm the maid! I got things to do! The beds! The dusting! The fires… Anyway, who's ever gonna mistake me for—"

"But we have to keep her end up! Don't we?" Timor's voice cracked with panic. "Until she comes back? Don't we?"

Gloria went to her room at the top of the house and lay on the bed, staring at the ceiling while rain hammered at the window. The thoughts in her head flapped around like birds and found nowhere to settle. It was probably a crime – a proper, written-down crime – to pretend to be the Suprema of all Afalia. Anyway, nobody would be fooled… It would be nice to wear expensive dresses – but then again, Madame had dreadful taste in clothes. People *ought to know* that Madame was visiting unfortunate people in the north! Why tell them any different? And what would happen when Madame came home and found Gloria Winnow pretending to be her? There would be hell to pay!

This draughty little room with its rattly windows was wintry all year round and it smelled of mould, and mice ate your shoes if you left them in the bottom of the cupboard. But Gloria loved it because it was hers and the only place she had lived since she left home. She didn't want to stop being Gloria and start being someone else – especially someone Gloria didn't like very much – in fact, someone Gloria was downright scared of. How could a person go around being scared of herself?

She heard Timor's footsteps on the stairs, but he did not

knock or open the door. He was waiting for her to come out and start learning how to be the Suprema. She got up quietly and went and looked through one of the slits in the door where the planks didn't join up. He was sitting on the top stair, his head in his hands. The fingers breaking through his hair were rigid.

"Where would I sleep?" she asked.

He swung round. "What?"

"Where would I have to sleep?"

"Good God, child, you can take impersonation too far! In your own room, of course! My wife would horsewhip you if she came back and found you had been sleeping in her bed… Obviously you'd have to go in there to dress… I haven't quite thought through the day-to-day… But don't let the dog in there, whatever you do. She leaves her hair everywhere. It's not for long. Just keep telling yourself: it's not going to be for long, alright?"

No, thought Gloria. *You're right. They'll see through me on the first day.*

Timor proved to be a merciless teacher. Gloria had no sooner got her vowels the right shape than he started lacing them together with consonants. She felt like a baby bird being fed screws and nuts and bolts: her mouth ached with chewing on them. He was never satisfied. "There's something you're not getting – something missing from the voice – honey, I think. Try to spread honey over every syllable."

It was a sweet thing to say, and Gloria thought how terrible it must be for him to be sitting here with his maid rather than his honey-tongued wife – missing her, wishing he, too, had caught that train…

"Now add the armour-plating," said Timor. "Studded with rivets. Think barbed wire in a party dress." (That sounded a little less romantic.)

Long before Gloria's efforts could win his approval, they ran out of time.

"Who's going to be there to see me sign this whatever?"

"Decree. It's a decree. Or an edict, if that's easier to remember. About twenty Senators, I should think. I'll sign the thing as soon as Kovet brings it, so you'll pretend to sign it, right? But you will have to learn to write her signature sometime soon. They may just watch and clap. If they start asking questions, stress that the gates won't be closed for long. It's temporary, say – also how fortunate we are that our forefathers built such mighty walls and gates to keep us safe. Something along those lines. Soothing. Use the word 'safe' as often as you like. We don't want them dwelling on the fact the rain hasn't stopped."

They stared at each other in mutual panic.

"I don't think I can do this," she said.

"Nor me. But we seem to be about to. Pretend you have

43

a cold. And if in doubt, just say, 'What is *your* opinion on the matter?'"

Two reporters from *The Voice* arrived at the gates of Foremost Mansion at noon and sheltered from the rain in the empty sentry box, which, on special occasions, held a soldier in fancy uniform. When the various Senators of State and lawyers arrived, the reporters managed to scurry through the gates behind them.

This time, there was no one to greet the visitors with umbrellas. Instead, Madame Suprema's lanky husband opened the door.

It seemed at first as if he was the only person at home. There were no lights anywhere, and rain clouds so shrouded the house that its elegant rooms were merely a stack of dark boxes. Here and there, the glimmer from a simple candlestick hinted at dead chandeliers hanging overhead.

"It would appear Madame has *lost her power*," Kovet observed and allowed himself a little smile.

"Rain got into the generator," said Timor, who had ensured darkness throughout the house. "This way, if you please."

No one was sitting at the Desk Supreme in the Audience Chamber – though it took some peering about to be sure.

"Where is she?" demanded Kovet rudely.

Gloria was in fact sitting on the stool in front of Madame's dressing table. Every few moments, fright turned a key in the centre of her back, winding her insides into tighter and tighter knots. She had used too much of Madame's perfume; the reek made her feel sick. The veil in front of her face reminded her of walking through a cobweb in the outhouse; spidery fear tickled her scalp. Her hair was much thicker than Madame's – it threatened to betray her by bursting suddenly out of the hat. The dark red lipstick tasted of oil. The clothes hanging in the wardrobes looked suddenly like headless, wicked girls, strung up as an example to others.

But even by candlelight, Gloria recognized the girl in the mirror all too well: it was the maid – the one who did nothing right, who regularly made Madame Suprema *ptach!* with irritation. On the wallpaper (Gloria knew without seeing it) was a faint red stain where Madame had thrown a pot of jam at her because it was not apricot. The stain looked like traces of blood.

Anyway, surely the Senators out there would recognize Gloria at once – she had answered the door to them often enough.

But the clothes fitted perfectly and someone ought to wear them. Also, Foremost Mansion had bars on the windows to keep out thieves or assassins or pigeons, which meant she could not climb out and run away. So Gloria buttoned up the jacket collar, found herself a really big handkerchief, pulled on the lace gloves and blew out the candle. The girl in the mirror disappeared. Only Madame Suprema Mark 2 remained to feel her way through to the Audience Chamber.

"Forgive be, gentleben, ladies. I have a cold," croaked the shadowy figure. Sitting down at the desk, she loudly blew her nose. Her handkerchief and the large white dog with her were the most visible things in the room.

Gloria waited for someone to speak, then realized that it had to be her. "Has the water come in at the gates?"

"Yes, Madame. Ankle-deep at the South Gate."

"Has it reached the War Memorial?"

"Yes, Madame. *Despite the weather forecast*," said Kovet with the hint of a sneer.

There was something very sneery about Mr Kovet altogether, thought Gloria. When, after Senate meetings, Gloria-the-maid brought him his coat and hat, he always checked the pockets to see if she had stolen anything.

"It bay be sunny toborrow, Senator Kovet, and we can open the gates up again! Weather is hard to get right."

"The gates will be temporarily sealed to make them watertight, Madame. We shan't be able to just open and shut them on a whim," said the Senator.

"Well then, let's not seal theb till we dow if they leak!" said Gloria more perkily.

"Can I ask, ma'am…?" One of the reporters knocked over his chair in jumping to his feet. "Can I ask – what news from up north?" The Senators, realizing for the first time that there were reporters in the room, began to mutter and moo, but the Editor had told them to get answers, so the reporter persisted. "We know they've got flooding, but now the telegraph lines seem to be down, 'n' with more rain, people want to know how the folk upcountry are doing."

Gloria thought: *I'll enquire, sir.* That was what Gloria-the-maid was supposed to say whenever visitors called at the front door. The phrase took shape in her head and wedged there. *I'll enquire, sir.* But she couldn't say that! They would recognize her instantly! So she said:

"Of course, sir. Senator Kovet is getting right on it. Aren't you, Senator?" Then she blew her nose again and bent over the edict to trace the pen nib over Madame's fake signature. She noticed how its looping letters trembled slightly as they stood surrounded by stark white paper. Clearly Mr Timor had been just as scared as she was now when he faked it.

Afterwards, the newspaper men ran for the shelter of the sentry box and waited there for the rain to ease off. Foremost Mansion stood on the highest hill in Praesto, so they could see the whole city laid out below them: all five smoke-belching factories, the silver tramlines like wire joining the factories one to another; the music hall and gymnasium; schools, water towers, the football stadium and polo field;

the circle of city wall and, beyond it, the gleam of water. Everywhere, water.

Water had swamped the city's river-port. Only cranes and one large cargo ship still showed above the surface; the rest of the harbour was submerged. The Furca River had ballooned into a vast lagoon with Praesto City an island in the middle. But instead of slowing down (as most floods do once they have overspilled their banks) the river kept on racing seawards at the speed of panic.

"I seen her flood before, but nothing like this," said one. "God help those poor souls upriver."

"I got family upriver," said his colleague.

"Oh. Sorry."

"The Suprema was feeling generous today, eh? She's never answered a newspaperman's question in all the years I been one. Even called me 'sir'!"

His companion snorted at a sudden funny thought. "Maybe the rumours are true. She really did flee the city, and this one's a stand-in!"

His mate laughed, too, then sighed disappointedly. "Nah. No such luck. You saw the dog. The Great Suprema goes nowhere without her dashed dogs."

CHAPTER FOUR

Parting Company

FOREST BEND, NORTHERN AFALIA

For a day and night Clem and his family sat on their roof. It was as if the whole world had drowned. They saw no one. In the distance, patches of higher ground rose out of the water like cruising whales. Their neighbours' houses were all gone, because they had stood on lower ground. Dead animals floated by – a cow – a horse – a pig – a parcel of rabbits. The strangest sight of all was a fleet of brownish boxes bobbing and banging against one another.

Coffins.

It seemed for a moment as if the graves in the graveyard had spewed out their dead. But these coffins were new and empty. The river had demolished the sawmill where Clem's father worked at making them... *Best coffins in Timberlake County*, he liked to say. Now they were on the loose, riding the flood, giddy-goose spinning as they went, and he watched them go by – his handiwork carried away down the river.

The family sipped their precious supply of fresh water and ate beans from cans split open with the axe, because Mama had forgotten the can-opener. Pa said that when the beans ran out, they would fish. He did not say what they would do when the fresh water ran out.

The rain, satisfied that it had done its job, stopped, and their clothes began to dry out, though Clem's father continued to shudder as violently as if someone was kicking him in the soul.

"We got each other." Over and over again Mama said it. "We still got each other."

Heinz stood on the end of the roof in the hope of seeing his piece of knotted rope float by.

Then rescue came in the shape of a rowing boat, and Mama changed her tune to "God be praised! God be praised!"

Three men, seven women and five children had already been picked up. Clem's father knew the men from his work at the joinery. "Many killed?" he asked.

"Enough."

The boat-handler was armed with a rifle and a handgun and wanted ten afal to take them aboard – "to pay for the kerosene". His boat *bang-bang-bang*ed against the roof, tilting each time, to the terror of those already in it. Heinz could smell that the bilges were a-swill with fear and misery.

Then the boatman said: "No dogs."

The youngest child in the boat burst into tears at the memory of leaving her pets.

Clem protested. Clem yelled. Clem said he could not leave without Heinz – said he *would* not leave without Heinz.

"He's like one of the family," said Mama.

"Please yourself," said the boatman, pocketing the money and making to push off.

"Get in," said Clem's father and slapped his son's head – a thing he had never done in his whole life. He looked to have aged twenty years overnight.

And that is how the mongrel Heinz lost his family to the flood: they got into a boat and were borne away, leaving him to run up and down the roof ridge – up-and-down, up-and-down, up-and-down, up-and-down, up-and-down – until their scent was swallowed up by the river's all-pervading stink.

CHAPTER FIVE

Shutting the Gates

PRAESTO CITY

The decree Madame Suprema (or rather Timor) had signed was read aloud through a loudhailer. The workmen standing by in readiness wished the Mayor would stop reading the decree so that they could get on with closing the South Gate. A surge of brown floodwater swirled eagerly through the gateway and washed the fake flowers off the War Memorial.

Gloria and Timor stood on the high steps of the gatehouse. A reporter from *The Voice* newspaper was taking their picture from a respectful distance.

"Why do we need to be here?" Gloria whispered. "Are we still keeping Madame's end up?"

"That's right," murmured Timor. "I'm sorry to be uncivil, but please don't speak if you can help it."

"Alright… I could go and help with the shutting. I'm quite strong."

The gate in question was thirty strides high and made of

bronze and copper. The copper had turned green, so that the figures decorating the gate panels looked like elves. Three hundred years ago, it had taken a team of elephants to close it.

"No need. There are pneumatic piston-hinges top and bottom, and a switch in the gatehouse. It will close automatically."

Further up the street, another cluster of umbrellas had been encircled by the Civil Guard in their horrible yellow uniforms. Placards sprouted between the umbrellas, but they were too far away for Gloria to read. And the rain all but drowned out the distant chanting: *"Let us out! Let them in! Let us out! Let them in!"*

The demonstrators seemed not to want the gate to close.

"They maybe don't like shut-in places," Gloria suggested. "When Madame shut me in the hall cupboard, I didn't like that on account of it felt like a coffin."

"Oh, do please keep your voice down!" begged Timor. As he stepped agitatedly from foot to foot, his shoes made rhythmical squelching noises. "They're protesting because they want to be free to go and help people on the outside if they're in trouble. They think north-country folk washed out of their homes might turn up here, looking for help, and not be able to get in… Though how they'd get here, I can't… She did *what?*"

Gloria shrugged. "I tripped and broke a vase. Fair dos."

Peering through the rain towards the protestors, Gloria suddenly wanted to join them. She could imagine her sister and brother, her mother holding the baby, Moony the cow, Grandpa with his bad leg, even the dog-that-had-died. She could perfectly picture them all standing up to their armpits in water, knocking on the city gate, but no one opening up, and them getting washed away. And they seemed more real than she did, standing on the gatehouse steps pretending to be a grown woman. A great sob of horror floundered up through Gloria.

Another dirty wrinkle of water rolled in through the gate. Floating in it were an oar, a bush and a nest of drowned rats. The wave carried them, like offerings, to the War Memorial steps and dumped them there, where the flowers had been. The crowd uttered a single bleat of alarm. Even the protestors stopped chanting.

Somewhere inside the gatehouse, an engineer threw a switch, and the vast gate jerked on its hinges… Jerked, but did not begin closing.

The engineer threw the switch again. A jolt. A curse. The workmen plunged out under the arch and began hauling and pushing with all their might on a gate that weighed tonnes. The photographer rolled up his trousers, pulled off his shoes and began photographing the men floundering about in the gateway. The watching crowd began squealing and groaning or protesting to the Mayor. The Mayor spread his hands helplessly: he had only come to read the decree – why would he know anything about sticking gates?

"They could try changing the grease inside the cylinders," said Gloria.

Another surge of water filled the workmen's wellingtons and made them sweary with panic. Daisy was barking encouragement.

"I'm sorry?" said Timor. "I couldn't hear you for the dog."

"I just thought they might want to check the grease in the piston-hinge things. My brother's a—"

"What, my *brother-in-law*?" Timor hissed, urgently looking round to see if anyone had heard. "The industrialist? Got killed falling off his polo pony? Remember?"

"Oh! Oh dear. Did he? How awful for…everyone." Gloria thought for a moment about Madame's lost brother. Then she remembered she was Suprema and rallied. "Yes, but *before* he fell off his horse, my brother knew about piston-hinges. Industrialists have to. They know to change the grease inside, 'cos it goes thick and blucky if you leave it too long, 'specially after a cold winter."

The reporter wading back to the steps forgot about the sock he had lost in the floodwater. "Hey, you in the gatehouse!" he called. "The Suprema says to change the grease in the piston-hinges!"

Ladders were fetched, but they reached only as high as the lower hinge of the gate. Engineers were sent up to the top of the city walls with tubs of grease and lowered on ropes to the upper hinge (which Gloria thought might have been fun but for the pelting rain).

Two hours later, the crowd of spectators had grown even bigger. To the embarrassment of the engineer in the gatehouse, they waved crossed fingers in the air, counted down from ten, then shouted, "*Pull!*"

The green, coppery elves jolted. The pistons sighed, and the beautiful ancient gate swung slowly, slowly shut. As it closed, it swished a swash of water far enough up the street as to wash the horrible yellow boots of the Civil Guards.

The city walls – and now the gates – seemed to reach halfway to the sky. By nightfall the city would be flood-proof. The protestors booed, but everyone else agreed: they had to stop the river breaking in.

And me getting back home, thought Gloria.

Timor pointed his bent elbow at her. She looked at it, puzzled. Was it some secret signal to skedaddle? "Take my arm, *Madame*," he said between gritted teeth.

"I couldn't do that, sir!"

Timor made a noise like a man cranking a motor car. So she slipped her hand into the crook of his corduroy coat-sleeve and together they paddled back uphill. Members of the public stepped aside and broke into applause as she went by. Gloria looked round to see whom they were clapping for. The elbow clamped her hand even tighter.

As they neared the protestors, Gloria asked: "Can I go and say something to them?"

Timor made a slight whimpering noise in the back of his throat, which she took for a no. But she could not help calling out to the nearest woman with a placard, "Harnesses! Harnesses on ropes! Hanging down the outside of the walls. Dangling down. So if people arrive outside – in boats, say – they can grab hold and we can haul them up! What d'you think?"

The reporter with a missing sock would have written it down in his notebook, except that the pages were shredding in the wet.

IN ATRAMENTO EST VERITAS

THE GREAT GATES CLOSE

For the first time in a century, the Great Gates have been closed. Despite problems, all four were shut and will not reopen until the crisis is past. The work of our forefathers may have saved us from chaos and loss of life. Heavy rain did not deter hundreds from watching, as the huge bronze doors swung shut, but the task took longer than expected when the hydraulics failed to function. A timely suggestion from the Suprema eased the situation, when she suggested an oil-change.

The Voice must ask why earlier weather forecasts were so wrong.

Your Editor writes:

The people of Praesto are to be congratulated on their bravery and good humour in the face of an historic natural disaster. *The Voice* salutes you. But with telephone lines being torn down by the flood, no news has reached me of the towns, villages and farms on both east and west banks. Anxiety grows for those in the timberlands and riverside communities. Have homes been destroyed? Have folk come to harm?

We would ask the Senate what measures are being taken to find out. Meanwhile, we can only hope and pray for our country cousins.

THREE SHIPS SUNK AS FLOOD SWAMPS PORT

Three of the four cargo ships moored in Praesto Port were

SUPREMA SAVES THE DAY

The Suprema attended the closing of South Gate. Her advice helped greatly when the gate jammed (see inside for more photos).

sunk by the river's raging torrent, leaving only one ore carrier afloat. Anchor chains broke and dock walls collapsed as ships were hurled about the dock. No one was thought to be aboard the vessels, but the hulks will be hard to salvage. Only the bulk carrier *Nickelodeon* survived.

TODAY'S ANAGRAM: MAMA MADE SUPER

CHAPTER SIX

Night on the Tiles

FOREST BEND, NORTHERN AFALIA

Heinz the mongrel had been left behind.

When, as a puppy, he had been taken away from his mother, he had cried for a week. But the ache had been eased by Clem. Now Heinz sat on the roof and looked out over an ocean of brown water, and no breeze brought him either the scent of Clem or the promise of rescue.

He had no choice but to find his boy again. Loneliness and cold made it harder to form a plan, but soon his wits would surely line up in the right order. Instinct would lead him back to Clem somehow. It must.

Heinz licked a spilled baked bean off the roof and lay down. Through his belly he could feel the house groaning and trembling. The flow of water boiling about the walls was flaying it of planks and gutters. The current was gouging soil from *under* the walls, too – little by little, scooping out gallons of oozing mud.

During the night he felt the house jolt and jar under him. By morning, the whole structure was swaying drunkenly and pulling itself to pieces.

It was the car that finished the job. The only car in the whole of Timberlake County.

The open-top Folly Tourer, its fold-down canvas roof sprung free of the windscreen, came sailing downstream. No driver steered it. No passengers waved. No steam rose from its bonnet, but it bore down on Heinz unerringly, and struck the corner of the house. The car was barely damaged – just one headlamp smashed. For the house, though, it was the last straw. Some beam broke within the roof, with a noise like a bough snapping off a tree. The right-angles of the building all folded inwards or outwards, and Clem's house staggered and disintegrated. The roof sprang from its moorings and tilted, vertical.

Heinz was no longer on it. He had leaped down onto the only surface that might take his weight – the roof of the Folly Tourer. The canvas received him like a hammock, folding up around him. His claws tore the fabric a little, but he lay so still, and wished so hard, that the car did not capsize. It continued on its exhilarating morning spin along the new expanded waterways through Timberlake County.

Over backyards and cabins, bicycles and warehouses, shrubs, mailboxes and baby perambulators, the Folly headed south. The whole moving water-world was, after all, heading south, towards the sea. Here and there, high ground welled out of the water, and on it were cattle and trees, sheep and horses, deer and pigs. Houses, even. People. But none of them was Clem. Heinz kept watch so intently that his eyes grew sore. Boats floated empty or upside down, like eggshells waiting to be smashed. But none of the boats was the one that had carried Clem away.

High above, a thousand birds wheeled and shrieked. Their nests were gone, their prey, their berries, their grain… But at least they were free to fly to the flood's edge, whereas Heinz was obliged to ride to his fate cradled in the roof of the Folly.

When it began to rain again, the wet gathered in the canvas folds and dripped through the hole torn by his claws. From beneath him came the sound of something lapping up the water eagerly.

Heinz put his nose and one eye through the split. And there, on the back seat of the Tourer, was a thing like a yellow bath sponge.

It was so small that it slid from one side of the seat to the other every time the car heeled over. It mewed like a cat, but since Heinz was not seized with a desire to kill it, he decided it was not a cat, but a very small dog.

"This your car?" he asked.

"My car."

And that was about it. Heinz, when he was warm and dry, could hold a hundred thoughts at a time in his head. But

"My car" seemed to be the top and bottom of this dog's conversation.

"My car," mewed the dog on the back seat.

"Breed?" asked Heinz. "Do you have a breed?" But whether the yellow sponge was a mutt or a pedigree, it had forgotten which.

"My car."

"Clem? You seen my boy Clem?" asked Heinz more urgently.

"*Mycar*," said the sponge.

CHAPTER SEVEN

Morning Glory

PRAESTO CITY

Next morning, Gloria was free to be herself. "I'm me in the morning," she told the dog. She fed Daisy, made the beds, prepared breakfast and dusted the ornaments. There were a lot of ornaments, all presented to Madame by foreign statesmen visiting Afalia. There were elephants, cats, horses, naked people, china flowers and photographs of the foreign statesmen in their best suits. Gloria had given all the animals names, but not the statesmen (who presumably had names already), and not the naked people, who she thought might prefer to stay anonymous.

Then she took Daisy for her morning walk. She no longer minded that her maid's uniform was too big for her. It was just so wonderful not to be Madame Suprema – not to peer through the netting of a veil or wear the fingerless lace gloves that made her hands look like chicken claws. She would have liked to have worn one of Madame's wool-lined raincoats, but maids don't have coats like that. So she was wearing one Cook had left behind in the hall cupboard. It kept the rain out better than her own.

From the top of Foremost Hill, she could see that the entire city was ringed with water, but that the gates and the walls were keeping out the swollen, rushing river. Rainwater was coursing down the gutter beside her, of course. But Praesto City was not drowning. The world thought of Praesto as a city built entirely of factories – "*World centre for the manufacture of cutlery.*" A pall of smoke from the five chimneys usually hung over everything, but today's low black rain clouds were swallowing the smoke. The rain had even managed to wash the soot off the statues and the white marble Senate Building. And Praesto also had its pretty patches of green – parks and golf courses and market gardens. Gloria would have liked to turn in their direction, but she had other plans today.

Daisy's favourite places were the graveyard and the park shrubbery where the dogs cocked their legs then chased each other. But today Gloria did not walk her to Pleasance Park as she usually did. Today they walked down into the city, where the smells were sharp as sandpaper in Daisy's nostrils, and the noise was even worse than at the railway station. When they stopped outside Factory One (Spoons), she sat down and licked Gloria's coat, savouring the cooking smells that clung to it.

"You can't take *that* inside," the gatekeeper told Gloria, pointing at Daisy. "Can't have dog hairs getting in the machines." His eyes remained on the people streaming into the factory, and a counter in his hand clicked as each worker passed through the gates. Behind him, the great dark building seemed to swallow them. The rumble of machinery starting up inside the factory sounded like a stomach digesting the first meal of the day.

"I don't want to," said Gloria. "I don't work here. I'm a maid up at—"

"So take yourself off," said the gatekeeper, *click-click-clicking*.

But Gloria had come hoping to catch her friend Higgy on his way to work. She needed to share her secret with a friend.

Higgy spotted Gloria from the end of the street and came running. His big grin already made her happier. As they talked, hundreds of factory hands streamed by to either side, as if the two were a boulder in a river. Or a city in a flood.

"Whatchya doing here?" said Higgy, his fingers raking through Daisy's sopping fur.

"There's something I got to tell you," said Gloria. "Someone, anyhow." Her heart sat painfully high in her chest and made her feel sick, but she absolutely had to share her secret with someone, and no one could be better than Higgy.

"Your woman did good, didn't she!" said Higgy.

"What?"

"Old Sourpuss Suprema. She only went and saved the day, didn't she? You live in the same house and you didn't know?"

For a moment, Gloria misunderstood – thought Madame Suprema must have come back; made lots of people safe in the north then come back home to Praesto.

Higgy rattled on in his big, bouncing voice: "I mean, all those things you said about her stopping your pay and calling you a… I thought she must be a real misery. But anyone who knows pistons can't be all bad, can she?" And he thrust a newspaper under Gloria's nose.

The black-and-white photograph of "Madame" – hat, gloves, husband, dog – flinched with each drop of rain that fell on it. Dark grey plops spread through the fabric of the paper and turned the Supreme Head of State spotty and blurred.

Should Gloria say it right out? *That's me in that photo. Madame's in the Lacha Mountains with Boz, helping people.* Would Higgy even believe her?

She had remembered, too, just how much he liked a laugh. Did he like laughing so much that he would run inside the factory and tell her secret to everyone he knew, just to see their faces?

Higgy snatched the paper back and put it under his coat. "Look, can't stop. Come and tell me lunchtime. I'm on the pumps today."

"Pumps?" Gloria, busy with second thoughts, was only half listening.

"In the basement. It's flooding, see? The fuel for the pumps ran out yesterday, so we're having to do it by hand. All the factories are desperate to buy up the old manual kind – man-powered, yes? Never seen one, myself. Before my time."

"But the city gates are shut now. Why is it still flooding? There's no—"

He laughed. When Higgy laughed, she thought he looked like a pumpkin with eyes, nose and mouth cut out and a candle inside. "It's still falling out of the sky, though – the wet stuff? *Uh?* It's still raining! We're in a dip here. All the factories are in the lowest bit of the city. The rain runs down, floods the factory basements. There's water coming up through the ground, too. There were mechanical pumps right up till yesterday, but the machine-fuel's used up now… So, yeah, it's like they say: 'All hands to the pumps'. Might be fun. Never been down the basement before, will make a change from polishing spoons… Got to go. You lose wages if you get here after the whistle. Not like you la-di-da maids."

The gatekeeper – *click click* – looked at his watch – *click click* – and put a silver whistle to his lips. Before he could blow it, Higgy was past him and inside the big black maw of the factory.

At the piercing sound of the silver whistle, Daisy took it into her head to run. She dragged Gloria half the way home.

The Voice

IN ATRAMENTO NON EST VERITAS

ALL HANDS TO THE PUMPS!

OUR GREAT FACTORIES NEED YOUR HELP

As soldiers are called up in time of war, citizens of Praesto are today asked to help our cherished city. From tomorrow, any person not told otherwise should report to the factory nearest their home.* There, a welcome awaits you, childcare for the young** and vital, valuable work. Training will be given, and you will have the thanks of all Afalia. SO! Expect laughter, comradeship and some jolly, energetic work!

Ask yourselves: where would we be without the Great Five?

LET'S PULL **Together!**

If you are NOT needed, you will receive a letter to say so.
**Pets will be cared for at a dedicated "Pets' Welcome Centre!"*

RABIES WARNING AFTER "HIDEOUS DEATH"

A pensioner was last night killed by a large pack of dogs in Castle Street. Civil Guards came to her aid, but could not drive off the dogs who, in the words of one officer, looked "raving mad, foaming at the mouth..." A vet found the dogs to be suffering from rabies, which causes swelling of the brain in those bitten. Infection leads to madness and (often) death. You are advised not to let children play out of doors, and to stay indoors unless absolutely necessary.

TODAY'S ANAGRAM: DONKEY MR TWO

CHAPTER EIGHT

Landfall

UPCOUNTRY

"Mycar."

The Folly Tourer crossed from Timberlake County into Friendship County without seeing any signpost to say so. Friendship County must have possessed several cars, because they sailed through rainbows of gasoline making whorls and swirls on the surface. The Folly needed no fuel, though, to speed on recklessly over lumpy ridges of heaving water. Shrubs snagged under the wheel arches, like food catching between teeth, so that pretty soon the automobile looked to be riding a raft downstream. But the heavy doors remained watertight.

"Mycar," said the sulky sponge on the back seat.

Heinz felt the *click-click* of breaking fibres and held very still; the fold-down canvas roof was tearing under his weight.

Occasionally the car entered an eddy and turned full circle before bowling on again. The steering wheel turned to right and left, as though in the grip of a ghostly chauffeur. With the sound of ripping canvas, Heinz finally slid unceremoniously through and plumped down on the passenger seat.

"Mycar!"

"Heinz," said Heinz in response. The gear stick trembled violently. The noise of water racing past the exhaust and drive-shaft was much louder here inside the car.

Every so often, flotsam would rear up out of the water ahead of them, so that the Folly seemed on course for certain destruction. Then the obstacle would sink down and let the car pass. Perched up on the front seat, Heinz stared ahead, as if by sheer concentration he might avert disaster. And it did seem, for the longest time, that he was succeeding. He even thought he glimpsed land up ahead.

But beneath the water lay dangers too great to wish away. The car passed safely between two telegraph poles. But trailing, unseen, beneath the surface were the wires that had once run between the poles. They snagged the bumper and then the tyres…

The car pulled up so sharply that Mycar flew over the seat-back and hit the dashboard, and Heinz was dumped into the footwell. A wave slopped in over the door. The car turned end-on-end to face upriver. Rushing water began to surge up over the bonnet. A floating bush scraped its way as far as the windscreen. Caught up in its branches was a dead swan, whose beaky head struck the glass and cracked it top-to-bottom.

"Out. Out *now*," said Heinz.

Mycar, though, was transfixed by the sight of the swan's head pressed up against the windscreen. It barked and barked. Drops of water welled through the crack in the glass like tears, then the whole screen split in two, and both bush and swan were in the car with them, and the car was filling up on all sides.

"*Out. Out now*," said Heinz and dragged himself over the door's rim as the Folly Tourer sank, hog-tied in telegraph wire. But in those brief seconds, a yellow blob the size of a bath sponge floated out of it and bobbed away. Heinz took it by the scruff of the neck and swam with it for the dry land.

CHAPTER NINE

Celebrity

FOREMOST MANSION, PRAESTO CITY

"I hate dogs," said Senator Kovet as he stood on the steps of Foremost Mansion, waiting for someone to open the door. He was looking at the sole of one shoe.

He held out a hand, and his assistant Myld was obliged to give him a fountain pen to scrape off the dog mess. "Sir has often remarked on it," he said as he took the pen back with two fingers.

"They serve no useful purpose, they are filthy and they eat too much."

"Quite, sir."

When the door opened, Daisy shouldered her way out to greet them and put white hairs down one flank of Senator Kovet's trousers. The Husband showed them through to the Audience Chamber to make their daily "Report on Behalf of the Senate".

Kovet sprawled extravagantly in his chair, looking

important and no-nonsense. Beside him sat "Milkweed" Myld (as Kovet thought of his assistant), making himself as invisible as a man can: knees tight together, elbows in, head lowered, cleaning his fountain pen on his handkerchief in readiness for taking notes. When the Suprema lit the spirit-lamp on her desk, it shone directly in Kovet's eyes through a hole in the shade, so that he could barely see her at all. It was almost as if she had done it deliberately to discomfort him.

Gloria had been practising doing Madame's voice half the night, but would have done better (she now realized) to have spent the time thinking up what to say to Kovet. "What's new?" she chirped.

Kovet smirked at her. "You will be gratified to know, ma'am, that our 'country cousins' have all been accounted for and rescued where necessary. All are safe and sound. Those trapped on their rooftops have been moved to high ground."

Myld scurried forward with a map and unrolled it in front of her. His voice was silky-milky and much friendlier than Kovet's. "These hills – here – and here – and here – are where camps and food stores are being constructed, ma'am, for those driven out of their homes. Hog Heights here. Breedon Hills here. The Round Mound here. The Ossian Hills. All well above water. The towns, of course, are mostly dry." Before Gloria was able to look for the camp nearest to her own home, Myld scampered back to the sofa, where he sat, stick-thin, like a praying mantis, clutching the rolled-up map.

Kovet relaxed and spread his arms along the back of the sofa: a man well pleased with the way things were going. "The local Army detachments will keep them supplied with food, water and…whatever, until the flood goes down."

"What about air drops by the Air Force?" said Timor, still holding the visitors' coats. "People will be needing tents… and warm clothing?"

Kovet looked round, as if surprised that The Husband was still in the room. "Exactly. Everything of that sort is in hand."

It came as wonderful news to Gloria. A rush of pure relief surged through her as she pictured her family sitting down to picnic on some grassy mountainside: a landscape dotted with alpine chalets and kindly soldiers bringing porridge in their helmets.

"Oh, that's so good! What, *nobody* drowned? Really?"

Kovet sat up a little straighter. "A few, possibly. Regrettably. Early days. Myld, do you have details of any deaths?"

"None at all, sir. Not since you took charge, sir. Some minor injuries but… No deaths as far as we know."

The light from her table lamp illuminated (for Gloria) her visitors' faces and the awkward figure of Timor beyond them, holding their wet coats. He was tilting his head, in exaggerated puzzlement. He mimed holding a telephone receiver to his ear.

"How *do* you know?" asked Madame Suprema. "I thought all the telegraph lines were down."

Kovet seemed startled. He made a great show, in fact, of being startled. "Well, we have our ways, naturally. We could not afford to be totally *cut off* by a little rain!" And he laughed, paused, then laughed again until he started coughing.

Myld passed him a handkerchief to stifle the coughs. "There is the Secure Line, obviously, Madame," he said. "In the offices of the Security Services."

"The Secure Line, yes!" said Kovet. "Couldn't think of the dashed name of it for a moment. The Secure Line. Used by the Security Services to keep in touch with the army bases in the north."

Gloria bounced up and down in her oversized chair. "So people will be able to telegraph these camp places! Talk to their family. That will be so cheering!"

"Of course not," snapped Kovet. "Now you are being ridi—"

Myld rocked forward hastily. No one who called the Suprema ridiculous could hope for a future in politics. "I regret, ma'am, the Security Services *never* allow ordinary civilians to use – or even know about – the Secure Line. I mean, not even Senator Kovet here has ever asked to use it. Imagine if it were kept busy all day and night by people… well, just *keeping in touch* with their families! It couldn't be used for its true purpose."

"But people want…" Gloria began, and was left looking for a word big enough to express everything she herself wanted, longed for. Her gloved fists banged gently on the edge of the Audience Desk.

"…*reassurance*," said The Husband from somewhere in the shadows. "People want reassurance. Names would be nice. Lists."

"Lists?"

"Lists. Of who's where," said Timor brightly. "Everyone accounted for."

There was a silence broken only by the wind howling in the chimney.

"The. Entire. Countryside. Population," said Kovet, setting each word down like a coin. "On. A. List." He laughed again. The glass of the unlit chandeliers overhead tinkled from the loudness of his laughing.

"Might I just say…" said his assistant shyly, hurriedly, "might I say how much you delighted the People at the closing of the South Gate, Madame Suprema? Your presence was a wonderful boost to morale! And your suggestion about greasing the hinge-pistons – well, it saved the day! Nothing less. Quite wonderful."

"Thank you!" If she had been standing, Gloria-the-maid would have bobbed a curtsey.

"I'm sure it would keep the People's spirits up if you appeared often like that – encouraged them in their daily work, you know? Work is a great distraction. It keeps us from brooding – don't you agree?"

Gloria did agree. Being a maid had never actually stopped her feeling homesick, but hard work had burned up the hours in a day and left her no time for brooding.

"Perhaps you would consider visiting each of the factories – you and Mr Timor and your beloved dog, of course. The workers would feel so…*appreciated.*"

Gloria pictured herself walking into Higgy's factory past the clicking gatekeeper, and the clicking gatekeeper not being allowed to stop her.

"My wife never—" began Timor, but he was too late.

"Of course, Mr Kovet. Love to," said Gloria. She could picture herself lifting her veil – only for a moment – and winking at Higgy, just to see his face. It was a happy thought.

But by the time Gloria stepped out of the limousine at Factory One (Spoons), she was rigid with terror, her veil tucked deep into the collar of her dress as she prayed that Higgy would be off work sick. Because he would surely recognize her! He would laugh and point and say, "Look who it isn't!" The gatekeeper would recognize her. Cook's daughter Lixi (who also worked at Factory One) would shriek, "She's not the Suprema! She works with my ma!" If Timor had not had her hand firmly clamped under his elbow, she would have turned and run back to the car.

Since she had last seen it, Factory One had sprouted roots – dozens of fat tubes rising out of the ground, that pulsed and throbbed, much as the arteries of her heart were doing. She had no time to see where the tubes led before she was indoors, having her hand kissed by the Managing Director of Spoons.

Stirring music was playing over the loudspeakers – patriotic songs and jolly brass-band marches. The same reporter from *The Voice* lifted his tweed hat to her and asked if he might take photographs.

"Oh, you found your other sock," she said, without thinking. "I am glad," and left him staring at his feet.

Entering the machine hall, she could feel herself shrinking – as spinach does in cooking – almost to nothing. The massive room made mere people look like chess pieces. The chess pieces all turned to look at her, women patting the hairnets covering their hair, men removing their caps. A ripple of excitement could be heard even over the roar of the machines.

Daisy recoiled, leaning back on her haunches, and her tail swung under her belly. If it had not been for Gloria's strong grip on the leash, nothing would have kept that dog from running back the way they had come. The smells were of oil and hot metal, and the noise was a spiked club hitting her skull.

A girl came up with a bunch of flowers, and curtseyed. Gloria smelled them and *mmm*ed, then thrust them at Daisy. The pollen ran riot through her nose and she sneezed and sneezed and sneezed – she had to spread her four legs just to keep her balance. Then the whole room seemed to be laughing, and the girl was reaching out a hand… Daisy rolled on her back and offered her belly for stroking, and the whole workforce gave a single, sighing "Aaaah!"

The floor throbbed and vibrated, but Daisy came, after a time, to associate it with being stroked and admired:

"*…such a lovely dog…*"

"*…such a beautiful creature…*"

"*…so fluffy!*"

She lay on her side, one paw stretching forward, tail gently swishing…

"*…who's a good girl, then…*"

"*…like a dandelion clock…*"

…and watched the world through half-closed eyes.

Plumes of spoons spurted from the mouths of monstrous metal machines and tinkled into troughs. Beneath her, the floor trembled to the snores of other monsters below ground. A young man holding a box flashed bright lights at Daisy's beloved Gloria, but it did not seem to hurt her. In fact, Gloria seemed happier with every passing minute.

They moved on to the polishing rooms:

"I heard it takes sixty rubs to get a shine on a teaspoon and a hundred rubs for a tablespoon," said Gloria. Over the months, she had heard everything Higgy knew about polishing spoons. The workers gasped with astonishment that the Head of State should know such things. Even the Supervisor seemed impressed.

Behind her veil, Gloria was smiling now. She was no longer spinach in the bottom of a pan. She was Madame Suprema, pleasing the crowds like a juggler on a tightrope with clown shoes and exploding trousers. Of course, their eyes were on the dog most of the time, but that was all the better. Even when a daringly cheeky woman asked if Madame wasn't "hot behind that veil", Gloria, flushed with confidence, replied, "Yes, but I *never* take it off, you know. Not since I passed fifty. Am I terribly vain? ...Can I see the new pumps?"

Suddenly, the management looked panicked, glanced at their watches and suggested it must be time for Madame to move on to another factory. Someone steered the photographer away in the direction of the entrance. But the workers were eager for the Suprema to see the basement, and Gloria was drunk on the smiles and applause and laughter. As she gave the flowers and Daisy to Timor to mind, he leaned forward and said something. But amid the din she caught only "*—ability*". It added to the delight singing in her chest to know he had noticed her ability to please. Clutching up her skirts, she descended into the gloom of the basement.

Even the chance of an encounter with Higgy could not scare her.

Until she saw him.

She barely recognized Higgy in his vest, dirty and sweat-soaked. He and dozens of other men and boys like him stood below a row of hinged wooden beams, hauling each one down as far as the water, then letting it rise up again to the ceiling. There was a slurping, sucking noise each time a beam came down and water was sucked into a hose and carried away. Then the beam rose up again with a thud that jerked Higgy's shoulders in their sockets. His hands were wrapped in rags and, standing under that jutting slat of wood, he looked like a boy waiting to be hanged. Despite the men's efforts, the water still seemed to swill thigh-deep through the basement. Gloria could not climb more than halfway down the ladder.

At the sight of her, Higgy's face brightened so much that her heart slammed and she thought: *Of course. Game over. He knows me.*

"Psst!" Higgy leaned sideways to speak to the man pumping alongside him. "I know the girl who works for her. I know her maid. We're good friends, me and her maid." He said it furtively, but loudly too, clearly hoping others would hear and envy him his link with fame.

And Gloria found herself wanting all over again to call, *Hey! Look! It's me, Higgy! Me – Gloria!*

Instead, she started back up the ladder, clutching her skirt in one fist. "Thank you, gentlemen, for all your hard work," she called back, remembering to get her vowel sounds just the same as Madame Suprema's.

In the entry hall, the Director of Spoons presented her with a gold-plated carving set – knife, fork and sharpener – in a velvet-lined box. He tucked a teaspoon inside as well, explaining that, although it did not really belong with a carving set, he was a Spoons man through and through, and hoped she would enjoy happy memories of her day at Spoons.

It was the most valuable thing she or anybody in her whole family history had ever owned. She only remembered in the nick of time not to say so.

In the car, Timor did not speak or even look at her. His cheekbones were mottled red and white and he kept his eyes fixed on the back of the chauffeur's neck. No – she understood: they must not talk about her triumph while the chauffeur was listening.

They visited Factory Two (Knives) and there, too, the music blared and the applause rattled, and she left to the sound of three hearty cheers. It was thrilling and baffling. How could they not guess she was a fifteen-year-old housemaid? She knew that the workers *thought* they were seeing the Supreme Head of all Afalia – and spent more time looking at the dog – and yet she wanted to believe it was *her* they liked, *her* they cheered, *her* they talked about afterwards, calling her a "nice woman", "so natural", "just like one of us almost".

Never since she had come to Praesto to work had she felt special or important. Even at home in Sawmills, no one had treated her like a queen or gazed at her, bright-eyed and delighted. So naturally she left behind her a dozen promises to visit again. Only that horrible flooded basement and the sight of Higgy at his pump could graze her shiny memories of a perfect day. That and Timor's total silence.

When they reached Foremost Mansion, she thanked Appis the chauffeur (so that he would like her, too) and prised Daisy off the floor of the car where she had fallen asleep, exhausted. As the front door shut behind her, she laughed out loud in sheer relief. "Did I do good, sir?" she asked and turned to look at Timor.

He had both arms clamped over his head and his knees bent, as if the ceiling was falling on him in large chunks. "What possessed me? What kind of bull have I loosed into a china shop? As I believe I told you earlier," he whispered through clenched teeth, "you, miss, are an *utter liability*."

But *The Voice* newspaper did not call her a liability when, next day, they spread her praises over five pages – one for each of her visits to the Five Factories. A caption to one of the photographs called Daisy "The Mascot of the Workers".

Timor threw it directly into the bin, unread. But Gloria retrieved it, smuggled it upstairs to her attic room and pushed it under the bed – just in case one day she might be able to show it to her family and say, *That's me there. It is. It was. Honestly.*

CHAPTER TEN

Rubbish Island

UPRIVER

Heinz was mistaken. It was not solid land he had spotted from the car – only a mat of litter tangled into a floating island – a raft of rubbish. Like him, the island had been born at Forest Bend. The giant trees that clutched it were oaks cut down to try and stop the river bursting its banks. The raft within the trees was made up of coffins. On its journey downstream, weed, rubbish and dead things had attached themselves.

The whole island revolved and buckled as it sailed downriver, but held together. Whenever some new casualty collided with it – a dead sheep, a cart, a table – that, too, became part of the fabric. And everything was welded together with rotting filth.

Birds perched on it, feeding on drowned animals. There were rats, too.

Heinz was a good ratter, but even he was fazed by the

number here. Flies hung over everything, outnumbering the birds a million-fold. Their maggots squirmed in every nook and cranny – they were the rice side-dish to every mouthful Heinz ate.

Cats, too, had found their way aboard – cats that had lost their fear of dogs, as Heinz discovered. They stood their ground. They hissed and arched their backs. Their claws were permanently out, so that their feet snagged wherever they prowled.

Those cats were vicious, but the rats were organized. They seemed, now and then, to knit their thoughts into one. They would turn, all at once, on a single target, hurling themselves at the enemy. Like black rocks they bombarded a vulture ten times their size, then tore it to shreds. They brought down a pouncing cat in mid-air. When they turned their attention to Heinz, he knew that courage was not enough to save him.

Crowding towards him, so tightly packed that they scrambled over each other's backs, the rats leaped at him three and four at a time. As he cowered down among vegetable peelings and broken glass, he could hear Mycar, king of the castle, still yelping – "*My muck! My muck!*"

The rats had Heinz surrounded, near the edge of the raft. One sank its teeth into his hip.

At that moment, a tree jutting up out of the water, once firmly rooted, lost its grip on the wet soil, and toppled. It struck one corner of Rubbish Island, launching a clutter of coffins into open water and scattering a mob of black rats. Myriad flies were whisked away by the swipe of twigs and leaves. The skeleton of a goat fell to pieces. The whole island wallowed.

Then the splash subsided and the uprooted tree joined itself to Rubbish Island, which floated on downstream.

Floating free in mid-river, in the bottom of one of the coffins, Heinz hunkered down, listening for the scrabble of rat claws. Fellow coffins banged and scraped against his, but there was another noise as well, closer, much closer. Something else had seized the chance to escape aboard Heinz's coffin.

"My box! My box!" said Mycar.

CHAPTER ELEVEN

Found Out

Gloria began to think she had been split down the middle with cheese-wire. In the mornings she continued to put on her maid's clothes and the cook's coat and walk Daisy. People in the street recognized the dog and stopped her to say how much they loved her – the dog, that is – and how much they admired "that Madame Suprema". Cyclists rode past and splashed Gloria's skirts and feet with water from the gutter. Shopkeepers and shoppers complained to her about the weather, the shortages, the way the Civil Guard helped themselves without paying.

Then she went home and put on the brocade or velvet or slippery satin, the hat and gloves and veil, and became Madame Suprema, who waved from a limousine to the same people in the street, and who had delicious food delivered to her house by a special van.

After one such morning dog-walk, Gloria left Daisy to dry

in the yard, took off her muddy shoes and, still in Cook's coat, ran upstairs to change into Madame Suprema. She was drying her hair with a towel when she remembered that Timor had still not had any breakfast and ran down to make toast. As she stood at the range, the kitchen door opened behind her.

There was a flustered apology, a timid, fearful whisper. "Didn't know. Beg pardon, ma'am. Just come back for me coat, begging your pardon, ma'am. I'm working in the factories now, and it gets proper cold, what with the damp."

Gloria turned towards Cook's familiar voice and smiled. "You're safe. It's only me."

But Cook's face tied itself into a reef knot as she looked Gloria up and down, up and down. "Ooo, you wicked little minx," she breathed. Gloria, too, looked down at herself. Paris fashion, Italian shoes, and tresses of wet hair staining the satin and velvet. "So, this is what you get up to when you get the house to yourself, is it? There's me sacked for no reason, and there's you dressing up in her clothes and preening yourself, who never had cause to. Wait till I tell her! You just wait! She'll skin you alive, you little madam!"

The toast began to char. It seemed that all Gloria's crimes had crashed together, struck a spark and set light to the air. The black smoke was from all her wicked lies going up in flames.

"No! You can't. I'm allowed. Really. Listen…" But Gloria pulled up short and took a breath.

Putting on someone else's clothes was bad behaviour. But impersonating the Suprema was probably high treason. She pictured firing squads and blindfolds for her and Timor…

"Let's go and find Madame," said Gloria. "She can tell you. She's just in the orchard with Boz. Your coat's in the hall cupboard. I'll get it for you."

Cook followed after her, of course, fingers pecking at an organza frill, a velvet bow, a strand of wet hair. "Same as stealing, that's what it is…"

Gloria opened the hall cupboard and stepped inside. "It's green, isn't it, your coat? I'm sure it's in here…" The cook bustled in behind her and pushed at the garments hanging there. The coat hangers shrieked along the rail.

And Gloria simply stepped outside and locked the door.

"I'm sorry. I'm SO sorry," she called in answer to the protests and the thumping.

Thinking time. All she needed was thinking time, and she would come up with a solution to Cook being held captive in a cupboard.

Timor came out of his office, still holding the newspaper he had been reading, and stared at the cupboard door. He looked almost as if he had been crying.

"Those weather people have been arrested," he said.

"Why? What did they do?"

He referred back to the paper. "'Conspiracy to mislead the Senate and endanger lives'."

"But they never… Did they?"

"Of course not. They told the truth. It was my wife who… Apparently, they lost their jobs a week ago. Now they've been arrested. All my fault."

"No, it isn't."

"I have to speak up for them!" But then his voice trailed off. "If there were an appeal, the court would want to call Madame – to give evidence."

"They wouldn't have much luck then, would they, sir?"

"And if it all came out…they could arraign her," said Timor.

Gloria had no idea what that meant. It sounded like being made to stand out in the rain, something Madame had done once to Gloria. "How could they? She isn't here!"

The look Timor shot her strongly suggested she keep quiet if she had nothing helpful to say. He nodded towards the rattling cupboard door. "What is that? Is it the dog?"

"Yes, sir," said Gloria. "Definitely."

"Let me out, you little madam!" said the dog-in-the-cupboard.

"You *have* to believe me, sir," Gloria insisted and looked him squarely in the eyes. "It's the dog."

Timor nodded and turned back towards his office. His thoughts seemed to be swimming upstream towards his wife, but against a current that was far too strong. She noticed how extraordinarily thin his wrists were and that his hands were shaking. When he dropped the newspaper and all the pages came apart, it seemed too hard a task to put them back together, and he left them lying on the floor.

CHAPTER TWELVE

Found and Lost

God, when she created dogs, gifted them different Virtues. Heinz had intelligence. Mycar had not been so lucky. It seemed to have been made so small that there was no room left in its tiny head for brains. It was not the dog's fault, but it made Mycar a bit of a trial to live with in an open coffin on a sickening swirl of river.

The river, for all its writhing, seemed strangely dead. There were no live ducks or swans or water rats ploughing their V-shaped tracks through it. For much of the time it felt as if Heinz and Mycar were the only living things left in the world. The half-dozen coffins that had escaped Rubbish Island gradually parted and were separated by the current. Some sank to the bottom with a belch of bubbles.

Breedon Hills came into sight to the south, the three mounds looking like monsters surfacing, brown and spotted.

The brown was grassy hillside churned to mud. The barnacles were people.

Dozens of gig boats had rescued hundreds of families from their rooftops and brought them here. None of the rescue boats were moored by the bank now. Their owners had set off downstream to look for somewhere better. Because anywhere was better than Breedon Hills.

On the hilltops, clumps of trees, like harpoons sunk in a whale's hump, offered firmer ground and shelter from the rain but not from the wind. Women and the elderly sat up there, holding children in their laps. Some were in their nightclothes. None had more than one bag of belongings. Down by the river, hundreds of men and boys ankle-deep in mud took it in turns to try and salvage things from the water – wood to burn or build into shelter, something dead that might make a meal. Anyone blessed with a length of string and a safety pin had turned it into a fishing line. They slithered and fell on their faces, lost their shoes in the mud, lost heart as, day after day, no one came to their rescue.

On the other side of the hills, a swamped landscape stretched away to the south. Some survivors had already set off that way, in search of food or help – without knowing where the water would be too deep, where wild animals would be lying in wait. Perhaps no such route to safety even existed. The people who opted to stay were pinning their hopes on being rescued. An end must surely come to this relentless misery. In the meantime, they were cold, wet and hungry.

So, when they saw the coffin coming downstream, they thought *firewood*. Whether or not there was a dead body inside it, they meant to have its timber. Men and boys crowded recklessly close to the water's edge, branches at the ready to hook it ashore.

"No lid," shouted one.

"Newish," shouted another.

"My babes could sleep in that!"

Heinz had been forced to lie down. He was too tired to resist the pitching motion that slid him and Mycar up and down the length of the coffin. But hearing voices, he jumped up, paws on the side and barking. *Clem? Clem?*

Clothed and masked in mud, the creatures on the bank were a terrifying sight to a small dog in a crate. They were wielding branches, slapping at his boat until it rocked even more wildly. Twigs broke off the branch tips into the coffin.

But on the slope behind them, another mud-boy came skidding down the hill on the sides of his feet – running and sliding, shouting and waving his arms. *"Heinz! Heinz!"*

Too far, too far out to reach, the coffin hit an eddy in the water and began to spin on the spot, round and round. Heinz circled in the opposite direction, trying to keep his eyes on the running figure.

Startled by the sudden appearance of the dog, the men laughed for the first time in a week. But their feet were on the brink of the flood. They dared not lean further out.

"I'll get him!" shouted Clem. "He's mine! He's my Heinz! It's Heinz!" And he ran straight through the slopping ripples and into deep water.

"Don't be a fool, boy!" shouted a man, but he stretched out his branch, all the same, for Clem to hold on to. Deeper and deeper Clem went, climbing out along the branch – "Don't let go! Please don't! It's Heinz!" – until his feet were off the mud and the cold was clutching him, body and soul. He reached out, touched wood, snatched for the rim. Heinz's head brushed his fingertips; a tongue licked a scab on the back of Clem's hand…

"Look out!"

A dead stag, heavy antlers holding its head underwater, crashed into the coffin, jolting it out of the eddy and sending Heinz sprawling. Clem let go of the branch and made a lunge for the coffin again and missed. He sank from sight. Underwater, the stag's antlers caught him and shovelled him back to the surface.

The men, confronted with the chance of venison for dinner and saving a boy from drowning, forgot firewood and lent all their efforts to dragging boy and stag ashore.

Heinz watched them do it, paws on the stern of his fragile little boat, one ear still pricked, the other already despairing. Within the length of a howl, he had both found and lost his beloved boy.

It was lucky for Mycar that it found nothing to say, or Heinz would have torn it into fish bait.

CHAPTER THIRTEEN

Problems, Problems

PRAESTO CITY

For about a year Gloria had been reading the cookbook to Daisy in the evenings (thinking that dogs probably preferred recipes to stories). Since Cook's sacking, this had come in useful, because it meant she knew how to prepare meals for Timor. Fortunately, there were fewer visitors: Timor had suggested only Mr Kovet came to Foremost Mansion to discuss affairs of State on behalf of the whole Senate. That way Gloria did not have to remember all their names.

That night Gloria, when she could finally hear Cook snoring, set a tray with napkin, finger bowl, sesame bites, a torch, a mug of tea and spicy Afalia rarebit on a gilt-edged plate, with apple crumble for afters. She fetched a chamber pot, too. Then she unlocked the hall cupboard, shuffled the chamber pot inside with her feet and set the tray down by Cook's head. On leaving, she banged the door loudly enough to be sure Cook woke and got her meal hot.

"I'm really, really sorry," she whispered through the door. "I didn't know what else to do." Cook was in no mood to forgive. She sat eating and complaining, slurping tea, making threats and calling Gloria names, saying how she must – absolutely *must* – get back to the factory… Gloria felt obliged to sit on a stool outside the door and listen, wincing. Fortunately, Daisy came and licked sweet, jammy apple off her fingers, which was a comfort. Fortunately, too, Cook bedded down early to sleep.

Not Gloria. All that night she lay awake, wondering what to do about Cook. At two o'clock she had decided to bribe the woman into silence with one of the ornaments on the mantelpiece. (Some of the picture frames were real gold.) No.

By three o'clock she was trying to work out ways of moving Cook to another room higher up the house, without her escaping. Impossible.

By four o'clock, thoughts of murdering Cook and burying her in the garden were flitting through her head like black bats. No!

By five, packing a bag and running away seemed much the most sensible thing.

So that is what she did. Stealing out of the house in her maid's clothes and own skimpy coat, Gloria walked downhill to Higgy's house, crying all the way because she would never see Daisy again; never sit by the kitchen range reading to her about hotpots and noodles; never brush her fur till the dog fell asleep standing up; never feel the roughness of her paw when they shook hands.

The streets were utterly empty. In the bus garage, all the buses were sitting down on their naked wheel-hubs – not a tyre in sight. *How would people get to work without the buses?* she wondered. And still she did not remember.

She sat on Higgy's doorstep, shivering, waiting for sun-up – not wanting to wake the family in the middle of the night: working people need their night's sleep. At least it wasn't raining. What would she tell Higgy to explain about running away? Would she spill her secret in his lap and beg him not to tell a soul? Or could she pretend that Madame Suprema had sacked her for doing something stupid. Yes! That was it. She would say she had scorched Madame's silk nightdress while ironing it, and had been banished.

There was no nightlight in any of the windows. Not one window in the whole street was lit. And still she did not remember.

She could hear the drumbeat of the pumps in the factories. Were people *still* standing under those wooden beams with water up to their knees, hauling and heaving? She dozed for a moment and dreamed of them all, a line of men and boys stretching out from here to ever, all pumping – and woke, hands clenched and with a pain between her shoulder blades.

Only then did she remember. Her weary brain finally

recalled the newspaper summoning everyone to report to the factories.

But surely that had only meant for them to work shifts? Not for daytime, night-time and seven days a week! Surely it didn't mean *everyone*? Mothers and fathers and children? Round the clock? Surely these friendly little houses on Mountview Street were not all empty now, the beds unslept in, the stoves all cold, their owners gone? It made her want to hammer on Higgy's door.

She was stopped by the soft sound of a rubber-tyred wagon toiling up the street, pulled by an elderly mare, hooves wrapped in cloths. The wagon was painted a sickly yellow. Down from the footboard jumped six Civil Guards, armed with metal rods. Gloria crept under a tin bath lying upside down in Higgy's yard. For the first time, she was glad she had not stolen Daisy and brought her along.

In twos, the Guards set about forcing open the front doors of houses. After a few minutes they re-emerged carrying furniture – tables, chairs, carpets. No lights came on. Yes, alright, there were power cuts happening all the time, but there was no sound of people protesting or clinging onto their possessions: no one was home. Within half an hour, the men were gone, bouncing back down the street on their soft, rubber tyres.

Gloria crept out from under the tin bath. She pushed open the splintered front door of Higgy's house, but there was no one in there – just a mess where moving the furniture had dragged carpets out of place and a toy box had been tipped over. Higgy's dad's rowing oar had gone from over the fireplace, and the sewing machine, too. She wanted to ask Higgy, was it true? Had the Five Factories swallowed up everyone in Praesto – even postmen and teachers and bakers and shopkeepers? But Higgy was not there to ask.

So she went back up the hill to Foremost Mansion, because she could not think what else to do. And at least Daisy was there, even if all the problems were as well.

But as the sun rose, it woke something in Gloria that was neither fright nor guiltiness. Who had given the order for everyone to go to the factories? Not her. How dare the Civil Guard ransack her friend's house, and what would the Suprema do about it if she were here? What would *Gloria* do about it if she went on being the Suprema?

"You know what, Mr Kovet?" said Gloria when the senator arrived to report on "The Situation" (as it had come to be known). "I'd like to know who decided for everyone to go to the factories and stay there?"

Kovet looked at his assistant, whose face expressed nothing. Kovet seemed more surprised than she had been expecting. "Well, *you* did, Madame." He snapped his fingers at Myld, who applied to his attaché case and produced a sheet of stiff white paper without crests or seals or any fancy decoration – except for the Suprema's seismic signature. He read from it.

"*In the event of a risk to the economic infrastructure of Praesto, the seamless continuity of future viability of production must be maintained at all costs.*"

It was a moment of scalding embarrassment. She felt her face burn red. "Right," she said. "Exactly." Tears were gathering behind her nose, aching, looking for some way out. "I did, I know. But I did not want to be hated for it – or you – or any of us to be hated. And that's why…everybody has to be happy about it. It has to be done right."

"I thought it all went very smoothly," said Kovet, glancing at his assistant in case Myld knew any differently.

"We could do better!" Gloria squeaked. "For instance, I think carpets would help. And some tables."

"I beg your pardon, Madame?"

"Knick-knacks, too. They'd make the machine rooms more homey. But carpets most of all, because they'd make sitting down warmer. Also mattresses and pillows for sleeping on."

Kovet looked at her in bewilderment. "You can't be asking the Treasury to *furnish* five factories with beds and tables! It would cost a—"

"Oh no! It wouldn't cost one afal!" Gloria broke in. "Just

tell the Civil Guard to take everything they've nicked from the houses, and deliver it to the factories. Every last thing. Then I won't have to shoot them… What's your opinion on the matter?" Her audience were too startled to respond. "We could just shoot them, I suppose. It is shooting for looting, isn't it? *SHOOTING FOR LOOTING!* What a good slogan! Put up *lots* of notices in the barracks. *SHOOTING FOR LOOTING!*"

Kovet breathed in his own spit and started to cough. "You surely trust your own Civil Guard, Madame!"

"Oh, of course I do, Senator, and it's a crying shame people hate them as much as they do. But this way everybody can stop worrying about thieves and robbers dressed in yellow uniforms breaking into their houses."

"Remarkable!" gasped Assistant Myld, round-eyed with admiration as he handed Kovet a handkerchief to stifle his coughing.

Gloria's plan was taking shape even as she spoke. "Of course, the factories won't have room for absolutely *everything*, so you can tell the Guards to take the rest back to *exactly where it came from*. Then I can send a nice letter to them from me saying how glad I was to see them taking the trouble to *fetch people's things to them*. And in the middle of the night, too, when they could have been warm and dry in the barracks! So kind of them! Something like that. I think they'll get the point," said Gloria and lined up the pens on her desk in a neat row.

After opening the door for his senator, Myld pattered back across the hall, put his head back inside the audience room and surprised the Suprema as she was trying to juggle pencils.

"May I ask, Madame, how you know that the Civil Guard have been looting?"

Gloria went to tap the side of her nose, but the veil reminded her not to. "I have my spies," she said, and Myld giggled loudly and clapped his hands.

"What the hell was all that about?" said Timor as the front door closed behind the Senator for Home Affairs. He had been eavesdropping, naturally.

"The Civil Guard are breaking into houses and stealing things. I don't think they should be allowed, that's all."

"How d'you know that?"

Gloria considered telling him about running away – about the snails on the inside of the tin bath she had hidden under, about the rags muffling the horse's hooves... Then she said, "I found your binoculars in the hall cupboard. I could see them from my window. Anyway, it's really and truly true."

He looked at her sideways, as if unsure whether to fire her. At last he said, "I don't believe the word 'nicked' ever passed my wife's lips... But it was a good ploy. Please, do warn me the next time you think one up. My nerves can't take many more surprises."

Gloria promised. She was just glad she hadn't had to admit to running away. Looking back, running away suddenly seemed craven – childish, even.

IN ATRAMENTO NON EST VERITAS

CIVIL GUARD MAKE FACTORY A "HOME-FROM-HOME"

The Civil Guard were yesterday praised for making our Factory Heroes a little more comfortable by fetching furniture, bedding and ornaments to the workplace. The strain of work eased a little as the Civil Guard fetched treasured items to those who are currently working to save the Great Five Factories.

In their free time, the Guards travelled to and fro to homes all over the city, fetching rugs, bedding, knick-knacks and pictures. "I call it my cure for homesickness," said one Sgt Morbek, as he returned a teapot to Miss Shival of Forge Avenue.

We salute their kindness.

COMPETITION TIME!

The Voice is offering this splendid pocket watch to the lucky winner of our monthly Workplace Hero Award. Supervisors will decide the cheeriest, most hard-working man or woman of the last month.

The winner will be chosen at random next Tuesday.

RUMOURS OF ROSE CITY CULT

Rumours have reached us of a "cultish frenzy" in Rose City, where inhabitants have turned to pagan witchcraft. The Cult leader claims to have "fetched down" the rain in vengeance for the city's loss of water when Big Rock Dam was built one hundred years ago. And how did he do this? By sacrificing day-old babies and "the dry-skinned" (old people). After the flood, Afalian law will fall heavy on such horrific crimes, but in the meantime we can only hope and pray the rumours are untrue.

TODAY'S ANAGRAM: CUR YELLED AFAR

CHAPTER FOURTEEN

Rescue Mission

PRAESTO CITY

For a day, Cook yelled at Gloria. For a day, Cook would not speak to her at all. On the third day, Cook heard a man's footsteps pass by, and begged a favour.

"The woman in the hall cupboard wants a treacle bun for her tea," said Timor. "May she have one?" He was standing in the kitchen doorway, one sleeve rolled up, one flopping, his napkin still tucked in his belt from lunch, and his feet bare. He had not shaved, and looked too crumpled to get his thoughts straight.

"Open the door, then lock me in," said Gloria. "I'll talk to her."

"I hope you haven't 'set her by' for us to eat when the food runs out?"

"No, sir. And she thinks the Suprema is still somewhere about."

"Good. Well, mollify her, will you? Or we're up Furca Creek without a paddle."

"Yes, sir… But please, sir – you won't forget to let me out again, will you?"

Cook had emptied the umbrellas out of their barrel and turned it upside down to be a seat. She perched on it now with the tea tray on her lap. Gloria sat cross-legged in the only remaining space, pressed up against Cook's knees.

"That rarebit you done me – my daughter puts a dollop of chutney on hers." Cook put the treacle bun in the pocket of her dress. "That's for her." Tears streamed effortlessly down the creases between her nose and the corners of her mouth. "Be rock-hard by whenever I see her again, but it's better than nothing. She loves a treacle bun. Can't hardly bear to think of her waiting back at the factory, not knowing why her ma's not come back. She'll think the dogs've got me, see?"

"What dogs?"

"It gets so cold at night in the factories! Cold and damp. There's only the floor for sleeping. I needed my coat for Lixi, and maybe a mat to lie on?"

"So people really can't leave the factories at *all*. Not even if they need to, and ask nicely?"

"There's hardly a soul left outside – 'cept for the Civil Guards, curse 'em. And the rich, of course. Businessmen.

Senator toffs. There's people in them factories now as haven't never been inside one in their life – couldn't work the machines if they was paid (which we're not). There's all this water coming up from the ground and running down off the hills – the pumps gotta be kept pumping day and night. And they say it's easier to feed people at work. I know we got to pull together for the good of the country 'n' all," said Cook, "but when there's children mixed up in it, it's hard... It's the wet I worry about. Going to her chest. Lixi's delicate."

The Wet, yes, thought Gloria, and pictured, for a terrible fleeting moment, the circular walls of Praesto City full to the brim with water. What good would spoons be to anybody then?

"Oh, we's not making *spoons* no more," said Cook. "Just pumping. And making pumps. If we don't, the water might come right up and wreck the machines... You gotta let me go, Gloria. If it was just me, I'd stay here happy as a hippo – what with the food and real tea – but I gotta get back to Lixi. I only snuck out to fetch some warm clothes...and maybe a mat or two and a bun."

"You make it sound like prison!" said Gloria. "They have to let you out – you haven't done anything wrong!"

"Oh, they's just keeping us safe, kinda thing. Security said it weren't safe for me to leave – on account of the dogs – but I said I'd bring 'em a bottle of whisky if they let me out for an hour. Madame wouldn't grudge me a bottle of whisky, would she? Where is she? I han't heard her coming and going. But I gotta get back. Lixi will be frantic, thinking the dogs've got me!"

"What dogs?"

"If that woman had a heart inside her – rabies or no rabies – I'd ask her on bended knee: get my Lixi outta that pond of a place…let us have a job here, her and me. We wouldn't want paying – we don't get paid a thing at the factory – they say we're doing it for the Common Good. Me and her could sleep in here."

"But it's like a coffin!" said Gloria unthinkingly, appalled all over again at shutting Cook in.

"Call this a coffin? You should see Spoons. May be big and roomy, but so's the North Pole. *She* should do a visit – like last month. Madame should see the state of it now."

Gloria nodded and stood up, taking off her apron. "I think I should," she murmured, and her vowel sounds had already begun to change shape in her mouth, like sucked toffees.

"We were not expecting the honour, Madame…"

The Owner of Factory One (Spoons) was at a meeting over at Factory Three (Forks). So were the Manager and Deputy Manager. So it fell to the Shop Floor Supervisor to welcome Madame Suprema. He did so with blushes and apologies and the expression of a hunted rabbit. He snatched off his spectacles as if it would make him more presentable.

"I said I'd visit again," said Gloria. "And here I am!"

The smell of metal and oil had been replaced with a stink of damp and mould. She must find Higgy! She had to find Higgy!

By cutting through the polishing room and walking really, really fast, Gloria was able to keep ahead of the Supervisor – even Daisy had to break into a run. She headed directly for the hatch leading down to the basement where she had seen Higgy. The noise of pumps seemed to be pounding *inside* her head. The jolly marching music playing on loudspeakers only added to the unbearable din. From the polishing room came the new noise of sawing.

"We've gone over to making pumps…as you'll know, I suppose, ma'am," panted the Supervisor, struggling to keep up. "Beam-pumps and hoses. Just temporarily. Till things are back to normal."

The hatch leading to the basement was shut, but rattling in its frame, as if prisoners were trying to break out from below.

"Please would you…" She stopped herself. "I shall visit the men down there now," she said, pointing at the hatch.

The hatch lifted a little of its own accord, then thumped shut. Water spurted out from under it. It was afloat. "Oh holy… *Have they all drowned?*"

The Supervisor was so startled by her shriek that he dropped his spectacles. "No, no! No, ma'am. The water level…well it kept on rising, didn't it? We had to fetch the pumps up from the basement. To ground level, yes?"

And so they had. The machine rooms were a-clatter with pumps pumping and pipes sucking the water away. They took up most of the space between the vast, silent, useless cutlery machines.

Men, women and boys were now heaving on the hinged beams. An open door to a side room revealed a nightmare tangle of snaky rubber coils, knotting and twisting. In amid them were girls with cloths covering their faces. The air was acrid and full of smuts. For a moment, Gloria thought she was fainting, because her sight was blobby with black shapes. But the air was simply snowing smuts of rubber.

"Hoses," said the Supervisor, hastily shutting the door. "I am proud to say we have met our quota most days. Last week we made more hoses than either the Knives factory or the Forks.

Of course! The tables being taken away in the night. The buses with no tyres on their wheels. Gloria suddenly understood. The factories needed all the rubber and wood they could get – rubber for hoses that would carry the floodwater as far as the city walls, and wood for making into pumps. Pumps and hoses! Had she accused innocent Civil Guards quite wrongly then?

To her relief, Gloria could also see cushions and pillows, clocks and knick-knacks, toys and musical instruments – all horribly in the way, but definitely "homey". When she stopped to admire a painting of a horse balanced against the wall, the owner whispered to her: "Them Civil Guard swine went on a looting spree. But afterward, someone musta had a word – twisted their arm. Had to give it all back – the lot! They had this off my parlour wall – but I got it back, look!" Gloria's answer was a shocked gasp...but she felt a lot better for knowing she had been right about the Guards.

Daisy unclamped her tail from between her legs and broke away from Gloria's side. She had scented a friend among the pump-men. It was Higgy. She drew Gloria's attention by barking loudly.

Without Daisy, Gloria would never have recognized her friend. His round, plump face had sagged into dents and dips like a punctured football, and his hair was three shades darker. His belt was buckled as tight as it would go, and still the waistband of his trousers sat on his hip bones within a breath of falling down. Daisy, when she laid her paws on his chest, almost pushed him over.

He let go of his beam and hugged the dog like a lifelong friend. He and Gloria looked at one another, he at a densely black veil, she at a friend.

In that moment, Gloria knew the she *must* take him home with her. She could not leave him here. She would make him her Private Secretary! Yes! Why not? The factory could spare one boy from among the hundreds it had put to work on the pumps. Anyway, they would not dare to refuse a request from the almighty Suprema!

"She's a lovely dog, ma'am," said Higgy. "You keep her safe indoors, or those others'll take her apart. Soft as butter, Daisy is."

His boy's voice had broken! Gloria wanted to laugh and say, *Who's the grown-up man, then!* "Soft as butter, yes."

"We're good mates, aren't we, Daze? Your maid Gloria, ma'am – she and I, we know each other." And his bloodshot eyes shone brighter with pride.

You don't know her at all, Gloria said, but not out loud. What she did say was: "Take the day off. Everybody! Please tell everybody they can take the day off, Mr Supervisor! It's a holiday!"

As in a draughty hall a rug lifts and ripples along its entire length, the news rippled through the factory. *Clack clack clack...* The pumps fell silent one by one. The words multiplied a thousand-fold, louder and louder, to clamber over the raucous music. Hammering and sawing stopped. Gloria waited for the cheering to begin.

But none came. Little by little, the noise started up again: the pumps, the sawing, the hammering and welding.

The Supervisor coughed anxiously. "That's a kind thought, ma'am. But folk would be scared to leave the factory. What with the dogs."

"*What* dogs?"

"The rabid dogs, ma'am. The ones with rabies. On the loose. Roaming about. Killing things." He looked down at his broken spectacles. The tone of his voice was less respectful now. It hinted: *Everyone knows about the dogs.*

"Course none of them's *our* dogs, ma'am," said the woman bringing her a cup of tea in a silver-rimmed teacup. "Ours have all gone to the Welcome Centre. Cats. Dogs. Rabbits. We had to bring them here with us, then the Civil Guard came and took them there – somewhere near the zoo."

A teenage girl, thin as a tangle of hair, came clambering out of the hose-room. She was wearing a summer dress that had once been pale blue and was utterly unsuited to the cold. "*I'll* take the day off!" she said. "She offered, and I want to!" Her face dared anyone to forbid it.

"Are you mad, girl? What about the dogs?" said Higgy. "Don't you read the papers? You couldn't pay me to leave here."

"Don't care," the girl said. "There's things I got to do!"

The Supervisor flapped his hands at her and looked around for somebody from Security.

"Actually, that reminds me…" said Gloria. "I need a maid to help with some of the many things I have to do. This girl will do, Mr Supervisor. I'm sure you can spare her. Come along, you – and bring Daisy."

With the same speed as she had come, Madame Suprema

left Factory One (Spoons), followed by Daisy dragging a wisp of a girl along by the lead.

All the way home in the car, Gloria peered into the shop doorways, down alleyways and into gardens, trying to spot rabid dogs. She must read the newspaper every day in future.

Then it occurred to her that she had not glimpsed a newspaper in days. Perhaps they were only being delivered to the factories these days. Of course! The delivery boy would have been sent to work there!

"Appis, please may I ask you to fetch me a copy of *The Voice* every morning?"

"Very good, Madame," said the chauffeur.

"Appis, have you ever seen these rabid dogs people are talking about?"

"Oh yes, ma'am. Plenty of 'em."

And to think she had sat all night on a doorstep while savage dog packs roamed the streets, foaming at the mouth, lurking in the parks, killing things! It made her sweat with horror. Her heart would not stop thudding.

"I can't work for you today, lady," said the stick-insect huddled in the corner of the back seat. Her obstinate sulk suggested fourteen. Her jaw jutted in readiness to defy even the Suprema. "I have to find my ma."

"No, you don't," said Gloria.

"I really do."

"You really don't, Lixi. I already did."

CHAPTER FIFTEEN

Feral

UPRIVER

The coffin was filling up. Heinz was belly-deep in water, holding Mycar in his mouth, when the box ran ashore and snagged under a tangle of tree roots. It took the two dogs a deal of scrabbling to climb up between the roots onto the bank.

Now he was ashore, Heinz's instinct was to turn back the way they had come, towards that brown hill and Clem. But just as the river had decided where to let them ashore, the lie of the land dictated where they could go. They were in pathless, foresty wetlands. This was lizard land, wolf and boar country, snake and fire-ant territory. No matter which way Heinz turned his nose, his hackles rose.

The peacock, though, was a happy surprise.

It must have strayed from some villa garden or zoo and been chased by the flood into this wetland wilderness, like a jewel washed into a drain. Right now, it was dragging its finery through a nettle patch. Mycar threw itself at the bird, biting into the back of its head. But the peacock ran and kept on running, with Mycar on its back. Heinz followed behind, pouncing on the tail. It was not until they entered a clearing that the peacock came to a halt. And neither of them had halted it.

The pack of dogs confronting them was twelve strong. Every one of them showed bared teeth, flattened ears and ferocious snarls. Wild dogs – feral dogs – thinking as one – or rather they had given up thinking altogether and simply obeyed the pack leader.

They tore the peacock into an explosion of colour. Mycar was knocked aside. Heinz sat down at a distance, stock-still, tail between his legs. The rat-bite in his hip opened up again and wept warm blood. He did not roll on his back submissively – there was too much bloodlust in the air. He simply held back. *Yours, all yours,* said his polite posture. *I am not hungry.*

The peacock did not make much of a meal – all feathers and little meat – but afterwards the pack behaved like conquering heroes, tails straight up, heads cocked like pistols. Mycar, who had not been allowed one bite, still joined in the victory parade. Strutting in front was the pack leader, of course: No-Name. With no fur covering his smooth, grey, rippling skin, he looked like a newborn monster. Since his eyes were much the same grey as his body, he had the stare of a ghost.

"Feral," said No-Name. It was a challenge.

"Is that right?" said Heinz. They took the measure of each other. There was more of No-Name to measure than there was of Heinz. A lot more. From his stub tail to his scissor-bite, he was the size of a calf.

"Free dogs," said No-Name. "Chains gone."

Heinz idly scratched an ear.

"Top pack. Toppest," said No-Name.

Heinz stretched luxuriously.

No-Name threw him against a tree stump and stood on his ribcage. His scissor-bite rested on the mongrel's throat. "Join us?"

The teeth were pressing so heavily on his throat that Heinz could not make a sound. Saliva was drizzling through his neck fur and it was not his own saliva.

Mycar trotted up to Heinz's tail-end and sniffed. "Wejoin," it yipped. "Wejoin."

No-Name's pack had little to say for itself. The leader spoke for them, while they got by on snarling. Heinz was not that breed of dog. He could not abandon thinking. He could not forget Clem. He was a family dog, and these hooligans were not his family.

Even so, the feral life had its appeal. The blood of his ancient ancestors began to sing in Heinz's veins. Dogs running as a pack are brothers and sisters, comrades and allies. Besides, the food was good…

…And the hunting was joyous – the chorus of baying, the chase through flickering light-and-shadow, racing each other, as well as the prey. They pursued their meals through briars, brambles, nettles and shallow water before peeling off to left and right and surrounding it. Then No-Name would pounce and after that, the rest would pile in for the kill. The taste drowned out even the thunder overhead.

On a diet of raw meat, Heinz soon felt better, fitter, less sick with worry and weariness. He would find Clem. All in good time. Meanwhile, the flooded wetlands were a playground where a dog could thrive.

CHAPTER SIXTEEN
Judgement Day

PRAESTO CITY

Released from imprisonment in the hall cupboard, Cook did not seem to bear a grudge. After all, Gloria had brought home Lixi. She was positively impressed that there was more to Gloria than the chance of a supper tray in the hall cupboard.

But with Cook to prepare breakfast and Lixi to serve it, Gloria did not know quite what to do with herself at breakfast time. She was hovering in the corridor between kitchen and morning room, wanting to get some bread and jam, when she heard herself being discussed in whispers.

"Where's the *Real* One? Did they do her in, d'you think? Bury her in the garden?" said Lixi.

"Gloria got you out of Spoons, Lixi. The Real One wouldn't have rescued no one."

"But now *she* knows that *we* know she's play-acting the Suprema! So she'll maybe want to kill us both! To keep us quiet – keep her secret a secret."

"Daft duck. She could've poisoned my supper and left me in the cupboard, couldn't she? But, no, she let me out – says I needn't go back to the factories. And she did like I asked and got you out, and here we are, safe and sound. That bedroom she's put you in, that's the same four-poster they put the Samian ambassador in when he came for the Jubilee!"

"They're just buying our silence," growled Lixi.

"They don't have to buy mine, darling. They can have it for free. Look, I don't care if The Husband chopped up the real Madame Suprema and ate her on toast. She was prune juice, that woman. Sacked me for no reason, and no back wages. If she'd kept me on, we need never have gone in the factories. *This* one brought you home to a warm bed. Now stop fussing and eat your bun."

Gloria crept away from the kitchen, knocked at the morning-room door and let herself in. She sat down at the table, but said nothing, not knowing where to start.

"We have staff again, I see," said Timor without looking at her. "That's pleasant for us." Somehow each night's sleep made him look more tired and angry. Dark rings bruised his eye sockets and he seemed to have given up on cufflinks and clean shirts.

"Yes, sir. Lixi is Cook's daughter. I brought her home from Factory One."

"Like a souvenir?"

"Like a scarecrow. They've not got much food there.

And it's cold. I thought Lixi could be the maid!"

"The *second* maid, you mean."

Once again, the little green shoot of pride growing up through Gloria's chest shrivelled and died. She might be Madame Suprema in the factories and Audience Chamber, but Timor would always know she was just a maid wearing his wife's veil, shoes and gloves.

"And should we make Cook and Lixi *au fait* with our situation?" asked Timor.

"Pardon, sir? I don't under—"

"Do we tell them what's going on?"

Gloria winced, unwilling to annoy him even more. "They seem to already know, sir." The expression on his face made her hurry on. "But they're alright about it! Honestly! As long as we didn't murder Madame, which we didn't."

Timor threw his butter knife at the fireplace. It cracked one of the ornamental tiles. Then he sank his face into his hands and said nothing at all for what seemed like four days.

Someone had to speak. "Everyone's pets have been put in the Welcome Centre while their owners are in the factories. Can I go to visit them today? The pets, I mean, not the factories. Cheer them up. If you think it would, I mean – cheer them up." She waited another fortnight or two. Where was the Book of Manners that told you what to do if a grown man attacked the fireplace then wept his heart out right there in front of you? Desperate not to say the wrong thing, she fell back on Timor's own advice. "What is *your* opinion on the matter, sir?"

Timor rested his hands on his knees and leaned forward across the corner of the table until his nose was almost up against hers. "I have no opinions."

She was genuinely startled. "Really? What none at all?"

This in turn startled some of the black fog out of Timor. He got up and went to stare at an oil painting of Foremost Mansion hanging over the sideboard. "You see this place? It used to have mice. When we moved in, they were everywhere. The lofts were riddled with them. It's an old building and the last Supremo was very live-and-let-live about mice. But mice were not to Madame's liking. She strongly disapproved of mice. Within a week they were all gone. Similarly, I used to have opinions. I was riddled with them. They were not to Madame's liking. They were exterminated."

From behind the mantel clock he pulled the creased and six-times folded letter which the meteorologists had delivered into his wife's hands. Unfolded it. Read it. Put it in his breast pocket. "Go and visit the dogs, Gloria. Just don't *adopt* anything or anyone today. Understood? Take the limousine. I don't want Appis driving me to the courthouse. It's better if I walk. On no account tell him where I've gone. What have I just told you?"

"No bringing anyone home. Don't tell Appis you've gone to the courthouse."

Gloria glanced at the newspaper on the breakfast table and suddenly understood why Timor was off to the courthouse. The headline trumpeted:

TRIAL OF WEATHER PEOPLE BEGINS TODAY

Gloria had no sooner pressed the electric bell that summoned Appis than he arrived outside in the car. It was uncanny. Everybody usually has to finish what they are doing before they get up and do something else, but not Appis. One ring and he was there at the door, his car purring beyond the gates.

"I would like to go to the Welcome Centre for Pets, please," said Gloria, climbing in.

There was an awkward pause. "And that is where, ma'am?"

"Somewhere near the zoo. If you drive around, we're bound to hear barking."

"I have very little fuel, ma'am."

Gloria sat tight. She had absolutely promised Daisy they would visit the dogs.

"You have a new maid, ma'am," Appis said, adjusting his cap in the vanity mirror. "She answered the door."

"Yes. Her name's Lixi."

"Has she been vetted?"

"Vetted?" Gloria pictured dogs getting checked over for

fleas and hard-pad. "I don't think so."

"All staff must be vetted. For your own safety, ma'am. They could be anarchists. Spies. Trouble-makers."

"I know that." Gloria knew she must not show her ignorance by asking questions. Unfortunately, ignorance is like a petticoat that slips down little by little in public places. She could feel it slipping now. "Have *you* been vetted, Appis?"

The chauffeur looked at her in the rear-view mirror. "I am Secret Service, ma'am. It goes without saying."

"Oh! Are you? ...I mean, I know that, but I forgot. Sorry. To Timmy and me you are just Appis." A geyser of nervous giggles tightened round her windpipe. She found herself wanting to wind down the window and sing:

If you're Appis and you know it, clap your hands.

If you're Appis and you know it...

Mustn't! When did Madame ever get the giggles? Never, never, never. Gloria reached a finger inside her veil and bit down hard on it. "The Centre for Pets, if you please."

"With all due respect, ma'am, I think that would be most unwise."

Quite suddenly, Gloria had had enough of being in the wrong. The giggles gave way to a small, angry buzzing inside her, as though she had swallowed a wasp. "Are you calling me unwise, Appis. Like *stupid*, Appis?" And, at last, her pronunciation was perfect: razor-wire in a party frock.

Appis drove her around for an hour. Even with the windows wound down, they heard no roaring, trumpeting or birdsong as they passed the zoo. Finally, the chauffeur said, "I do apologize, ma'am. I simply cannot find the place." And he set off for home without waiting for her to agree.

Daisy kept nudging Gloria's hand – *nudge, nudge, nudge,* – wanting to be stroked. Something else was nudging at Gloria's conscience: what was happening at the courthouse? Even now, Timor was probably showing the letter the meteorologists had delivered. The whole silly mistake would be put right. Wouldn't it? No one would go to gaol.

Nudge, nudge, nudge.

But what if they were proved innocent? Who would the court blame instead?

As Appis drove past the Inns of Court and University of Law, the car came to a halt with the pretty ticking noise of a fuel pump that has run out of fuel. Gloria had the feeling it was the first thing all morning that had genuinely happened by accident.

While Appis went in search of petrol, she and the dog got smartly out of the car and disappeared. Suddenly there were far more important things than zoos and other people's pets.

The courthouse was only just around the corner. The ceiling of its entrance hall rested on fluted pillars at the height of low cloud. It was painted with pictures of foreign gods and goddesses wearing too few clothes for the weather. Gloria sat down on a bench, checked that no one was looking, took off her hat, let down her hair, put her coat on inside out. *Nudge, nudge, nudge* – Daisy was hungry and Gloria had no treats to give her.

What if "Madame Suprema" was called to give evidence, and Gloria had to pretend?

"Were you or were you not wearing the wrong spectacles on that day?"

"Of course not. I was lying," Gloria would have to say (because people who give evidence in court have to tell the truth or they burst into flames and die. Higgy had told her that). *"I wanted the gates to stay open so I could catch the last train out."*

"But I put it to you, Madame, that you did NOT catch that last train" (the judge would say) *"because here you still are in your silly hat and frilly frock and nasty chicken-claw gloves."*

And then the really true truth would come out.

And Timor would be arrested for pretending his maid was the Suprema. And as for the wretched, traitorous maid herself...

While Timor pulled the sky down round their ears, Gloria had chosen to go and pat some dogs.

"I put it to you, wretched, wicked maid," (the judge would

say) *"that you have pretended to be the Ruler of All Afalia, which everyone knows is high treason."*

"HEY, YOU!" The angry shout echoed hugely in the cavernous hall.

Her first instinct was to raise her hands in surrender. Instead, she sat on her hat and gloves to hide them. "You can't bring that animal in here!" raged the usher, pointing at Daisy with a clipboard. "Out with it! This is a court of law!"

She fled, head down, feigning a sort of reeling, rolling limp so that no one would mistake her for the Suprema. Daisy followed on in her lollopy lope. But footsteps came after them – faster and faster, to catch them up. A hand gripped Gloria's upper arm.

"Does Appis know you're here?" said Timor in her ear.

Gloria's heart was so far into her throat that she could only shake her head.

Timor had dressed smartly for his visit to court, but still looked so hunted and guilty that it just made the nice coat and shoes look stolen. Even his hair was sweating.

"What happened? Did you explain about Madame's spectacles?" she asked.

But Timor had had no chance to explain anything: to show the letter, to excuse his wife's lies, or to save the innocent meteorologists. Apparently, *The Voice* newspaper had made a rare error.

"The trial happened *yesterday*."

Apparently, the prisoners had not even been brought to court. They had sent in a plea of guilty from their prison cells. No one had given evidence on their behalf. They had been condemned, in their absence, to fifteen years' hard labour.

"Did you ask to visit them?"

"I was told that was impossible."

"Why would they plead gui—" Gloria was talking to empty air. Timor had set off to walk.

They climbed home in total silence, Gloria trying to restore her disguise, and running to keep up. Gradually their footsteps fell into time with the dull thudding noise of the factory pumps. Praesto City's heartbeat was getting louder every day.

In the afternoon, Gloria changed into her maid's uniform and cleaned the mansion from top to bottom. Cook left a supper tray outside Timor's office door, but it was still there at bedtime, untouched until Daisy accidentally ate it.

Fifteen years? That was the entire time Gloria had been alive. As she lay in bed, she thought through all the things she had been, seen, done during fifteen years of life. How could she possibly sleep? The weather people would not be sleeping. She tried to imagine their future filled up with Nothings, day after day. No family. No home. No dogs. No weather. Why would anyone plead guilty to something they didn't do...?

There was no sleep on either side of her pillow – not in her whole little bed. She changed ends, but it did not help. Fifteen years! The best thing to do would be to sleep every minute away, but the prison warders and their "hard labour" would make sure the weather people never slept…any more than Gloria could sleep now.

Madame's hat and clothes hung from the hook behind the door, sulky and silent.

"*You* could do something, if you just wanted to, prune-juice woman," Gloria told the figure dangling behind the door.

There was lamplight creeping under the office door. The hall clock said 4.15.

"It's alright! I know what to do!" she called, hammering on the door. "I can make it right!"

No one was allowed in Timor's office. Ever. Not maids. No one. When he opened the door, the mess inside proved no maid had ever sneaked in to tidy. She had not realized (until she went looking for him in the master bedroom) that Timor actually *slept* in his office, on a spartan little bed, below a window with bars on it. Right now, the bars seemed particularly grim.

Timor leaned against the doorpost. "Stop. Will you just stop?" His face was creased, like bad ironing. He was still fully dressed, so his clothes were creased, too. "You may stop pretending. I should never have asked you to do it… Listen. This is how it goes… Are you listening? Yesterday, Madame Suprema threw herself off the city walls, saddened beyond bearing by the sufferings of Praesto City and her part in them. Her lie about the letter was simply 'a silly attempt to keep everyone hopeful and happy'."

"Threw herself…?" Gloria had watched the floodwater boil dizzyingly past the city walls. The same dizziness overtook her now. She could perfectly well picture Madame, in her turquoise-and-green silk dress, plunging like a kingfisher into the river. "No."

"Go to bed, Gloria."

"You mustn't lie – not about something like that. And you don't have to. I can beg their pardon!"

"What?"

"Well, I don't know quite how you say it, but it's got a 'pardon' in it. I'm the Suprema. If I say I forgive them, people absolutely have to let prisoners go, whatever they've done. Don't they?"

Across the hallway, in the kitchen, Daisy woke up and began noisily pushing her enamel bowl around the floor, thinking it was morning. Even so, above the noise, Gloria could clearly hear thoughts *tick-tick-tick*ing through Timor's head like the fuel pump in a motor car. She willed him to understand.

"Grant them a State Pardon, you mean?"

"That's the one! I knew it had a 'pardon' in it! That way, you don't have to say she lied. Just that I forgive them…I mean *Madame* forgives them. And grants them a pardon. Yes?"

She did not think she had ever seen Timor smile before – not *really* smile. It was like when the tilting windows on the top floor swung open and caught the sun. He ran down to the cellar and fetched back a bottle of champagne, which he opened with gallantry and flair and a torrent of pale foaming gold.

"I don't drink alcohol, sir."

"Neither do I. But just look how happy those bubbles are! A moment ago, they were trapped in blackness and now they've been let loose! Wake Cook and tell her to cook something. Two somethings. And find some slippers, girl. Your feet must be frozen."

The champagne was soaking darkly into the carpet. Gloria felt it with her toes.

"How were the dogs in the Welcome Centre, by the way?" asked Timor.

"What dogs?" she said. "There's no dogs."

The Voice

IN ATRAMENTO NON EST VERITAS

METEOROLOGISTS GET 15 YEARS FOR WEATHER LIES

Sinister forces may have been behind the weather forecast delivered to the Senate some weeks ago. Intelligence Services have discovered that the two highly regarded meteorologists were "bribed to lie" in the hope of the city gates being left open and the Five Factories destroyed.

Today, both the Professor-in-Chief of the Society of Meteorology and the Head of Forecasting from the Institute of Weather Sciences were condemned to 15 years' hard labour for conspiring with Enemies of the State.

Those same enemies are thought to have escaped aboard the last train out of Praesto. The finger of doubt must surely point at Rose City, that uncivilized and grubby community which has long defied Law, Order and the Rule of the Senate.

Did this woman lie?

COUNTRY COUSINS KEEP FEET DRY!

Afalians driven from their homes by flooding anywhere between the mountains and the sea will be given temporary shelter in prefabricated sheds in Breedon Hills and six other sites high enough to promise safety from the swollen river. Rescue Services said: "Where necessary, there was an orderly evacuation of villages, hamlets, farmsteads and plantations. There was no panic. Neighbours have been helping each other in the true Afalian way!"

The situation is being monitored by planes of the Afalian Air Force.

Senator Kovet is doing his best for you!

TODAY'S ANAGRAM: NUTTY BROODS

CHAPTER SEVENTEEN

Biter Bit

UPRIVER, IN THE WEST BANK WETLANDS

With every triumph, No-Name tightened his control over the pack. It was he who chose what to hunt, who made the kill, who ate first. It was he who decided:

now we attack,

now we move on,

now we sleep.

The bitches loved and feared him equally. The males simply feared him...but revelled in the victories. The swamped west bank of the river stretched for a hundred lambits to the south, but in his own mind, No-Name already owned it all. The rest accepted that he had the power of life and death over the entire wet world.

In one valley, the floodwater reached the eaves of the empty cottages: the dogs had to swim from roof to roof. Further on, the water shallowed again, and the trees and pathways were no more than muddy. Hundreds of eels wriggled to and fro, unable to find the ponds they had returned to every year since birth. No-Name ate the eels to pass the time, though the rest of the dogs did not. Wriggling things. Too snaky.

When a full-sized hawser snake came out of the river, there was good reason to be scared. It wrote a whole alphabet of coils and kinks on the bank. While the rest of his troops scattered, No-Name simply stiffened. He ordered the pack to surround the snake, but they hung back – which so enraged No-Name that he raced among them, teeth bared to the very top of his gums. Foolish little Mycar strayed into his path and was kicked like a ball in the direction of the snake.

Heinz only ran to get Mycar back – it was more of a "fetch" reflex than a rescue mission. But No-Name, in his frenzy, took it into his head that Heinz was intending to claim the kill. Hurling himself at Heinz, he missed his mark, and found himself wound round and round with yellow coils. Snake-scales scraping over that hairless grey skin made a strange sound.

The snake sank its fangs into the top of the dog's head.

Heinz, being so close, bit into the snake. Scales came away in his mouth, and the creature's flailing lifted him clear off the ground, but Heinz hung on. Mycar nip-nip-nipped away at the monstrous reptile which – to everyone's surprise – suddenly died.

The pack dined on snake but, as the excitement of the kill drained out of them, noticed how bad it tasted and wandered away. No-Name ate nothing at all. The snake's venom was only poisonous enough to kill rats and water voles; still, it made the big dog shake and stagger and vomit. None of his army came to lick his head wound or lie down beside him. They dared not. No-Name had clothed himself in bristling menace.

Anyway, it was Heinz and Mycar who had killed the snake. It was their "dog day".

A knobbly range of hills poked up out of the flood, like dreams rising out of deep, dark sleep. On one small hill stood a barn cut off from its farmhouse. And in the barn was a single piebald plough-horse. She might easily have swum to join her fellow farm animals, but for being hitched with rope to the wall of the barn. She had eaten everything within reach – straw, hay and half a sack – then gone hungry. The pile of manure behind her was proof of her long wait. Finally, she had lain down to chew on her rope tether and starve. Misleadingly, the white markings round her mouth were in the shape of a smile and made her look clown-cheerful.

The dogs formed a half circle in the doorway of the barn. The horse lurched to her feet in terror.

To No-Name, she was simply meat. Tethered with a rope,

she would make easy pickings. Ironically, it was the rope that was his undoing.

The tail-end of the halter hung from the corner of the horse's mouth, with a big knot at its end. It reminded Heinz of his favourite toy and his beloved boy. Clem loved horses. On their walks together, he had always stopped to talk to the plough-horse on the potato farm.

So Heinz placed himself in front of the mare. Part of him wanted to kill and eat just as much as the rabble in the doorway. Still, somehow pity had reached painfully into his chest and skewed his emotions. He felt obliged to protect the mare.

Mycar, cocky, boastful (and stupid), sat down beside Heinz. "Mydog," he said.

That confused the pack. They hesitated.

Through a haze of headache, No-Name saw rebellion stirring. His eyes went blank, his thoughts turned to boiling pitch, and foam frothed between his jaws. He knew nothing, except that he needed to kill something.

Heinz was no fighting dog. He did not stand a chance against the crazed hound. He fled behind the pile of dung, thinking to draw No-Name away from the horse. Faint hope. One huge leap carried the beast half the length of the barn. The impetus carried him further than he meant, skidding on wet slime into the muck pile.

A hundred thousand glittering green flies rose up in a crackling cloud. Mouthfuls, eyefuls, earfuls of buzzing flies.

No-Name's next breath inhaled a hundred, blocking his nostrils. The next breath filled his gullet with a hundred more. His paws sank into the soft brown muck as he clambered upwards and shook himself, head to tail, gulping for air but finding only flies and more flies. The horse, eyes rolling, ears flat with terror, defended herself the only way she could. Her head went down, her rump went up, and she kicked out backwards.

No-Name landed on his back, eyes wide, stone dead, his head so close to his rival that Heinz could see the pink insides of his grey ears. The flies spread out through the barn in a spangling green haze.

The terrified horse wrenched loose the bracket that had fixed her halter to the wall, but her escape was barred by the dogs in the doorway. She moved to the back of the barn, trembling violently.

The pack of feral dogs turned towards every point of the compass. They were silent. The great, grey hound had threaded them together. Now the string had broken. No-Name was gone.

Heinz picked up the knotted rope – always his favourite toy. It comforted him instantly. The fact that there was a horse attached to one end was not enough to make him let go. He and Horse and Mycar walked out of the barn into bright sunlight. The pack pelted him with questions as he went by.

"So now are you, maybe…?"

"Now the boss has gone…"

"Is it you…?"

"…in charge?"

"Or one of us?"

Heinz kept walking. Three or four of the bitches started after him, but the heels of the mare were still too frightening, and they turned back.

The mare did not look round. It is said that horses don't believe that the world behind them even exists. But perhaps they just know when to be done with it. Who can tell with horses?

CHAPTER EIGHTEEN

Pardon?

PRAESTO CITY

"I'd like to—" said Gloria.

"I *wish* to."

"I wish to give a pardon—"

"Grant."

"I wish to grant a pardon to the weather people."

"Meteorologists."

"Metrologists."

"Mete-O-rol-ogists."

"Mete-O-lorogists."

"Alright. Weather people," Timor conceded.

Since the early hours, Gloria had been practising how to give a direct order to Kovet – also how to sign Madame's name for when she had to do it in front of him.

"Keep practising," said Timor.

Gloria had big, open, childish, readable handwriting. Madame Suprema had a signature like a seismograph when there's an earthquake – a sudden violent squiggle spiking in the middle. It was not just a matter of getting the shape right (Timor said) but of pouncing on the page and stabbing the thing to death. "Make the S sharper. More irritable."

"How do I make an S irritable, sir?"

"I don't know. You'd have to ask my wife. Just do it."

Gloria cheered herself up by thinking about the weather people. She imagined them clutching their prison bars and sobbing as they struggled to glimpse a little patch of sky. The door would open and the guard would say, *You are free to go. The Suprema has fixed it.* How happy they would be!

"Why didn't they ever just say, 'The Suprema didn't read out what we wrote'?"

"I'm sure they did, but no one believed them. Who would doubt the word of the Suprema, after all?"

"It's awful not to be believed," said Gloria decidedly. "It's like when the chandeliers were being cleaned and the candles went missing, and I said Boz ate them, and Madame didn't believe me and said I stole them and stopped my wages for a month."

"And did Boz eat the candles?"

"Of course! He'd eat anything. Shoes. His bed. Daisy's dinner…"

"Yes," said Timor thoughtfully. "He was a horrible dog."

The bell rang, out by the gates – gates that had been locked shut to keep out dangerous dogs. It was the newspaper boy.

147

They heard Lixi yelp as she fetched the paper indoors and read the headline.

DOGS DESTROYED
TO SAVE LIVES
RABIES OUTBREAK "CALLED FOR
INSTANT ACTION" SAYS DOG CENTRE

An outbreak of rabies among dogs at the Pet Welcome Centre made it necessary last night to...

Gloria sat on the sofa in the Audience Chamber with Daisy on top of her. She was comforting the dog after gently breaking the news to her that all her fellow dogs had been put down. Daisy sprawled there, in cheerful ignorance, and licked the ink off Gloria's fingers. Gloria would not let herself think about the massacre – mad dogs foaming at the mouth, men with guns... Who could imagine a city without dogs? It would be as if every child with red hair or all the blossom trees had suddenly disappeared. She tried to think of the Civil Guard as heroes, like it said in the paper, but it was hard.

"I suppose *that's* why Appis pretended he couldn't get me to the Welcome Centre. He probably knew all the dogs had rabies. Him being Secret Service. 'Unwise' he said, but really he meant it was too dangerous and horrible." Then she hugged the dog again – "At least I've still got you, Daze!" – and gave herself over to crying.

Timor looked at his watch. "Kovet will be here at any moment, *Madame*."

"Madame was gravely upset about the dogs business," said Timor, to excuse his wife's absence from her desk. "She is collecting herself."

Kovet and his assistant sat on the sofa. In the gloom of the Audience Chamber, Kovet had not realized the cushions were snowy with dog hair when he sat down, but was gradually finding out. "It was necessary for public safety," he said tersely.

"But very sad," murmured Myld and smiled wanly at Timor.

Screwed up in the wastepaper basket were eight pages of notepaper covered in signatures like seismic explosions. Timor could not get them out of his mind. "What's the latest news on the weather?" he asked.

Kovet did not bother to disguise his impatience. "Oh, God knows. Fire and pestilence, for all I know. Do you own a clothes brush?"

At long last "the Suprema" entered, wraithlike, and sat down at her desk. She was virtually invisible, having put on black mourning clothes in honour of the dogs. "People must be very upset," she said. "Is there anything I can do?"

"Not at all," said Kovet briskly. "They understand the need. Who wants to die of rabies?"

"It was very sudden, ma'am," whispered Myld, looping his hands around his knees. "One moment the dogs were cheerful, the next they were tearing each other to pieces. The symptoms are very terrible." He sounded on the brink of tears.

Kovet recoiled as the glowing white shape of the dog emerged from under the desk and headed his way. "There *is* something you can do!" he exclaimed, suddenly brightening. "You can set the people an example!"

"What of?"

"Of courage, ma'am! Of solidarity. Of bravery in the face of sadness! The Senate thinks you should give up your own animal." And overcoming his disgust, he snatched hold of the dog's collar and hung on. Lixi had just entered. "Fetch me a dog lead, girl," Kovet told her.

"*NO! Don't, Lixi! You can't! You mustn't! Don't!*" shouted the Suprema, her fancy vowels bursting like soap bubbles. She moved to rescue Daisy.

Timor intercepted her at the corner of the desk – "Now, now, my dear" – and he crammed her head against his chest, whispering words of comfort so tender that no one else could hear: "*Pull yourself together. Do you want to get us both hanged?*" His grip on her arm left bruises.

Lixi brought the spare lead, and Kovet made to leave with his prize.

Timor called: "Before you go, Mr Kovet, there are matters on this morning's agenda more important than dogs. This is, after all, a Morning Briefing and no affairs of State have been discussed."

"What?" snapped Kovet. "Yes, but *you* should not be here when we discuss them, sir. Kindly remember you are just The Husband."

"I am currently Madame's Private Secretary, in the absence of the last one."

Hair was tumbling out of the back of Gloria's hat where Timor had bent it out of shape. He tried surreptitiously to push it back without disturbing the veil. "Pardon, my dear?" he said, as if Madame had spoken. "*Pardon?*"

Madame Suprema became still and took a deep, shuddering breath. "Yes." She stepped back behind her desk. "Yes. I wish to grant a pardon to the two meteorologists, Mr Kovet. Timmy has typed the words, but I think you have to see me sign it, don't you?" Then her pen nib pounced on the white space at the bottom of the page and stabbed it to death.

Kovet and his assistant looked at each other, more puzzled than astonished. "I'm afraid…" said Kovet, but he clearly had no idea how to go on.

Myld collected the document and took it over to his

senator. They exchanged whispers, their mouths hidden behind its white parchment.

"I'm afraid," said Kovet, "that the two people you mention attempted to escape from prison this morning. They were shot dead." And he gave Madame a look of genuine bewilderment. "I thought that you…" Then he broke off, at a loss for words.

"…that you would have been informed straight away," said Myld, finishing the sentence.

Kovet left, hauling an unwilling Daisy behind him. Timor immediately locked the chamber door to prevent Gloria going after them. Even then, with his hand over her mouth, she kicked at the door panels.

"My dog! My Daisy!" she whimpered, as the front door shut and Timor took his hand away.

"Not yours, in actual fact."

"You let them take Daisy! You just let them! I hate you. I wish I'd never…"

"And I wish I had never asked a fifteen-year-old girl to impersonate my wife. But there you go. Right now, the meteorologists aren't too happy with the situation either. Damn you, Mogda!"

A head-and-shoulders sculpture watched them smugly from the sideboard. Timor punched it so hard that he left a hole where the rosebud lips had been.

"Sixteen," said Gloria. "Actually, I'm sixteen now. Today's my birthday."

The doorbell rang. They heard Lixi answer it and give another of her gasps. There was a knock on the chamber door. "Please, ma'am. Mr Whatsisface – the skinny one – he's back."

Myld stood on the doorstep, elbows drawn close to his sides, ankles tight together. And there beside him was Daisy – beaming, tongue lolling, shedding fluff like a dandelion clock and panting as if she was laughing.

"Oh!" said Madame Suprema. "Oh!"

"I reminded Mr Kovet that Daisy is the 'Mascot of the Workers'," said Myld. "I suggested the People might not like to think of her being thrown off the city walls." He handed over the lead with two fingers and, as he did so, winked at her conspiratorially and gave her the sweetest of smiles.

CHAPTER NINETEEN

Help

The horse made a pleasant companion – she and Heinz rubbed along well enough. But she moved slowly, or stood still to graze, whereas Heinz dashed about chasing smells. Mycar, meanwhile, would wander off in search of things to own. When it found one, it sat on it defiantly, despite the fact that nobody else *wanted* the rotten sack, the broken wheel, the fallen mistletoe.

Often, it rained. Sometimes the clouds dropped sleet. But sometimes the sun shone, even warmly enough to raise steam, and the wetland vegetation looked like spinach stewing in a pan. All the scents were stronger then.

More and more often now, the scent of People hung snagged on the boughs, the bushes, the flattened reeds. The wetlands were not a People kind of place, but large groups had plainly passed this way, all heading in the same direction. Sometimes deep water might drive them off course, but before long the scent trail always turned south again, always south. Heinz listened for the noise of tramping feet, but the roar of the river muffled all other sounds.

At night, he lay beside Horse, chewing on the knotted end of her halter, until he fell into a slurry of troubled dreams. But his nose never stopped sorting through the smells around him, searching, all the time searching, for the one that mattered: the one that said,

"Clem".

Heinz urged Horse to move faster; the smells were stronger now and he was sure there were people close by – just a little way ahead – just half an hour's run. But Horse was so much bulkier than a dog, and needed wider gaps to clamber through. She made hard work of steep slopes.

Strange spires of rock stuck up out of the drowned forest. Heinz climbed one of them for a clearer grasp of his position. Even from halfway up, he was rewarded with a spectacular view. The river had expanded into a sea so wide that he could not even see as far as the other bank. Yellow plaits of water showed where the current was strongest.

There were threads of smoke, too, rising up from the landscape – campfires? So they were close! People truly were close by! Heinz determined to catch up with them before dark.

Out on the river, a fishing boat was being swept downstream. The currents had tight hold of it and had long since bitten off the rudder. There were people in it, too – Heinz could just see their backs where they were crouching in the bilges.

Then suddenly – hail. The hailstones were small at first – grapeshot that felled whole flocks of birds. Then they were bigger – white explosions that wounded any living thing out in the open. Out on the river, the boat was suddenly laden with a cargo of hail, heavy as coal. Lower and lower it sank, taking in water over the sides before it disappeared under the weight of ice.

Heinz and the plants around him were quickly scoured off the spire of rock, and tumbled to the ground. Grazed and winded, he lay yelping with pain as the hail hammered bruises into him. Finally, he wormed his way into a groove under the rock and watched the hailstones pile up outside, walling him into his hidey-hole.

As quickly as it had begun, the hailstorm stopped. With panicky paws, Heinz scrabbled his way out of his prison. The frozen wall gave way to reveal Mycar licking the scattered hailstones.

But Horse had taken off in terror, looking in every direction for relief from the pain. Her panic took her towards the river; it was easy to follow her trail – easier still when she started shrieking.

Horse had ploughed into deep mud up to her knees and was sinking deeper with every frantic effort to break free. Heinz circled the mire, looking for a way to help without becoming trapped himself. The sight of him calmed Horse a little – he had rescued her once and might again – but her trust in him only made things worse: now Heinz would have to achieve the impossible. The rope from her halter lay lightly on the surface of the mud. It had not sunk in. The knotted rope tempted Heinz out onto the soft mud to retrieve it. The great ragged river sent waves slopping ashore, making the mud even softer. But one washed the rope-end closer. Heinz darted forward and grabbed it. Then he was heaving on the halter, in the desperate hope of dragging Horse to safety. She put down her head, stretched her neck towards him – and the halter slipped clean over her ears and off. Heinz somersaulted backwards onto dry ground.

He had to fetch help! And his view from the rocky spire had told him help was at hand. He set off to run in the direction of those plumes of smoke. With his travelling companions no longer holding him back, he sped through brush, briar – any gap wider than his shoulders. Out of the corners of his eyes, he saw drowned badgers, vultures eating carrion, squirrels, porcupines and the red filigree of the blood vessels in his own eyeballs. Smells of the wetlands streamed through his nose and out of his tail: he was full of them. When his breath ran out, he was still left with the smells rampaging through his bloodstream. He was running to find Clem. (Horse was almost forgotten.) Clem would be there! Clem would make everything come right...

Light was fading. Evening was dropping through the tree branches like leaf-fall. He could hear voices, smell a camp fire, rabbit cooking, human sweat and damp clothes... Clem would be here. In fact, that boy there, his back turned to Heinz and his face towards the fire: that might be him! It must be him! Heinz chose to see nothing else. The stench of sadness and fright was all around. But he could give comfort! He was a dog-of-many-Virtues! Bounding over to the boy, he jumped up and rested his front paws on the bent back. His friendly bark of welcome came out oddly fierce: *You left me. You went without me...*

It was not Clem.

The boy gave a roar of panic and jumped up. A girl nearby screamed.

"*Ferals!*" shouted someone. "*Ferals!*"

A man snatched a burning branch out of the fire; another grabbed a garden hoe.

But one had a gun.

The boy was in the way; the light was poor; the rifle

wavered in hands trembling with weariness and fright. The travellers drew together, mothers gathering children into their arms. The shot went wide. Another bullet dropped into the gun's chamber.

Heinz scooted in a circle and fled for the trees. Giant nettles splashed into his face and left their scalding hairs in his nose. Another shot, and still Heinz was running. He thought the bonfire itself must have pursued him into the forest, with all its heat and sparks…except that everywhere was suddenly very, very dark.

CHAPTER TWENTY

Whispers

Gloria was determined to comfort the people whose dogs had been slaughtered because of the rabies.

Strangely, Timor did not object when she said she was going to visit the factories again. "Don't make waves," was all he said. "I mean it. For everyone's sake, don't make waves."

She had expected Timor to take the news of the weather people's deaths very badly. The news of their arrest had left him limp and helpless. But the news of their deaths seemed to have stiffened him – literally made him rigid. Like an unreliable ironing board, he might just collapse and slam shut on you. Even so, it would take a real struggle to put this new Timor back in the ironing cupboard if he didn't want to go – there was just too much steel in him.

Appis arrived driving a horse and cart – to conserve fuel, or so he said. Perhaps he hoped the Suprema would scorn to ride in it and decide not to go to the factories after all.

That way he would not need to act as her bodyguard – a difficult job now that places were so overcrowded and full of discontent. He could not have been more wrong – horse and cart were all Gloria had known before she came to Praesto… And Gloria was fairly full of discontent herself.

But Kovet had been right about the dead dogs. When Gloria and Daisy got to Factory One (Spoons), there was no great weeping and wailing for the lost pets. The workers had worse things to worry about.

In the yards all around the factory, tendrils of rubber piping now curled and coiled like the forest around Sleeping Beauty's palace. There were chains with padlocks on the factory doors. No one was allowed to leave "for their own safety". The dogs at the Welcome Centre might have been put down, but, of course, the rabid strays were still on the prowl in the city.

It said so in the newspaper.

The noise of pumping was louder still, because so many more pumps had been built. Though the water outside the city walls had risen five fathoms, the water under the factories was no deeper than before, so the pumps were doing their job. Or rather the people working the pumps were doing theirs. Night and day.

The air inside was so damp that it condensed into water droplets on walls, machinery and faces. It was much colder indoors than outside. Coughing added to the symphony of noises – baby coughs and child-sized hacking, women's tinny coughs and men's barks, deep as elkhounds. The workers' clothes were all torn under the armpits, from heaving on the pump-handles. Thanks to Gloria, layers and layers of carpets had been fetched in by the Civil Guard, and the children sat on carpet-islands (though these, too, were damp). There was no more running about; it seemed all the children's energy was used up on coughing.

Gloria arrived during a change of shift. Exhausted pumpers were replaced by others and freed to sit down. Men wearing dirty butchers' aprons brought in bowls of stew.

"Meat! There's meat today!" exclaimed a woman. "Don't know how they got hold of it, but by heck it's welcome! Look, ma'am, meat! A banquet!"

Astonishingly, Daisy did not even try to shove her nose into anybody's bowl or wag her tail in their faces while they were eating. She simply stared at them with big, brown, sad eyes, then rested her head on Gloria's shoes and flumped down.

But as the news of the visit spread around the factory, other people came hurrying in from other rooms. They crowded around the Suprema in such cheerful numbers that *somehow* Factory Supervisors, Management – even Madame's chauffeur – were jostled aside, parted further and further from Madame and her dog. It seemed the workers could not wait to stroke and admire Daisy. Then, all mixed up with the coughing, faint whisperings began.

"Get the children away, ma'am!"

"Please, Madame!"

"…even if we can't leave…why not the children?"

"…place isn't healthy…"

"My boy's chest is that bad."

"…hear that coughing?"

"…get them out of here? Somewhere out of the damp?"

"Somewhere warm?"

"…home…"

"…sleeping at home in their own beds."

"…home…"

As Supervisors elbowed their way through, the tide of people drew back, afraid of getting into trouble. Their eyes lingered on the Suprema, pleading with her not to betray them.

Gloria looked around for her friend Higgy. But perhaps he was in another machine-room. That chap there might *just* be Higgy's father – same eyebrows, same chin, same flowerpot body and string-thin legs. But it could not be Higgy. For surely, this was an old man: wrinkled grey face, thinning hair, slumped asleep against the damp wall, with a bowl of stew half-eaten in his lap. His calloused hands lay open on the floor beside him, like two dead crabs. Daisy assured her this was indeed Higgy.

When the Clerk of Works asked for her autograph, she tore another page out of his notebook and wrote a separate note, which she folded up small and pushed into Higgy's curled fingers. He was so deep asleep that he did not even stir. The note said:

The maid Gloria sends her love. x x x

"You shouldn't be here, Hig," said Gloria under her breath. "No one should."

Outside, the chauffeur Appis asked if she *insisted* on visiting the rest of the factories. He strongly advised against it. She wanted to go, just to spite him…then thought of Timor's "*Don't make waves*" and let Appis take her home.

Oh, but she would make waves soon enough. She meant to kick up an absolute storm. She had made herself a solemn vow to get the children out of the factories if it was the last thing she did. Better still, she would get *everyone* out – close the factories down and, if need be, let the machines drown.

Daisy, peering between the planks of the cart at the road bowling by, simply wondered why the factory people (generally so kind and loving) should have taken to eating dogs. One smell of their food bowls had told her of butchery on a vast scale.

CHAPTER TWENTY-ONE

Banquet

PRAESTO CITY

When Timor looked at the diary and informed her of the Annual State Banquet, Gloria foresaw a huge problem.

"How do I eat?" she wailed.

"With a knife and fork, I imagine, and acceptable table manners."

"But I'd have to lift my veil to find my mouth!"

Timor could not say how his wife had overcome this snag: the Suprema had never taken him with her to banquets. "I shall say you have a sore throat. That way you need neither raise your veil nor make the traditional speech. Or eat."

"But I *want* to speak!" she protested. "I want to tell them to close down the factories and let everybody go home!"

Timor closed his eyes – whether out of impatience or sorrow, she could not tell – and said, "That might surprise them, seeing as keeping-the-factories-open-at-all-costs was the Suprema's idea. Remember?"

Gloria was only briefly deterred. "I might have changed my mind! I might have seen the error of my ways!"

He narrowed his eyes at her.

She corrected herself. "I'm sorry: *the Suprema* might have seen the error of her ways and felt sorry about all the hardship."

"And sheep might roar and lions bleat. You're meant to be impersonating her, not improving on the original."

The tears that had been aching behind Gloria's eyes wilfully spilled out and betrayed her as a young girl out of her depth in a deep, dark world. "*Why* can they not go home, sir? They're not making anything! They're just pumping and pumping. *Why* do they have to be there? It's like a punishment, but they haven't done anything wrong! I don't understand!"

Timor did not shout. He sat her down and absent-mindedly poured her a brandy, as he would have done for his wife. To be polite, Gloria took a swig. It exploded inside her head like shrapnel. Timor sat down opposite her.

"The whole economy of Praesto – well, Afalia really – depends on the factories. We keep the world supplied with cutlery. Take the factories away and what would we have? A bit of agriculture. A lot of forestry. Shipping – though what would we ship if it wasn't cutlery? Praesto City is very rich – the rest of Afalia not so much, but the city is. If you ever find yourself running a country, Gloria, don't let it depend on just one industry to bring in the money, because if you lose that, what are you going to fall back on?"

"I'll remember, sir," said Gloria obediently (though running a country was not high on her list of ambitions).

"And don't build your core industry in the most low-lying part of the city, which is liable to flood."

"I'll remember that too, sir."

"And don't depend on commodities like strip-steel and nickel that you have to fetch in from another country."

"Right."

"And don't make it something that causes large numbers of people to spend tedious lives in horrible conditions making something that, fundamentally, the world could do without."

Gloria recoiled from the anger in his voice. "Actually, sir..."

"*Actually?*"

"I was just going to say that actually, I don't think your opinions were extermerated like the mice. You still have lots."

Timor shut his eyes and breathed deeply until he had reefed in his temper. Then he went back to explaining the need for pumping:

"The Great Five Factories pay for everything we need here in Praesto. So we need them to outlive the flood, d'you see? So the machines have to be kept dry, so that they'll still be in good shape after the flood goes down, yes? The owners would have needed an ocean of fuel to power the pumps with generators… So, when they ran out, they needed man-power to pump out the water, day and night."

"Still…I don't think it's worth it, not with all the coughing and blisters and damp…" said Gloria obstinately.

"*You* may not. But you are not my wife. *You* may well have different ideas. So might I. But don't let's get our opinions out in public or we might both end up on the gallows… Now go and decide what you're going to wear to this damned banquet, will you?"

Gloria went obediently to the door – even as far as the foot of the stairs. A smell was coming from the kitchen, of garlic and rosemary, and of chocolate cake baking. She turned back, stood in front of the State Office door for a whole minute, then opened it just a little way and talked very quickly through the crack. "The pumping people work harder than we do. It uses up more energy, pumping, doesn't it? So they need more food. And we don't need as much. So people who aren't pumping ought to send some of their food to the factories."

He snatched open the door and Gloria leaped backwards. "There are 60,000 souls in Praesto City, girl. Probably 59,000 of them are in the factories right now. It would take a miracle for the few to feed the many." He gave a grunt of frustration and ran both hands through his hair. "Look…I'll do a deal with you if you'll just go and get changed."

And they settled for sending a note to each and every Senator, every Senior Officer in the Armed Forces and Person of Influence, asking them to send half of their food rations to their nearest factory.

"*We* will…but *they* won't, will they?" said Gloria sadly.

"Hope springs eternal, girl. Now do me a favour. At this banquet tonight, listen with your ears and do nothing with your mouth. Understand?"

In the event, eating in a veil was not a problem at all. For nothing could have induced Gloria to eat the food she was served.

It had intrigued the guests – bankers, factory owners, builders and lawyers – to discover what the chef would serve up for dinner, given the food shortages. When the Senator for Food and Farming invited the guests to turn over their menu cards, there were cheers, hearty laughs – even a round of applause.

Menu

To start
*Breast of penguin thinly sliced
with remoulade of chickpeas.*

Entrée
A choice of:

*Fillet of giraffe
on a bed of braised bamboo
or
Carbonnade of lion
with sunflower seeds and
pulpe de poisson d'or**

Sweet
*Blackberry ice-cream made from
the milk of tigers
golden carp

Down in the basement of the Banqueting Hall, the carcases of sixty more zoo animals were hanging in the dark while their meat matured. The guests were invited to view them, but few accepted – they preferred their food neat and tidy and on the plate.

Gloria would have preferred it still to be walking about in the zoo, and wept silently behind her veil. She wanted Timor to find out who had authorized the killing of the animals, but dared not ask him. When they summoned the chef from the kitchen for the Suprema to thank him in person, Gloria inclined her head politely and refrained from hurling dinner knives at him.

The guests all knew each other, but they did not know Timor. Madame had always come alone before. They seemed wary of him. Timor explained, politely, that he was acting as his wife's Private Secretary. Laying a firm hand on Gloria's shoulder, he explained that Madame was suffering from a sore throat, and found eating and speaking painful, so would not be making a speech. When people started to talk business, he made notes, as any Private Secretary would. But the Senator for Security snatched the notebook away, wagging a finger in his face and tut-tutting. "A pleasant evening between friends. No interest to anyone outside this room."

The guests drank huge quantities of wine. Some became happier, some sadder, some noisier, some angrier. Their respectable good manners and polite conversation gave way to shouting, asking questions, but never listening to the answers.

"My workers aren't happy," said the Manager of Factory Two (Knives). "The dog meat is helping to keep them fed, but still, it's all I can do to keep control."

"Surely, keeping control is your job," said the Senator for Trade and Industry. "If you cannot do it, you must be replaced."

"Oh, I'll manage, sir!" said the Manager hastily. "Of course I'll manage. I was just..."

Squabbles erupted. Fists thumped the table, whose white cloth was, by now, splattered blood-red with blackberry stains. The Head of the Federation of Directors seemed to think a speech was called for, even if the Suprema was unable to give one.

Clutching a slopping wine glass in one hand and waving the other, he said, in slurred tones, "I think we can all agree that whatever happens, it is vital for the future of this country that we keep the factories in working order, the machines dry and the people...*contained*, where they can't make trouble. While we feed them, they eat. That's all it takes. *Containment*. Also, come what may, certain *crucial public figures* must get through this...this...*unpleasantness!* The linchpins, yes. Them as can get the city back to what it was before the flood!"

"Us, you mean?" said someone.

He looked around, as if surprised. "Of course us! Yes."

"Thank goodness for Noah's Ark then," muttered the Governor of Afalia Bank.

Those two words Gloria heard repeatedly, spoken in lowered voices: *Noah's Ark*. Each time, the words were met with a nod of the head and a glance towards her.

"Key people like us – best brains...indispensable...be on Noah's Ark."

"...can't risk losing people like us...Noah's Ark."

"...if the worst comes to the worst...Noah's Ark."

"Anyone know how many they could take? Noah's Ark?"

"Herself must know – it was her idea..."

"What's Noah's Ark?" Gloria whispered to Timor. "Should we ask?"

Timor shook his head. "They seem to think you already know. So, no."

CHAPTER TWENTY-TWO

The Old Man of the Woods

UPRIVER WETLANDS

Heat. His waking sensation was of heat, and Heinz could smell burning. He tried to raise his head – to look around him – but found he was parcelled up in grey, unable to move for the creaking grey fibres binding him round. His legs were bound against his body. Struggling was impossible. The only other colour seeping through his eyelids came from below: the yellow and red shifting glimmer of flames. He was being roasted over an open fire.

The grey cobwebby fibres clung tight to his fur and to each other. No amount of wriggling could loosen them. Only his snout was free to gape, and he panted faster than even his heart could keep pace with. Smoke filled both mouth and nose. It was all he could smell. Every other scent in the universe had been taken away from him, and that was worse than blindness, because without smell no dog can get his bearings. The grey cobweb bound his chest too tight to let him breathe. He could not remember what had brought him to this torment.

Like a cooked joint, his captor lifted him down from over the fire and laid him on a fragrant bed of leaves. There was the sound of a knife blade being sharpened. Then the knife-tip sliced through the grey fibre trussing Heinz from nose to tail. It fell away like the flesh from a peach stone, and a hand unfolded his legs – one, two, three, four. Perhaps Heinz was cooked and ready for eating.

"Sweating done. Time to put back the wet." And a hand cupped cold water to Heinz's mouth. "Reckon you ran yourself inside out and upside down, puppy dog."

When the old man spoke, his long beard flicked against his chest. He talked to Heinz and he talked to Mycar. He talked to Horse, who he had rescued from the mire. (How he had managed it even Horse did not know.) None of the old man's guests answered him, but he talked anyway. It put Heinz in mind of Clem's mama talking her way through a recipe as she cooked supper.

The trees around them seemed to lean in and listen – seemed to have grown old and bearded, listening, for their trunks were hung with the grey cobwebby moss. When the wind off the river ruffled them, the trees, too, seemed to be talking, their long grey beards flickering against their chests.

The bullet had grazed Heinz's back, but not enough to slow him down. Though near collapse, he had run full-tilt into the domain of the Old Man of the Woods.

"You wild or a home-lovin' dog?" the man asked, mixing up tree sap and herbs and honey to daub on the bullet-burn. Tame or feral, the man would have thought no less of Heinz. It did not seem that "human" or "animal" made much difference to him either. The river flood had brought huge numbers of both kinds migrating through his terrain in search of safety. Each time the river spread itself, the Old Man would shift ground a little, but no further than necessary. The river brought him the fish he ate, the water he washed and cooked in, the flotsam that furnished his open-air home.

"Maybe the world's ending," he told Horse as he rubbed her down with fistfuls of grass. "Probably not, though – just Nature kicking up her heels. No point running from The End anyways."

Though the Old Man seemed to care very little about surviving, he took the greatest care to remove all the bones from the fish he fed Heinz and Mycar – even the tiny little hairy ones. Then he pulled Heinz onto his lap and fondled his ears.

Love recuperated in Heinz. It had fallen sick thanks to the rat bite and No-Name and the bullet and the running… Now, as he slept on a bed of grey moss and dreamed of Clem and of picnics, all his best Virtues crept back to him. And best of them all was Love.

But the Old Man of the Woods did not like guests to outstay their welcome. One day, he fetched Horse and, having seen Heinz's devotion to the knotted rope, put it in the dog's mouth and told him to go. "Go. Go on. Go. Leave me in peace."

Heinz looked back at him with big uncomprehending eyes. What had become of Love? Of baked eel? Of tugged ears and elderly fingers grooming him for fleas? Mycar set off cheerfully enough, but Heinz waited a long while at the edge of the clearing, hoping he had misunderstood. The Old Man kept his back turned and concentrated on weaving iris leaves into a sleeping mat.

When he heard them crash away through the woods, he laid the mat aside. Under his breath he cursed all dogs for the hold they take on a man's heart.

Strange beasts roamed the banks near Big Rock – giant geckos, shellfish that climbed the trunks of trees to tinkle in the boughs like bells, woolly deer, dragonflies as big as birds and rats in every colour but blue. Fire ants floated across streams, locked together into red rafts. Owls hooted in the daytime and frogs glowed in the dark. What was more, the place told lies.

Because of the cliffs, sounds kept bouncing about. Because of the purple lizards spraying poisons at their prey, smells got tangled. Sometimes Heinz would catch a scent of human travellers or hear distant noises, but he could never be sure where each came from.

The sun came out; the wetlands glistened. He was confronted by a landscape gently sloping up towards a blue sky and, at its feet, a sweet-smelling field of hyacinths. A parcel of rabbits sat on a log among the hyacinths, huddled together beneath a cluster of ears. Best of all, beyond the hyacinths, a group of people were in plain sight, toiling uphill.

The knotted rope was suddenly wet with spit – the rabbits had reminded Heinz how hungry he was.

I am hungry, too, said a voice behind him. It was Hound Death. Heinz shivered from nose to tail. His legs crouched, his tail swung in under his body.

"Do you feel it, too?" Heinz asked Horse. "The danger?" Horse did not understand the question and took a step forward, but would not tread on the flowers.

Mycar, though, had seen the rabbits.

"Don't?" said Heinz uncertainly.

"Myrabbits," said Mycar and ran out across the hyacinths.

They were big, sturdy plants and Mycar was a tiny dog. For a good long way, it kept going, sneezing at the pollen from the flowers. Then it stepped between two flower-heads and was lost from sight.

They watched for him to reappear on the far side of the

hyacinths, yapping. A breeze blew. The rabbits, on their log, shifted sideways. Or, rather, the log they were sitting on moved sideways. The flower-heads jostled. Darkness showed between.

Water. Both hyacinths and rabbits were afloat in deep, dark, flowing water.

For a long time, Heinz waited and watched for Mycar to come gasping to the surface and topple the swamp rabbits off their log.

The landscape lay still. The only sounds were of the frogs singing and Horse heading off in search of a safe crossing place. And whether a lizard or pike or water snake had snatched Mycar, or whether the little dog had simply drowned, they would never know.

My Mycar, said Hound Death in Heinz's ear. The tone was not spiteful or gloating. It was gently good-humoured.

"That dog can be a real thorn in the paw," Heinz warned. "Are you really sure you want to take it?"

Don't worry. All are welcome. My Mycar now.

CHAPTER TWENTY-THREE

A Rosy Solution

PRAESTO CITY

Gloria looked at herself in the mirror and crayoned dark red lipstick onto the reflection's mouth as if she was writing graffiti on a wall. She did not like the woman in front of her. That woman there had been chosen by the people of Praesto to be Head of State. They had voted her into power and let her live in this big house and given her Appis and his limousine, and free groceries, and naked statues for her mantelpiece. "She should have stayed and made everything alright."

"How, exactly?" said Timor. "She was only human. She had no magic powers. And please don't write on the furniture." He was sitting cross-legged on the floor, stitching artificial autumn leaves onto Madame's hat. "The Suprema" could not afford to look shabby.

"But it's awful. You didn't see! If Madame saw those places, she'd shut them down and let everyone go home."

"And let the machinery drown? Machinery worth millions?" said Timor.

"Machines don't matter as much as people."

"To some people they do," said Timor. He held up the hat on the tips of his fingers to examine the effectiveness of his sewing. "Look at the banquet. Every soul there thought that machines matter a whole lot more. You heard them: keep the machines in working order. Keep the people *contained*."

Gloria was annoyed that Timor was not more upset, more angry about what she had told him – of the cold and the damp and the whispered pleas for the children to be spared any more suffering. And yet with his cuffs buttoned, his eyes narrowed and an expression on his face of someone who is doing long division in his head, there was something about Timor that forbade argument.

At long last he stood up, handed her the hat and said, "So. Careful does it today."

Gloria's heart gave a thud of alarm. "When? Why? What about?"

"When you tell Kovet to shut down the factories. You're right – people are a lot more important than spoons. Don't worry, I'll give you a script."

"Close down the factories? Impossible, dear lady!" said Kovet with a chortle and a shake of the head. His tone was that of a jovial uncle patting a child's hair.

And she had learned the words so carefully that Timor had written down! She had spoken them all in her best Suprema voice. Now the words lay on the desk like dead flies – Kovet had simply swatted them. "The wealth of the city depends on the factories. Without them, what is the purpose of Praesto? Afalia *is* manufacturing. Afalia means cutlery to a world in need of cutlery! Ninety per cent of the population of Praesto make their living from cutlery! Praesto City *is* manufacturing!"

Gloria could feel herself flushing red with anger under her veil. "No! Afalia is people!"

Some of the jolliness gave way to impatience. "Oh nonsense. Without wages how do people buy food? And who puts the wages in their pockets? The factories!"

"But they're not making cutlery any more! And the owners aren't *paying* them wages either! Didn't you know?"

"Well, of course they aren't. The owners can't ship *in* nickel and they can't ship *out* any cutlery. *And* they've had the expense of building all those pumps. Anyway, why do the workers *need* money while there's nothing to spend it on? They're getting fed and watered, aren't they? Really, Madame, am I talking to the same woman who last year lowered the school leaving age to thirteen so that the factories would have more workers? Why this sudden wish to be *liked*? Your politics have always been so…*pragmatic* in the past."

Gloria tore a leaf of paper off the jotter and scribbled on it.

Kovet straightened up in his chair, clasping the arms. "Let us turn our thoughts to more important things."

Gloria felt a flicker of daring. "What? Noah's Ark?"

Kovet half rose from his chair in panic and looked around him for eavesdroppers. "Shshsh. No! No, no. I'm sure it won't come to that. Where's your husband – Private Secretary – whatever…"

"Fetching whisky for you and Mr Myld."

There was a chinking of glasses outside. Myld sprang up and locked the doors. The sound filled Gloria with a longing to be on the outside.

Kovet said: "I must ask you not to discuss affairs of State with your husband. He is not a member of the Senate."

Gloria had been wearing the Suprema's clothes for too long – she knew just how to reply. "Don't worry about Timmy. I make the decisions around here. He does as I tell him."

Kovet smiled. "Then let us get on with ending this confounded flood."

Myld was by the desk in an instant, spreading out the map in front of Gloria, pointing out landmarks. He smelled of cologne and pink soap. His breath, when he spoke, was toothpastey. "Many thousands of years ago, the river bifurcated here, at Big Rock. Scientists think an earthquake opened a split, you see, and—"

"Skip the geology, Myld," snapped Kovet, and Gloria took

the opportunity to write *bifficated* on her notepad.

"So, one single river split into two: firstly our bit – the Furca – that's Latin for fork…"

"I did go to school, Mr Myld," said Gloria, hoping he might think she knew Latin.

"And this other leg was called the Rose River."

"What's that Latin for?"

Myld smiled. "Apparently the water used to be pinkish, from the red sandstone. But as you know, of course, seventy years ago, a dam was built here, at Big Rock, to redirect *all* the water down past us here in Praesto. Genius engineering. The extra water scoured out the riverbed and made it much deeper. So the ships bringing nickel and oil and suchlike could safely sail upriver to here from the sea. And the cutlery ships could set sail from here without running aground."

"Genius, like you said."

"Genius." Myld's voice was as soft as the velvet plush of his waistcoat. "Of course, the dam put an end to the Rose River. It ceased to exist. Unfortunate, but necessary. The fruit trees and crops died, so the Rosies (as they call themselves) mostly came here and got work in the factories. That *also* benefitted the economy!"

"Enough of the history lesson," snapped Kovet. "The Suprema knows all this."

"Of course. I do beg your pardon, ma'am. Now, if we were to *remove* the dam, the river would split into two again – half this way, half that way. Hey presto! The amount of water pouring past Praesto will be half what it is now!"

"Excellent!" Gloria actually clapped her chicken-claw hands with delight.

"Isn't it," said Myld tenderly, modestly, as if the idea might have been his own.

"And the people of Rose City will be so happy to get their water back!"

"Mmmm," said Myld.

"If there's anyone still living there, I mean. Is there?"

Kovet jumped in. "Hardly anyone. Lowlifes. Immigrants. You know the sort."

Gloria noted down on her pad: *What a snob.* "About how many?"

Myld and Kovet spoke at the same moment:

"Three hundred?"

"A thousand?"

"But how *would* you? Get rid of the dam, I mean," asked Gloria.

"Bomb it, Madame."

"Ah. Right. Excuse me, gentlemen," said Gloria, and left the room, in haste, by the door to the document room. Hitching up her skirts as high as her drawers, she ran up the back stairs two steps at a time. As she had guessed, Timor, shut out of the Audience Chamber, had found the next best place to try and listen – the office directly above.

"Word problems?" enquired Timor, who had had little success in eavesdropping.

Gloria nodded and read from her piece of paper. "*Bifficate.*"

"Bifurcate? Good lord! Split in two."

"*Pragmatic.*"

"Practical. Doing what's needed without wasting time wondering if it's right or wrong."

Gloria screwed up the paper. "Kovet wants to bomb the dam at Big Rock and bifficate the river back into two. Is that a really brilliant idea…or not? Mr Myld says '*mmm*' and Mr Kovet looks shifty."

Timor closed his eyes to think. The veins pulsed in his forehead. It was as if she was seeing thoughts travel through them. "If they wait until after the flood goes down, it may be a good idea. With the river like it is…" His eyes opened. "…it would wipe out Rose City and everyone in it."

"It doesn't have city walls like ours?"

"It doesn't have any kind of a wall."

"But just think: if it can stop the flood, and people don't have to work the pumps all day long and live in the factories! The workers say the Rosies set light to firemen and kill each other – they read it in the newspaper! And Kovet says they're all lowlifes and there aren't many of 'em anyway…though how he'd know, I don't understand. Or the newspaper, come to that. How do they know?"

"While you work that out, kindly consider: the people of Rose City are citizens of Afalia, Gloria, and as such it is the Suprema's duty to protect them. And even if they weren't, just what price do you put on one 'lowlife' newborn child?"

"Well, anyway," Gloria suggested, trying not to get distracted, "couldn't they maybe move out of the way till the flood's over?"

"That's supposing anybody warns them ahead of time. And how exactly would anyone do that, given that the telegraph wires are down. And who—"

"Aeroplane!"

"—And who *agrees* to having their entire city destroyed? Don't be naïve, girl."

"Is that like being stupid?"

"Close enough. Just don't be it. Drown 16,000 men, women and children to save ourselves? That's not pragmatic, that's a massacre."

"16,000? Not 300?"

"16,000 men, women and children."

Gloria checked her outfit in the mirror then hurried down the back stairs again.

"I'm sorry, gentlemen," she said as she returned to her desk. "Where were we?"

"Sending a plane to bomb the dam at Big Rock," said Kovet impatiently and pushed a State Decree across the desk for her to sign.

Gloria looked at the velvety soft paper with its gold deckle-edges and beautiful handwriting. The Clerk of the Senate had made it look so pretty, what with the big swirly capitals and all the lines the same length and all the tall letters standing tall. And all so that the Suprema could give the order to drown 16,000 people. There was even a special pen to sign it with: a fountain pen made to look like an old-fashioned quill feather. A peacock feather.

"Ma used to say it's unlucky to bring a peacock feather indoors," she remarked, and went on staring at the paper.

"Perhaps you should take your hat off so you can see to *sign your name*," growled Kovet irritably. Daisy had just come along to share her drool with Kovet's trousers.

"No. It's alright, thank you." Gloria set down the pen. "I don't think the workers in the factories want lots of people getting drowned. They must remember being down in the cellars, pumping, and the water just coming up and up… No. They told me, they just want their children to be safe and warm and clean and not hungry… Until they get that, I can't think about anything else."

While his assistant began to gather up papers, Kovet rocked on his haunches like a volcano thinking about erupting. He stared at Gloria, open-mouthed. "What they *want* is not to have the walls fall in on them and the flood to wash them all to kingdom come!"

But then Myld opened his blue eyes very wide and spread his long fingers, inspired by an idea. "Why not *ask* them?" he said. "Let us find out what the people think! This is a democracy after all."

Kovet stared at his assistant. "*Ask* them?"

"A ballot, yes, sir! I shall organize it myself… Give me two days… But we must not take up any more of the Suprema's time. Let me help you on with your coat, sir."

Kovet stalked off across the hall, muttering and swiping at his fluffy trousers. Myld waited until his boss was out of earshot, jogged Gloria lightly with an elbow and whispered, "I say! Well played, ma'am! Well played!"

When Gloria told Timor about Myld's plan to "ask the people", he frowned and stared out of the window for a long time. "I hope he won't."

"Why? They'd never say yes to knocking down the dam with people in the way!"

"They're scared," he said. "When people are scared, they tend to take their brains out and put them on a high shelf for safe-keeping."

"Oh, still! They're good people. They wouldn't drown anybody on purpose!"

Timor continued to look out of the window. "Good People. I've heard it said that 'Good People' is an oxymoron."

"What's that? A really stupid ox?"

"It's two words that don't belong together. Like you and me."

"MORALE IS WONDERFULLY HIGH"

After a visit to the factories yesterday, Madame Suprema declared morale to be "wonderfully high" among the workers. "I so admire their cheerfulness and energy. They are giving it everything they've got, and it is hard, hard work. They seem like the members of one family,

pulling together to get through a troublesome time. They must be tired, but labour on as if they have the strength of Hercules!"

ZOO ANIMALS ESCAPE

A landslide, caused by months of rain, allowed dozens of animals to flee Praesto Zoo yesterday.

Cages buckled and aviaries collapsed, as sodden soil turned to slurry. The missing – pandas, lions, tigers, snakes, hippos and bears – may number up to 600. A zebra and three chimpanzees were killed "by fellow animals". Crocodiles and alligators were among the first to be seen on Praesto's streets. Zoo Director Mikka Pogg said that all species were "proving hard to capture". The Civil Guard have been armed and instructed to shoot as necessary.

Anyone not living within the safety of the factory walls should stay indoors until all danger has passed.

THE THREE CHIMPS KILLED LAST NIGHT

CHAPTER TWENTY-FOUR

Trust Nobody

FOREMOST MANSION, PRAESTO

Gloria threw the newspaper on the floor. "Lying scribble! I never said morale was high in the factories! Every day it's full of lies!"

"Do you even know what morale *is*?" said Timor.

"No, but I'm guessing it doesn't mean wet and cold and miserable. I don't believe a word this paper prints."

"The Editor is a woman I greatly respect," said Timor with a warning look which Gloria failed to see.

"The other day it said dog poo can kill your eyeballs. How am I supposed to believe *that*?"

"Then never make me a sandwich when you have just walked the dog. It is perfectly true," said Timor.

But her sudden anger could not be quelled. "Well…I don't believe there ever were rabid dogs roaming round the streets. I don't believe the weather people were even put on trial; I think they were just shot. There never was a Welcome Centre for Pets – they were all just killed and cut up for meat to feed the workers."

It was as if she had just taken off the Suprema's tight-fitting corset and her whole body had breathed deep with relief. For days and days she had been trying not to believe a lot of things, and suddenly she couldn't try any more. The truth had overwhelmed her. "What? D'you think I didn't hear that factory man at the banquet? The workers are eating dog-meat! 'Escaped zoo animals'? They never broke out yesterday, 'cos you and me know those toffs at the banquet had already scoffed them! I think the newspaper just makes things up!" Timor looked dangerously pale and annoyed, but Gloria was every bit as angry. She swallowed hard. "And I don't know why you're defending them!"

Timor stood up. She thought he might be going to throw her bodily out of the window. "The Editor of *The Voice* is a brilliant, principled woman. I have known her almost all my life. She is utterly incorruptible. She would never publish lies."

Gloria's temper refused to subside. It kept jumping up inside her like a yapping dog. "What if she was bullied into it?"

"Believe me, Professor Hecuba Lightfoot is not a woman to be bullied."

"Why would she be different? Everyone gets bullied!" snapped Gloria. (It was one of those fearful moments when truths lurch up out of nowhere, like vomit.) "The workers get bullied. Mr Myld does, by Mr Kovet; Boz bullied Daisy… Madame bullies everyone – me, Cook, her Secretary, you…"

Timor snatched the paper out of her hand and threw it in the general direction of the fireplace. A terrible silence blotted out whatever else she might have said. At last he said, "Show me what you're talking about. I doubt you will prove to me that my dearest friend is fabricating the news." But his eyes held a glimmer of doubt.

Gloria went to her attic room to fetch the newspapers…and found someone in there already – someone who was her. When the person turned around, it made sense: Lixi the maid was wearing Gloria's clothes. In fact, all Gloria's clothes were lying in a heap on the floor. Lixi had been trying them on.

"What are you doing?"

"Trying to find something wearable. You don't even have electrics up here, do you? Don't suppose it worries you though, does it – *backwoods girl.*"

"I gave you my wool dress."

"It itches. You have the dreariest clothes." Far from looking embarrassed, Lixi seemed glad Gloria had walked in on her.

"That's my harvest festival dress. I went to a barn-raising in that," said Gloria.

"It shows. You're *such* a peasant… What's the matter?

You've got all that satin and lace to wear now. What d'you need these for?"

"Because the fancy ones aren't *mine*."

"Isn't that the truth! You're just thieving them. How would it be if someone *knew* the maid was dressing up in the Suprema's clothes? That's treason, that is. They could shoot you for that. Tie you to a post and blindfold you and the soldiers would line up and load their rifles and that's when you'd wet yourself 'cos you're so scared, and then *BANG!*" She clapped her hands in Gloria's face. "So, you mustn't be greedy. You can't wear those *and* these, can you? So I'm having these. And you can give me a go at the Suprema's silk undies. I'm not wearing your knickers." Her eyes were bright with daring. "It's silk drawers for me from now on. And lipstick. A pink one." She went on plucking at the small heap of clothes on the bed.

"Oh, not the gingham dress! Ma sent it me at New Year! I haven't even worn it yet!"

"So why's it so creased?" (Gloria said nothing, rather than say she slept with it under her pillow, hoping to dream of home.) "Never mind. You can iron it for me."

"No! You can't have the gingham. Please."

Lixi put her hands on her hips. She looked as if she had practised doing it many times in front of a mirror. "What you going to do about it, *Ladyship*?" And she left with an armful of clothes – even Gloria's sister's nightie that had been a leaving-home present.

It was true. What could Gloria do? What choice did she have but to give Lixi whatever she wanted or be unmasked and shot? What choice did she have but to go on being the Suprema and wearing the Suprema's fancy, fussy clothes? When had she honestly thought she was going to wear her gingham ever again?

Timor was waiting, so she left the mess for later and pulled all her copies of *The Voice* out from under the bed. And there was her picture on a front page – *Madame Suprema visits Knives* – her face blotted out, of course, by the black veil.

The two of them spread the papers out over the big rug in the Library to examine them in date order – a big, white, crinkly sea of news. Then they crawled over them, looking for…

"What are we looking for, sir?"

"Mistakes. When they began. The Professor never tolerated mistakes, or downright lies, obviously. 'Tell the truth and shame the devil,' she used to say. It made her a terrifying school teacher but a very good newspaper editor. We dined together often after I left school. My wife would not join us – she loathed clever women. She also loathed me going anywhere without her. Finally, the Security Services informed me it was an 'unsuitable friendship'; that being the Suprema's husband, I might 'give away State secrets to the Press'. So. No more suppers with Professor Lightfoot."

"If she taught you at school, she must be a very old lady now. Old ladies do make mistakes."

"Do you mind! How old do you think I am? She's probably about fifty…fifty-five."

"Like I said. An old lady." Gloria bit her lip. "Please, sir…"

"Yes?"

"When can I *stop* being Madame Suprema?"

Down on his knees and studying the article in front of him, Timor seemed not to have heard.

"When can I stop…?"

"I'm afraid I didn't think that far ahead. At the beginning. I'm sorry. It was a spur-of-the-moment thing. As you know."

"So…does that mean…for ever?"

"Good lord, no!" Timor sat back on his heels, appalled at the thought of having Gloria around for ever, pretending to be his wife. "Till the flood is over, and you can get out of the city…or my wife returns, of course. Don't worry. I expect we'll be found out long before that and shot. Joking! I'm joking!"

They returned to scouring the newspapers for… something, without knowing what. Gloria was very sorry she had got so angry about the lies in the paper, because Timor clearly thought the world of Professor Lightfoot – and what did it matter if a stupid daily newspaper invented news now and then to fill up spaces?

Even now, he was saying: "She's fiercely intelligent. A real stickler for getting things right. In school, we used to mimic her behind her back: 'Yes, boy, but it is *true*.' 'I don't want your *opinion*, boy. Is it *true*?' But looking back, she's… unforgettable. Utterly devoted to Latin, Greek. I think, if she could, she would be printing *The Voice* in Latin. You've only got to look at the crest under the banner to know everything about Hecuba Lightfoot. See? *'In atramento est veritas'* – 'The Truth is in the Ink'."

"So…what does the '*non*' mean?"

"*Non?*"

"Yes. In this one, it's *'In atramento non est veritas'* – and this one – and this one."

He snatched the paper she was holding, scuffing on all-fours across the others, rucking them into a mountain range of newsprint. "Dash it. Dash it. Dash it."

"Why? What does it mean?"

"It means 'There is *no* Truth in—'"

There was a knock on the library door, and Lixi (dressed in Gloria's blue gingham) announced Kovet and let him in without waiting for permission. The Senator for Home Affairs stood in the doorway and surveyed a room strewn with newspapers, The Husband down on his hands and knees. Timor was caught so unawares that he could not immediately get up.

"*Carpet moth!*" called a voice from beyond the mahogany desk. "You have to put down newspapers to stop them laying their eggs in the carpet!" Only the back end of the Suprema's purple gown was visible. "I can't *abide* carpet moth, can you? The way the eggs hatch into those horrible white maggoty things? It's a job for the maid, really, but she is *such* a useless article, I can't trust her to do *anything* right. Timmy is just as bad – he gets cramp. Timmy, take Mr Kovet Somewhere Else, and don't come back till you have stopped having cramp."

After they had gone, she stayed for a long time curled up in the kneehole of the desk, her teeth chattering with delayed fright, and wondering where she had left her hat. When she rested down one hand, it squashed a dead moth.

Timor was not gone long. "Kovet and I are sharing the one car, to save fuel. Kovet wanted it this evening, but when he called at Appis's cottage across the road, neither Appis nor the limo were home, so did I know when he'd be back? Clearly our chauffeur has a private life after all."

"I prefer the horse and trap anyway," said Gloria. "I'm good with a horse and trap."

Timor sighed. "No. You're not. Must I tell you again? The Head of State does *not* drive around the streets in a horse-drawn vehicle, like some rag-and-bone merchant. Please try to remember." He began stacking the newspapers in their right order. "I telephoned Hecuba at her home. And at *The Voice* offices. Both lines were dead. Maybe we've lost the telephones within the city now, too." A puzzle in the paper caught his eye. "Can you do anagrams?"

"I never tried, sir. What are they?"

"Puzzles. You have to move the letters around to read something else. Hecuba enjoyed that kind of thing. I could never do them myself." He showed Gloria the front page – the one with her own picture on it. Her face had been torn across, but the puzzle in the corner was still readable: MAMA MADE SUPER.

"That's *Madame Suprema*," said Gloria. "Easy."

"Quite. So… Whenever you have a moment, solve the rest, will you?"

"Why?" said Gloria.

"Because I asked you to? Is that not how this works? The Master-and-Maid thing? I ask? You do?"

Up in her attic bedroom, Gloria curled up tight in her narrow bed. She thought she would not sleep. For one thing, Lixi had stolen her nightdress, and she was cold. But dreams were waiting in ambush. They dragged Gloria into an inky pool of sleep and drowned her in terror. She dreamed she could not unfasten her dress – the buttons had disappeared – and that her hat was fused to her head. She kept asking people to help her, but all they did was curtsey and say "Suprema For Ever". She tried to explain who she was, where she came from, but her words turned into moths, trapped inside her veil, and began laying their eggs in her hair. *Suprema For Ever.*

She woke clawing at her scalp, her lips tightly clamped together. She had to light every candle in the bedside drawer before the dark recoiled as far as the foot of the bed and the dreams curled themselves back into the chamber pot. *Suprema For Ever and Ever and Ever...* She took out sheets of paper where, nightly, she practised Madame's signature. Then she took out the newspaper and began to puzzle over the anagrams:

BELL NOW TOOTING = WELLINGTON BOOT
LION SHUNS HEEL = HELLO SUNSHINE
MAMA MADE SUPER = MADAME SUPREMA
YODEL SPRUNG = GOLDEN SYRUP
EAT FAT LASS = SAFE AT LAST
EEL THROTTLES PLUG = LET'S PULL TOGETHER

Then the anagrams became harder and harder to find, hidden away on the inside pages in among the jokes for children and the book reviews. But solving them got easier the longer she did it.

CUR YELLED AFAR = READ CAREFULLY
DONKEY MR TWO = NOTED MY WORK (?)

Easier and more disturbing were:

NUTTY BROODS = TRUST NOBODY

The candle flickered. The dark moiled around the room, like black panthers circling.

HILLIEST SAILS = THIS IS ALL LIES

Outside, thunder rumbled its disapproval. Lightning scorched the whole room…

FOAMIER FIREFLY = I FEAR FOR MY LIFE

Then came torrential rain, and the skylight started to leak – *tip, tip, tip*…

WHELK YELL LIMIT = THEY WILL KILL ME

Gloria got up and fumbled in the cupboard for her smock and skimpy coat, but still shivered. As she wrapped herself in the bedcover, the last anagram she had been staring at – MOVE GRIEF – solved itself without use of a pencil. Lightning wrote the answer inside her skull:

FORGIVE ME

She made no noise going downstairs, for fear of waking Lixi in her luxurious great bedroom. She let herself into Timor's room and felt her way across it, colliding painfully with the desk. More lightning helped her identify where he slept.

"Excuse me, sir. Could you…" she whispered, without waking him. Trying for the most respectful way of disturbing him, she groped for a foot, but misjudged which end was which and put her hand down on his face, then had to move it to his mouth to stop him shouting out in alarm. "Sorry! Sorry! Sorry, sir! Don't shout at me. Lixi might hear. I've done the anagrams."

He lit the desk lamp and peered at the sheets of paper, seeing only his wife's seismic signature over and over and over. Gradually, he picked out the pencilled words in between. "*Golden syrup?* You woke me for *golden syrup?*"

Gloria pointed to the ones she had circled. "I'm so sorry, Mr Timor, sir. I think your teacher-friend is in awful trouble."

Timor left the house, telling her to go back to bed. But as soon as she had found herself a pair of rubber boots and Cook's dark coat in the hall cupboard, she ran after him. It was hard, what with the rubber boots and the length of Timor's legs and the rainwater cascading down the hill, but she caught him up.

"Are we going to the newspaper offices?"

"Go home."

"Or Professor Lightfoot's house?"

"Go home, Gloria."

"Hecuba's an odd name. I never heard of a Hecuba before."

"Do as you are told."

"Why would the newspaper lie about dogs with rabies and escaped lions?"

"So that no one will dare leave the factories. They won't kick up a fuss about having to stay there. The pumps can be kept pumping day and night. Now go home."

"If the Professor never tells lies, who d'you think is

doing it? Telling the lies, I mean."

"If she tells me tonight, I may share the news with you tomorrow. Now go."

Gloria persisted. "I wanted to say that I don't think *NOTED MY WORK* is right. *MY WORK NOTED?* It doesn't make sense."

"No. It doesn't. I believe it reads *Not my work. Ed.* 'Ed' for 'Editor'."

"Oh! That's clever! Sorry to get it wrong." She was breathless with trying to keep up. The boots were too big for her and rattled round her legs with a glopping noise. Cook's box of matches rattled in the coat's pocket. Rain spat in Gloria's eyes.

"No. No, you did well, Gloria. Thank you."

That silenced her, when nothing else could. In all her time at Foremost Mansion, the Suprema had never *thanked* her.

They walked to Hecuba's home through the park. The trees stood limbless, their branches all cut off for fuel or pump-beams. Bats flew by their heads, invisible, with a fluttery thrum like a faltering heartbeat. When the front door swung open at a touch, Timor drew a sharp breath.

"Oh, the Civil Guards broke into houses all over," Gloria explained. "I saw them do it when…" She stopped, sooner than confess to the night she had run away.

But nothing was missing from Hecuba Lightfoot's lovely

house. The bookshelves that lined every wall had not been ripped out for the sake of the timber. The lights did not switch on, but that meant nothing, what with the fuel shortages. Gloria struck a match. Four bone-white plaster heads loomed in the dark passageway – Aristotle, Cato, Pliny, Cicero – watching the intruders. Timor called Hecuba's name softly, unwilling to scare a sleeping woman alone in a big house.

But he could have called as loudly as he liked. The legions of ancient Rome could have clashed their swords against their shields and shrieked battle cries in Latin without waking Hecuba. Gloria struck another match.

The Professor lay dead across her bed, an industrial flagon of printer's ink by one hand, her mouth, tongue, cheeks, neck, hair and bedspread dyed inky black.

"Just like Socrates, eh, Hecuba? Poisoned by men too stupid to prize genius and too crooked to prize truth." Timor blew out the match. "Sleep soundly, friend. Wake in Elysium."

As he pulled himself to his feet and leaned against the big, dark wardrobe, the coat hangers inside it rattled like bones.

"What do we do? Who do we tell?" whispered Gloria.

He took a long time to answer. "No one. No one at all. Kindly assume that there is no one in the whole city you can trust. Not a soul. Understood?"

"Understood, sir."

CHAPTER TWENTY-FIVE

Making Contact

UPRIVER, BIG ROCK BEND

When they reached Big Rock Bend, Horse came to a standstill. Here, the river hit a dam head-on before swerving southeast and flowing onwards. It was almost impossible to think over the crashing sound of tonnes of water changing direction. A long steep hill led upwards to the full height of the dam.

On his own, Heinz could have climbed it in no time. But he knew that, without encouragement, Horse would simply turn back into the wilderness and be lost. Heinz could not abandon her. This was the route to safety – he was sure of it. That was why people were beating a trail southwards – because safety lay over this hill!

Heinz picked up the knotted end of Horse's halter-rope, studied the steep slope and, finding a zigzag route, started to lead her up it. Halfway up, Horse stopped. Too weary? Too afraid? Again, Heinz hauled on the rope to urge her on.

Again, she lowered her head and the halter slipped off and left him pulling only rope-and-halter.

Heinz turned his back on Horse and clambered on towards the sound of voices. So close! So close! Last time, the refugees had shot at him. These ones probably would, too. But the scent – even of sick, filthy, desperate people with guns – drew him all the way to the crest of the granite hill.

The refugees had sat down to rest. There was a sunset – a rare wonder after weeks of drizzle, hail and dour black clouds. In front of them, the old empty river gorge sloped down towards Rose City – a shock of colourful beauty, lit crimson by the setting sun.

Circling the city were ugly acres of tents, upturned carts, oilcloth hanging over washing lines to make roofs, water butts, baggage… Refugees had been finding their way there for weeks, imagining they were the first, only to find hundreds had arrived before them. There was so much to see from the top of the dam that it was a while before anyone noticed the dog standing behind them.

Heinz did not go any closer. He stood where he was, then turned and disappeared again over the cliff edge. He reappeared holding a rope in his mouth. This time he took a few steps more, before standing still. He was looking into the sunset; the figures in front of him were silhouettes. There might be guns in their hands – he could not tell.

They watched the stray dog turn and trot off again. It returned with a halter, put it down alongside the knotted rope and gave a bark.

Heinz saw every one of them flinch. *Shouldn't have barked*, he thought.

Someone picked up a rock and threw it.

"Don't," said a child. "'S a nice doggy."

"It's a mangy mutt," said the child's mother.

The rock terrified Heinz. He recalled the shooting, the pain, the fear, the world melting as he ran out of breath... But he did not flee. Horse was stuck on the cliff: she needed help. He was Heinz, dog-of-Clem, blessed with many Virtues, and he had come as far as any dog could be expected to go. He turned his back and sat down, facing the way he had come. A sitting target.

A man armed with a handgun walked forward and picked up the halter. He turned around – and promptly fell over his own child who had followed him. The child, who was carrying a big stick, extricated itself and ran towards Heinz. The father fumbled for his gun and cocked it, but his child was in the way.

"Doggy's all trembly!" called the child and, despite a chorus of "*Don't!*" began stroking the stray.

The bullet-graze was still sore. Stroking hurt. But Heinz did not move, because beyond the pain there was a much better feeling. Besides, he did not think he *could* move. For some reason he was trembling, like a whippet in a bucket of ice; shuddering so hard that he could hear his claws scraping the rock. The sky was filled with swirling clouds of starlings. Heinz put back his head and howled – a howl so long and grievous that the rising moon shivered like a great golden gong.

The child pointed its stick. "There's a horsey down there."

IN ATRAMENTO NON EST VERITAS

WORKERS BEG THE SENATE: "TAKE ACTION TO END FLOODING"

ANXIETY GROWS AS WATER LEVELS FAIL TO DROP

Despite less rain falling, the Furca River remains dangerously high.

Workers in all the Five Factories are beseeching the Senate to find a solution to the flooding, and to find it soon. Their fears are understandable. Though the weather has brightened, there is no sign of the flood outside the walls easing. Letters received at the offices of *The Voice* each day ask the same anxious questions, and the Editor finds herself powerless to answer:

"What if the city walls start to crumble?

"What if water-borne diseases – typhoid and yellow fever – find their way into Praesto?"

"How long before food supplies fail?"

"How much damage is being done, outside the city, to homesteads, farms, timberlands and animals?"

COULD THIS SAVE OUR CITY?

Geologists have suggested that if the dam at Big Rock could be demolished, the floodwater would be halved, thus saving our city at a stroke!

(Artist's impression.)

REFUGEES "BUTCHERED BY ROSIES"

News has reached us of refugees from upriver arriving at Rose City, hungry and distressed, only to be butchered by the cult which has taken control here. Unconfirmed reports speak of 150 deaths in the last month.

CHAPTER TWENTY-SIX

Ghosts

FOREMOST MANSION, PRAESTO

Gloria dreamed she saw Hecuba's ghost walking through walls and closed doors, her hair dripping ink, her mouth spewing ink as she spoke, in Lixi's voice: "*Give me your dresses. Give me all your money. Give me your hair. Give me your teeth! You don't need them now you're dead…*" Then the ghost tugged at her clothing. Gloria woke up, rending at her tangled bedding, and squeaking, "I don't have anything! There's nothing left. You've taken it all!" Her bedroom was as dark as the ink in the dream.

Once awake, Gloria could not sleep again. The normal creaks and breathings of the house suddenly sounded like ghostly feet on the stairs, phantoms ganging together… Or Lixi, perhaps, come with more threats and demands. Gloria slithered out of bed and hid in the cupboard. "Honest, I don't have anything! There's nothing left," she told the dark.

It was true. Every coin, every note, her propelling pencil

and hairbrush, even some of Madame's jewellery and perfume bottles had been confiscated by Lixi, amid threats and insults. And there were daily demands for money. "Steal it from Timor's wallet." "Get the combination to the safe." Lixi seemed to think anything and everything was within Gloria's reach.

Who to tell? Cook would not believe it of her own daughter, and Timor would say it was all Gloria's fault for "rescuing" Lixi in the first place. But she absolutely *had* to buy-off Lixi, who knew secrets that would get Timor and Gloria shot for sure!

The skirts of Madame's brown silk day-dress brushed her face and she shuddered. The cupboard was freezingly draughty. It was no more than a pair of doors blocking off a section of the eaves. At the back, a sheet of hardboard was all that separated it from the loft space beyond. Deciding she was too full of fear to feel any more, Gloria pulled off the backboard and peered down into the loft. Pitch-black.

She collected a candle, a coat hanger and a twisted sheet, and lowered herself into the loft, where she was literally walking across the ceilings of the rooms below. It was easy to locate Lixi's room in one corner of the house.

With the coat hanger she began to scratch on the floorboards – or rather, the ceiling above Lixi's bed. Pitching her voice so low that it hurt, she growled: "They don't belong to you. I seen you thieving. I seen it all."

Snores greeted her efforts. She scratched and scraped some more.

"I'm watching you, Lixi. I see your thieving. One night soon they'll come for you like they came for me. I was a thiever, too. Now demons beat me black-and-blue all day, and all night I have to look for someone worser'n me, so they'll leave me alone. Found one now, haven't I. I'll show 'em. I'll show 'em all those things you took…"

The shriek, when it came, was so loud that it scared Gloria into standing up under a beam, and she banged her head and a big spider fell down onto her hand. She had the presence of mind to blow the flame out before dropping the candlestick and violently shaking herself spider-free, or she might have burned down the house. She scratched for a little longer with the coat hanger and moaned deep down in the back of her throat, then she crawled back, over rafters and splintery floorboards, to her twisted sheet and the lesser darkness of her starlit bedroom.

Gloria ran downstairs and found Lixi standing on her bed, still screaming and staring at the ceiling. She was brandishing an ornament as a weapon – a wood carving of a Samian ibis.

"You screamed?" said Gloria, much as she might have said, *You rang, ma'am?*

"There's a something…up there!"

"Squirrels?" said Gloria guilelessly.

"Squirrels that *speak?*" shrilled Lixi.

The temptation for revenge can be powerfully strong. "Well, there's the *ghost*, I suppose," said Gloria. "Madame did say this place was haunted. But people only usually hear them the day before they die. And it's only usually bad people."

"*Liar!*" yelled Lixi and threw the carved ibis at her. Gloria caught it and put it back, with exaggerated care, on the mantelpiece before bidding Lixi a ladylike goodnight. "*Liar, liar, liar!*" The words followed her along the corridor. Gloria hurried back to the eaves room, in case Cook or Timor came up to investigate the noise.

In the morning, she found all her own clothes in a heap outside her bedroom door. The blue gingham was stained with slashes of pink lipstick and all the buttons were missing. But even Gloria's going-home money was there.

The Voice

IN ATRAMENTO NON EST VERITAS

SOLUTION TO FLOOD IS WITHIN REACH!

Senator Kovet lays before Madame Suprema a plan that could lower the river within days. Experts are confident it will work.

Today, you will be asked to vote for or against the bombing of the Big Rock Dam. If the dam falls, the raging river will spill much of its water into its old watercourse which, 80 years ago, flowed past Rose City and over the western border of Afalia. The map below shows the merits of the scheme and *The Voice* commends it to you. In your Editor's opinion, this should have happened weeks ago.

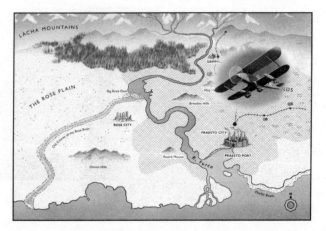

ROSE CITY SHOOTS DOWN PILOTS ON MERCY MISSION

Two of Afalia's finest young men have had their lives cut short when, in separate incidents, their planes were shot down while delivering blankets, food and medicine to refugees in the north. Squadron Leader Leon Swale and Flight Lieutenant "Hay" Stack volunteered for these mercy missions, despite hailstorms and the difficulty of finding dry landing sites. Their fellow officers expressed grief and anger.

It is thought the men were both targeted by Rose City militia as they flew upriver past the Big Rock Dam. They would have made easy targets, heavily laden with supplies, and flying low so as to spot refugees in need of help. The Senate and the Air Chief Marshal of the Afalian Air Force have expressed revulsion at their shameless murder.

Our sincerest condolences to their families, friends and fellow officers.

CHAPTER TWENTY-SEVEN

Voting Day

PRAESTO CITY

Reading in the paper about the dead pilots, Gloria felt a surge of hatred for Rose City and every soul in it. Shot down for trying to help homeless people? She could almost picture the flaming aeroplanes plummeting out of the sky, shedding blankets, food, clothes, toys, young men… It took the sound of Timor's anger to make her think twice.

"Look at it! Rose City looks like a village on here! And they've drawn it in the wrong place entirely! I know for a fact that it's hard up against the dam! Everything in here is geared to swing the vote. You have to get down to the factories, woman, before they read this rubbish and vote to bomb! Tell them… I'll write down what you have to say." And he began writing, on the back of a sheet of opera script, in tall angry letters that leaned forward as if they were charging into battle. Gloria knew she would struggle to read it. She knew, too, from him calling her "woman", that she was blurring into his wife.

Gloria was still caught up in the newspaper's lead story. "What about the pilots? They can't be invented – can they? People would know if their husband or their son was dead or not!"

"The whole page is lies."

"But...*this* time maybe it *is* true!"

"Did Hecuba die for nothing then? You started it, with your 'I don't believe a word'. And suddenly it's true now? Alright. Alright. I'll check on the pilots. But get yourself down to the factories and try to stop them voting to bomb the dam. Go!"

He was so angry that Gloria did up her coat buttons wrong as she ran for the door.

Daisy had grown accustomed to the noise and stench of the factories – had even enjoyed the fuss everyone made of her there. But when she arrived at Spoons the following day with Gloria, she sat down at the gate, resolved not to go a step further. Gloria had to send her home with Appis in the horse-and-trap. The trap-horse shared Daisy's instinct to flee.

Gloria shared it, too, but here she was with a job to do.

The Senate Printer, driving a horse-and-wagon, had just finished delivering the voting slips and crates of pencils. Gloria had the presence of mind to ask him to wait and take her to the other factories; that way, no one in the other factories would be able to vote before she got there.

The Supervisor, in a state of great agitation, dodged about in front of her like a goalkeeper trying to stop a ball. "Your ladyship! I don't think... It might not be..." From behind him a noise boomed louder than any football crowd. Management, themselves clutching voting slips, watched from the second-floor balconies outside their offices, nervous of the enraged factory hands crowding round the crates of pencils and voting slips.

"Please do not issue the voting slips until I have said a few words," said Gloria – she had to shout over the noise. "I want their full attention." Copies of *The Voice* were everywhere, strewing the floor, tucked into the hinges of the machines. When her arrival was announced on the tannoys, the workers rushed in, brandishing yet more copies of the newspaper. Even those working the pumps left their posts and added to the racket.

Angry, raging faces, haggard, wild-haired and sweat-soaked, converged on Gloria, shouting, their cheeks purple, their spit flying. Those crowding in behind pushed forward, until those in front were jostling Gloria, treading on her feet. She had no need to ask which way they would vote.

"Put a stop to those thugs in Rose, Missus!"

"...not human!"

"Animals!"

"Bomb 'em to blazes, Missus!"

They slapped their rolled newspapers against their palms like coshes. *The Voice* had brought them news of the airmen's death all mixed up with an answer to the flood.

"They got to be stopped!"

"Unforgiveable."

"What kind of people are they?"

It felt as if their hatred was directed at her. Factory Supervisors waded to her rescue, heaving workers roughly aside, ordering them back to work, but the hands were so angry that they barely noticed. The Suprema must make the villains pay! For the sake of those poor dead pilots and murdered refugees, the Suprema must make the skies safe again! The Suprema must switch off the flood.

"But it's not true," she said almost to herself. And then louder, "What if it's not true?" Over and over again: "What if it's not true?"

"It's in the paper! Why would the paper make it up?" they yelled, angry with her for not having already loosed an entire fleet of bombers on Rose City.

Had none of them – not a single one of them – solved Hecuba's anagrams and worked out that the newspaper was feeding them lies? She had come imagining *no one* wanted the dam to be bombed and thousands killed. Timor had written such wonderful words – once Gloria had solved his handwriting, she had cried at the beauty of them. But the speech required a wall-map, common sense and an audience sitting down and listening. She foolishly began to explain: "If we bomb—"

And that was where the sentence ended, for the word *bomb* exploded then and there, sending shockwaves through the factory which shook pigeons off the rafters and rats out of the basement. She caught sight of Higgy's face in the crowd, aged and scraggy, but not pallid any more, because it was purple with the effort of shouting, and his eyes were bloodshot. "*Bomb them! Bomb them!*"

The chant grew and grew. "Bomb them! Bomb them! Bomb them!"

The newspaper's front page had removed any possible pity for the people of Rose. Gloria considered slipping a note into Higgy's hand:

It is not true. It is all lies.

But she knew he would only be torn to pieces if he tried to repeat it. She wanted to shout: "*It's not true! How could the Senate know any of it? They're lying to you! They murdered Hecuba!*" But she knew that then *she* would be the one torn to pieces. And if the workers did not kill her, then the dark forces that had killed Hecuba would silence her tiny piping voice.

Anyway, the People were telling her to bomb the dam.

They wanted it. They demanded it. And it was her job to do what the People of Afalia wanted. Wasn't it?

And what if it was all true, and the pilots really were dead?

What if the walls *were* leaking and there was no other solution? She found herself standing on tiptoe. Her head was crammed with questions…and empty of answers.

Gloria stepped onto a stool. Then onto a conveyor belt. Then onto a steel-sheet feeder, then a steeping-tank.

At school, a million years before, Gloria's teacher had only had to raise one hand and with the other put a finger to her lips, and a class full of noisy, excitable, scrimmaging, shrieking children had fallen silent. Gloria raised a hand now. She put a finger to her lips, just like that teacher.

Forgotten, frightened, fretful small children trapped amid a forest of legs put their fingers to their lips and raised one hand. Their older sisters and brothers saw it and did the same, slaves to a half-remembered habit. Their mothers, remembering their own school days, did the same. One by one, ten by twenty, the hordes of people became a forest of hands. Gloria stuffed Timor's speech up her coat sleeve and waited until the only noise was of coughing. The Factory Cough.

"Alright. Listen up." She tried to look furtive, like a pantomime villain. Though it was an audience of hundreds, she lowered her voice and spoke only to the first few rows of the mob below. "Am I hearing right? Do you *really* hate the people in Rose City more than you love your own children? What's it matter what the Rosies do? What do you care? Rats to the Rosies. The newspaper says they're all arguing and fighting and killing each other. Let 'em. First things first. What about what *you* want? What do *you* want most? This is your big chance. Don't you see? I made a vow to get your children out of the factories. So help me do it! Tell the Senate you *won't* vote for bombing until the children are safe and warm. Three children died just the other day in Forks! You want that to happen to yours? Tell my Senate you won't pump the pumps or mend hoses or anything until they look after the children! Those airmen in the newspaper – they probably parachuted down and they're safe somewhere. They're only 'missing'. Think about yourselves for a change! You deserve it. Take a rest. Stop work. Pass it on."

The faces boggled at her. Cries of "What's she say?" "What's she saying?" came from the back of the room. The front rows passed the message back – a strange susurration of overlapping syllables echoing Gloria's words. Not that she had told them the truth – she had just done different things with lies.

The workers, many sick and feverish, had worked themselves into a state of hysteria. Even after they changed their minds, their blood was still on the boil. They began to tear up the little voting slips and throw them in the air. The hollow-eyed children smiled at the snowy confetti, so more and more adults tore up their voting slips and threw them upwards to entertain the little ones.

By riding with the Senate Printer and his blank ballot slips to Factories Two, Three and Four, Gloria each time caught the workers before they could vote. In each, she managed to turn bloodthirsty mobs into striking workers. But by Factory Five (Foundry), her chauffeur Appis and Myld had somehow heard what was happening and were waiting for her beside a horse and trap.

Astonishingly, they did not arrest her for treason or lying, or try to stop her entering the building. But she had no need to climb on another machine, address another mob. Since the factory gates had been locked to keep them in, the workers had been communicating with each other in semaphore, roof to roof. With flapping flags, Gloria's message had travelled from factory to factory: First things first. Think about our children; let's down tools and get what we want!

No more voting slips were needed. A strike had begun.

Even at the great age of sixteen, Gloria still expected to be smacked if she misbehaved. Now, she fully expected to be either slapped or arrested. But Myld only offered her a hand to climb into the trap. Keeping tight hold of her fingers, he leaned in close. "Well! What a splendid game this is turning into!" he whispered.

As Gloria rode home, her feeling of triumph began to waver. She had hoped to present her success to Timor like an ice-cream cone, but the ice cream seemed to be melting, and all she was left with was cold and sticky hands. What if the people stopped pumping and the water rose up now and drowned them all? What if the city walls fell in because she had stopped the bombing, and everybody got killed? What if she had wrecked the economy of Afalia for ever and ever?

Timor was in an odd mood. "Well? Any luck?" he asked, clearly expecting none.

"Sort of. Don't be cross. I didn't read your lovely speech…"

Timor gave a groan of despair.

"But I did get them to go on strike till the children are out of the factories. So they all tore up their voting papers."

He stared at her for a long time. "How… What an extraordinary person you are."

"I hope they don't drown, though, when they stop pumping… Oh – did you visit the pilots' homes? Bet they weren't really shot down. Bet you."

Timor chose not to answer.

CHAPTER TWENTY-EIGHT
Treachery

PRAESTO CITY

When the people went on strike and stopped pumping, an uncanny silence fell over the city. There was still the noise of the flood beyond the walls, but the interminable *thump-thump-thump* of the pumps was gone.

Along with it went the headache that had been plaguing Gloria. For the first time in months, she overslept. For the first time in days, she woke hungry for breakfast.

But in the kitchen, Cook and Lixi were talking in low voices, so she hesitated outside the door. Lixi seemed to be coming to the boil, like an overfilled kettle. Though she spoke in whispers, the whispers were as hot and hissy as steam. She was throwing things about and using swear words Gloria had never heard before. Then she went silent – so silent that Gloria kneeled down to look through the keyhole in case, by some wonderful stroke of luck, Lixi had fallen down dead. But the girl had her hands on her hips in that stance she so favoured. Quite suddenly she tossed her head and announced: "We're leaving! We're off out. I got things to tell!" The things she wanted to tell were not about ghostly whisperings or speaking squirrels or her attempts to blackmail Gloria. "I'm not stopping on here where I have to wait hand-and-foot on that scrubby, lying little *maid*. We're leaving."

"But—" said Cook.

"BUT. We got something good to sell, Mother. *We* know something that people will pay us to tell! The newspaper. Politicians. They'll give us a *big* reward – like maybe a house and a lot of money... People do that. They pay informers to tell things. And we got a solid gold thing! We can tell 'em their precious Suprema's just a scrubby maid from the backwoods. Him and Her are in it together, fooling everybody! You wait! They'll give me a medal for it, and pots of money."

To Gloria, suddenly everything seemed over – she could not move, and her cheeks were cold. But inside her head, her brain insisted on churning away, thinking, thinking, thinking, tedious, futile thoughts. She must go and tell Timor that she had done a terrible, unforgiveable, stupid, un-undoable thing.

The first thing Timor did, as she pulled up a chair, was to pass his breakfast to Gloria. That made it all the harder to speak. After all, it was she who had brought Lixi home to Foremost Mansion, like some deadly infectious germ. "I've done a really terrible thing, sir..."

"They will kill her," Timor said quite calmly, when Gloria finished explaining about Lixi's plans to betray them. "They'll shoot us, yes, but first they'll kill Lixi. A maid knowing something like that? It would make them look like fools. I can try explaining that to her, but I doubt she'll listen."

"I'd kill her, but I don't think I could bring myself to, 'cos of Cook. Even if I had a gun."

"Could you kill *anybody*, Gloria?"

"No, sir. Probably not. But you can see how sometimes people might want to when—" She broke off.

Cook had lumbered in to clear the plates. Her red eyes and nose were the only colour in her face, and the crockery tinkled loudly as she picked up the tray. "It's in the hall cupboard, sir," she said sharply.

"What is, Cook?"

"The traitor. I locked it in the hall cupboard. Gawd knows what we do with her long-term, but it'll have to do for now."

"Your…?"

The crockery rattled alarmingly and danced around the tray. "Love her to pieces, but my Lixi hasn't learned about politics yet. Not the *lived* kind. When she has, she'll know a good Suprema when she sees one. Right now, she doesn't have the brains. So she's in the hall cupboard, considering her options." Cook nodded violently in Gloria's direction. "Far as I'm concerned, this *here* is Madame Suprema, sir. She may not have the certificates, but she's got what's needed.

Parents all over'll say the same. So, all due respect to your wife, sir, it's *this* Suprema wins my vote." Mindless of the peril to the china, Cook drew the morning newspaper out of her apron pocket and slapped it down on the table. "This one here managed to get the kiddies out of the factories when no one else cared. Have a read of that and be thankful you got little Gloria and me working for you, sir."

The headline read:

MADAME SUPREMA DEMANDS HEALTHIER CONDITIONS FOR YOUNGSTERS

CHAPTER TWENTY-NINE

A Rosy Future

ROSE CITY

The refugees teetered nervously down from Big Rock Dam towards Rose City. In the sunshine, the city looked radiantly beautiful: houses built in pinky stone, wooden houses turned golden by years of desert dust. There were large old civic buildings, big paved public squares and campanile towers glinting with bells. A thousand garden-allotments had turned into colourful mosaics of tomato-red and sweetcorn-yellow.

Only the refugee camps circling the city were ugly. The figures moving among the mounds of rubbish looked like flies swarming. Amid the mess, though, there were hundreds of colourful Afalian flags facing the sky – as if to show passing birds the full extent of the Rosies' pride in their country.

It was hard not to hurry. Down there, loved ones might be waiting. Friends, neighbours, family members might also have reached here, and if that was possible, so was happiness.

Heinz saw nothing. He had been wrapped in someone's jacket and was carried in arms. When some jolt raised him near the surface of sleep, he caught sight of Horse. The knotted rope was in the hands of some lad…but no one who was Clem. Heinz had not thought hard enough, looked hard enough, travelled in the right direction. All the Virtues he had been born with had somehow escaped him on the journey, like precious belongings falling through the hole in a bag. Careless. Clumsy. And now he was too tired to look any more. There was nothing to do but sink, as Mycar had sunk, into the deep blackness of sleep.

The array of Afalian flags proved not to be there for decoration – they had been stretched flat over pea-sticks to give shelter. Under them sat little groups of the homeless surrounded by their possessions. They studied the newcomers with desperate eyes, in search of a face they knew.

"Where you from?"

"Snake Landing. You?"

"Bull's Creek. You met any others from Bull's Creek?"

"Sorry."

On the roadway into the city, an old man sat at a stall wearing the traditional Afalian straw hat draped in brightly coloured scarves. He held up his hand as they approached. It might have been a greeting or a command to stop – his eyes were too deep-set to read. "How many are you?" he asked. His accent was foreign.

Hope was instantly replaced by dread. They were not wanted! The patience of Rose City had been used up by too many arriving! What if they were just yet more unwelcome strangers, wanting, wanting, wanting…

The old man took a deep breath and began to recite the script he had spoken a hundred times before:

"Welcome to Rose City. We will do our best to help you. Where there are babies and elderly people, we try to find room for them in our houses, but almost every house is full now, so I must ask that only the very old, and mothers with babies— Oh! You have a horse! A horse is remarkable… Where was I? Ah yes… What Love can do, we shall do. We are honoured to meet you. Every stranger is a gift. I myself came to this blessèd land as a refugee from war. We wish we could do more. Meanwhile, we have bean porridge. Sit down. We will fetch it to you."

Heinz would not eat. Many others went without food and headed at once for the all-important Lists. Heinz followed them.

The Lists covered a long wall with the names of people who had arrived in Rose City. New arrivals ran there. On legs that had walked one hundred, two hundred lambits they ran, in the hope of finding the names of loved ones. Frantic refugees ran their fingers down column after column of names and, when they came to the end, began again in case they had missed seeing the one they were looking for.

Heinz stood among the clutter of feet and watched this strange ritual of stroking the walls with one finger. But he could not read lists – only smells. He knew he ought to be mapping the smells of this new place. But he was too tired. He resolved to find Horse – the only friend in the world he had not lost.

Horse, wearily and against her will, was giving rides to little children. Heinz walked behind her heels, seeing nothing but the prints her hooves made in the soft ground, smelling only the sweet reek of her droppings. He could not go on and on and on and on searching, like those frantic people scanning the wall with one finger.

A sharp movement made him flinch. One of the Afalian flags had blown off its stakes and bowled across the ground in a bundle. It enveloped Heinz in cloth. He was terrified. This dog who had faced down No-Name, who had ridden white-water rapids, fought rats and killed a hawser snake, was riddled with fear. There were feet running towards him. He could hear yelling. He set off to run, but the flag had snared him. He writhed and struggled and trembled and mewed. More running feet shook the ground, like feral dogs heading in for the kill. Heinz's legs scrabbled, but he was upside down and his claws were caught in the flag's weave and he hadn't a hope of escaping. His temperature soared. Hands began pulling at the flag.

"Gotta-gotta-gottabe!" roared a voice, ragged as a hacksaw. "Letitbe-letitbe!"

Scents swarmed through the sun-hot, sunlit cotton. A swill of remembered smells. Sawdust. Cats. Myrtle bushes. Rabbit stew. Fish bait. Clem. Knotted rope. Rubber balls. Clem. Water hyacinths. Hound Death…

Hands gripped the flag and tugged so hard that Heinz was tumbled out of it and rolled over and over. He got to his feet but was too dizzy to run, and keeled over.

"Naughty horse," whined a child's voice. "Come back! Where you going?"

Heinz opened his eyes and Horse's huge nose filled his vision. She sneezed wetly. Then she nudged him, as newborn foals are nudged into standing up for the first time. Heinz rolled onto his back and there was another face above him: the round dazzle of the sun; he could see nothing at all. Then hands lifted him and all those same smells came back: sweat, Clem, rope, Clem, home, ball, joy, Clem, Clem, Clem… And he put out his tongue and licked – and his tongue licked face and the face pressed into the fur of his neck… And sadness cracked like an eggshell and fell away.

As Clem stood cradling his dog, crying salt tears of happiness into its matted fur, Horse nudged him, too, as if to say, *About time, boy. About time.*

NOAH'S ARK OF SHAME

SCANDAL AS "FAT CATS" SCRAMBLE TO SAVE THEMSELVES

"ARK" WILL BE PUT TO BETTER USE

Shock details have surfaced of a plan by the rich and powerful to escape Praesto by ship, abandoning the rest of its citizens. Many notable figures in the city have been arrested.

Horror was expressed last night that bankers, factory-owners, celebrities, industrialists and even some politicians have been secretly preparing to set sail in luxury if the city walls should fail. "This is a scandal," said Mr Kovet, Senator for Home Affairs. "I am shocked and outraged that the very people who should be setting an example have sunk so low.

FAR BETTER USE

"The ship in question will be put to far better use. Close-hauled and securely chained to the city walls, I intend it to house the city's children. In times of danger, our first thoughts must always be for our innocent children, not ourselves."

GRANTING THE SUPREMA'S WISH

Madame Suprema has called repeatedly for the children of our heroic factory workers to be moved to cleaner, dryer surroundings.

Last night Senator Kovet, a father himself, agreed: "The factories are no longer a healthy place for young children. Let them be housed instead aboard this 'Noah's Ark'. Let them play and sleep, warm and safe, where those cowardly 'fat cats' planned to sit purring."

The Editor adds her own voice in praise of "Noah's Ark". Children are our future and if (Heaven forbid) the city walls should fail, those aboard the ship will be in the very safest place.

We also congratulate Senator Kovet on his knighthood, conferred last week by Madame Suprema "for services to the city and people of Praesto in time of need".

CHAPTER THIRTY

The Pied Piper

PRAESTO CITY

Gloria was outraged. She slapped the back of the newspaper as Timor tried to read it. "I shouldn't have had to read about this in *The Voice*! Kovet should have come and told me! I mean, I never ordered anybody to be arrested! Who's been arrested? How many? And I never knighted him! I don't even like him!"

"Need it be true?" asked Timor. "I see that 'The Editor adds her own voice' just here, which is remarkable, given that she's been so well and truly...silenced."

The crack in his voice fetched Gloria up short. What kind of sadness and rage must be battling inside him, while she threw a tantrum in his living room? Hastily, she changed the subject. "I didn't know *Mr* Kovet has children," she said. "He doesn't *look* like someone with children."

"Is there a look?"

"I'll bet *his* sons haven't been put to work in the factories."

"No. Their mother tutors them at home. Nice boys. They're the image of their father, but they have better manners. The rich and powerful are always exempt – or you and I would be working the pumps now. Count your blessings."

"Oh I do, sir. I really do."

Gloria tried to find a bright side to the situation. She was perfectly sure that Kovet would rather be sending airmen to bomb Big Rock Dam than giving in to the striking factory hands, and rehousing small children. "He must be better than he looks," she said, "to get so angry about the selfish toffs and their escape plan."

"Oh, he knew full well about Noah's Ark," said Timor. "At the zoo dinner and after."

"You think?"

"You said that when you mentioned 'Noah's Ark' next day, he looked panicky and stopped you saying any more. *He* knew what you were talking about, even if you didn't."

"Yes! Yes, he did! So…not very 'shocked and outraged' at all then?" said Gloria.

"No matter. It looks as if you won the battle of wills, girl. Congratulations. As Cook said, you got the children out of the factories. There is something, though… Something nagging away in here." He ruffled his hair, smoothed it again and looked back at the newspaper. "This makes it sound like a huge conspiracy…and yet we got no wind of it… No one came to tell *you* about it. It smacks of a putsch. A power grab. I'll get a list from the Prison Governor of who's been arrested. With luck, it's all lies and there was no conspiracy at all… And I must try and find out who is calling themselves 'Editor' of *The Voice* these days… Will you go and see the children settled into their floating palace?"

"Of course! It will be a happy thing to do," said Gloria, pulling on her hat and veil. "And I promise not to bring any home with me."

The bell rang in the hall, and a peep round the door showed Mr Myld beyond the coloured glass panels.

"Oh!" squealed Gloria. "What's *he* doing here? Don't let's let him in!"

Myld's eyes shone with enthusiasm. "…And so we thought your beautiful Daisy should lead the procession!"

Gloria, too, was excited by the thought of little children parading all the way to their "floating palace", led by Daisy. Myld's arrival, though, had thrown her into a panic. She had not wanted to let him into the hall, but he was so slim that he had sidled round the door the moment the latch was undone.

"I'll come with you! Just give me a minute to put my coat on," said Gloria, thinking to hurry him outside again.

Myld winced. "*Please* don't take offence, ma'am, but Senator Kovet *so* deserves the spotlight today. He uncovered the scandalous 'Noah's Ark Plot', as he calls it. And he thought up this *so*-much-better use for the ship. I know the old chap can seem gruff at times, but I am rather devoted to him. So I beg you, Madame, stay home today. Let him have his moment of fame...and let *Daisy* represent you in the parade! The Mascot of the Workers!"

"Of course! Yes! Tell Mr Kovet... Sir Kovet, I mean... Senator Kovet thank you from me." And Gloria opened the front door. She had no qualms about entrusting Daisy to the man who had already rescued her once from Kovet's spite. She knew he would bring her back safe and sound.

Just as the dog's lead changed hands, and Myld started down the steps, banging began in the hall cupboard – the noise Gloria had been dreading.

Lixi.

"Let me out. Don't go! They locked me in! I know things!" There was a bat-like noise of umbrellas being beaten to death against the woodwork. Gloria thought it was the noise of her own heart disintegrating.

Myld came back up the steps, looked towards the noise and raised his eyebrows. Gloria thought she was going to be sick and wondered how to do it without lifting her veil.

"Let me out and I'll tell you something! She locked me in 'cos I know too much about her!"

Myld gave a faint smile. "Staff problems?"

Gloria nodded so hard that her hair burst from her hat.

"The maid drank the cooking brandy. She went berserk! We had to put her *somewhere*!"

Myld gave this the longest consideration. "Would you like me to...*remove* the problem?"

"No! No! She's had lots of hardship, poor thing."

Myld tilted his head ever so slightly, as if faintly amused. Then, remarkably – astoundingly – he left, luring Daisy into his pony-and-trap with stale cornflakes from his pocket.

As soon as he was gone, Gloria headed for the attic room and Timor and Cook, to watch the excitement through shared binoculars. Having made it happen, she did not intend to miss seeing the parade. "I'll kill you later, Lixi," she remarked, kicking the cupboard door as she passed, and half thought she meant it.

The factory gates were even now unlocking, all the children under eleven marching in happy, high-stepping columns out of the Five Factories towards the city's port. Their parents and older brothers and sisters watched from within the railings; they were in holiday mood, waving as their little ones marched off towards the mysterious Noah's Ark. There was no wrenching sorrow at parting. (After all, the ship was not actually *going* anywhere, and *The Voice* had said that parents could visit in a day or two, when the children were settled in.) By all accounts, the liner had been turned into a palace fit for princes and princesses (though no one had actually seen it, since it was moored up behind the Civil Guard barracks). If the politicians and captains of industry had been planning to escape aboard it, it was bound to be comfortable. There was talk of school and games and bunks with feather pillows with no headlice in them! (Some, who knew the original story of Noah, feared the Ark might already be full of animals, but were assured that *their* Ark would be much more comfortable than the original. And just for them.)

Daisy did not know what to make of Mr Myld – he was a mixture of too many smells. She was drawn to Kovet by the tobacco he kept in his pocket, and his obvious fear of her only made her more determined to win him over. Myld's hair, though, was stuck down with sweet oil. His armpits smelled of nothing, and his trousers of starch and cornflakes. It was hard to know whether to lick him or find him a muddy puddle to roll in. She did not understand why Gloria had handed her over to him that morning, but was happy enough to go with Myld, for the sake of the cornflakes.

The procession wound through the city, watched by a handful of Volunteer Firemen, Air Force officers, two press photographers and a sprinkling of Civil Guards. The ship's Captain, in full dress-uniform, led the way for a while, then hurried off ahead, saying there was "much to do". (Though what a moored hotel ship needed a captain for, nobody quite knew.) So Kovet and Daisy were left leading the children out of the city's industrial thumping heart towards the city port: the Pied Piper and his dog. Brothers and sisters held hands, the older children led the younger... The Cutlery Brass Band was playing. The children pretended to march. Myld moved among them, encouraging them to sing. He looked like a long, thin spoon stirring bubbly soup.

"What a nice man he is," said Gloria, watching him through the binoculars.

There was something about the excitement, the brisk, bright morning, that made Daisy step out, head high, tail sweeping to and fro like a queenly wave. Kovet had been supplied with stale cornflakes by his assistant, but they stayed in his pocket. He could not bring himself to have Daisy snuffle them out of his hand. The grim gates of the Civil Guard Barracks opened onto a long corridor running clear through the building. On the far side, Civil Guards lined the stone staircase up to the city wall and saluted as Senator Kovet and dog struggled up the steps. Myld took three stairs at a time to catch them up, and there were cornflakes again!

The harness Myld put on Daisy, though, was downright alarming. So was the crying, when five hundred frightened children saw their hotel for the first time.

They had been promised a luxury liner stuffed with books and toys. Noah's Ark was a big ugly ore carrier – the one vessel left afloat after the port was sunk by the flood. Somehow, rope lines had been propelled aboard it by rocket, and it had been hauled closer and tied up hard against the city wall. Hidden by the huge, ugly barracks, it lay out of sight of anywhere else in the city. And it was out of sight of the crowds that the festival mood changed to a military operation.

White canvas chutes, like slides in the park, ran from the top of the city wall down onto the decks of the ship. More Civil Guards stood waiting at the foot of the slides. The children were invited to slide down. None said yes.

Then their eyes were transfixed by the sight of a white, fluffy dog flying out from the wall as a luffing crane swung her into mid-air and lowered her gently to the ship's deck. She barked up in their direction, asking to be rescued.

Through a loudhailer, Kovet asked: "Who's going to join Daisy? Who wants to go down the nice slide?"

A tough-looking girl, who wore boots instead of shoes and fists instead of hands, plunged onto the canvas slide. Her cronies followed her, shrieking. When the timid ones still hung back, ice cream was promised. And when that failed, Myld suggested, "Senator Kovet wants to go down the slide, don't you, sir?"

"Know your place, Myld. I want nothing of the sort," said Kovet.

So the Civil Guard stepped in and, one by one, the children were thrown, like sacks of nickel ore, onto the chutes.

Their yells were not the same as in the park playground, where Daisy had often watched children screaming with excitement. Hampered by the sling still circling her stomach, she began to run to and fro, barking. *Stop. Stop. Stop.* Something was terribly, horribly wrong. Where was Gloria to put things right? The water racing past the ship's hull spoke menace.

"When this is finished," Kovet told his assistant, "dump the dog over the side, right? That's an order. Is the Captain aboard? I can't see him."

Myld, too, scoured the deck and bridge for the Captain. "Engine room, sir?"

The cargo of children was being stowed in the forward hold of the ship. They were slid down more cloth chutes, like coal into a coal-cellar. No cabins, no bunk beds, no dining halls or deck games. No ice cream. Only a dark, hollow cavern of rusting metal, booming with their own screaming. When the front hold was full, the Guards filled the rear one. It was an operation performed with military precision. As the last child was stowed, the Civil Guard immediately began to quit the ship, swarming up hook ladders latched over the city wall. The moored, floating hotel was about to leave on an unscheduled voyage.

"Cast off all!"

The ship's engine gave a snore, a cough and shuddered into life.

"This, sir, will have the workers obeying your every command," said Myld to his boss, with a broad smile. "Here are five hundred reasons for the workers to do exactly as they are told. You have definitely played a winning card here… Oh, I almost forgot to say, sir, I took the liberty of fetching your little boys here earlier on."

"You did what?"

"Your sons. I gave them one of the crew cabins, naturally. Up near the fo'c'sle, sir. Perhaps you'd like to say goodbye to them?"

Kovet stared at his assistant – a thing he had rarely done before; at the fine, flaxen hairs on the top lip, the steely blue eyes, the archery bow of a mouth, the knife-sharp nose…

And all the while, Kovet could hear cold-hammers knocking out the cleats in the wall, letting go the mooring ropes, the ship throbbing into life.

"Not my boys, Myld!"

"Crew deck, fo'c'sle end, sir. See for yourself."

Kovet leaped onto the one and only remaining chute and slid down it, accumulating the dirt left behind by a hundred grubby children. Struggling to his feet, he shouted at the Civil Guard – "Stop! I forbid you to cast off this ship! Where's the Captain?" – realizing, little by little that they, too, had betrayed him; that they were Myld's men now. He ran towards the bow in search of his sons, stumbling along the deck and calling their names.

They were not there.

Another of Myld's lies? Or was he just looking in the wrong place? While he stood frozen by indecision, the huge ship swung away from its berth, floating sideways downstream and out of the shelter of the city wall. When the full force of the river hit it, it heeled over, but righted itself and sailed on. Beneath its hull was meltwater from the Lacha Mountains, ambitious to reach the sea. Aboard it were five hundred small children, one dog and Mr Kovet, now *Sir* Kovet, Senator for Home Affairs.

Gloria, Timor and Cook stood watching, through binoculars, the blank façade of the Civil Guard Barracks from the eaves bedroom. They saw the ship appear unexpectedly beyond the city wall and drift away and away.

"It's broken loose!"

"S'pose there was kiddies already aboard," whispered Cook.

"Don't say that! Say they're not on there! Say they're not!" said Gloria, clinging on to Timor's arm.

"The cables must've failed," he said.

Only one of the Foremost household knew for sure what had happened: Daisy. With her harness still hooked up to the luffing crane, she hung suspended, as the deck moved out from under her paws. A windlass struck her a blow; the deck railings snatched at her and set her swinging to and fro as the ship sailed by underneath her.

Seated at the controls of the dockside crane, Myld let go the harness and watched the dog drop onto the afterdeck. He had meant to drop her in the water but changed his mind. It had just occurred to him how much Kovet would *delight* in Daisy's company.

A fire bucket rolling across the deck struck her such a blow that she fell on her side, and only the deck railings saved her from sliding overboard. Up on the city wall, Myld groaned in an ecstasy of pleasure.

CHAPTER THIRTY-ONE

Liquefaction

ON THE FURCA RIVER

Aboard the MS *Nickelodeon* were five hundred small children, one dog, Senator Kovet, Senator for Home Affairs...and – surely! – a crew.

Kovet struggled to think clearly. Of course! He could see one of the sailors even now, up on the bridge, wrestling with the ship's wheel. All he had to do was instruct the crew to turn the ship around and go back. The thought of Myld seizing power was unbearable. Still less bearable was this boat ride. He had never realized how flimsy a 15,000-tonne vessel could feel. It was as if the ship was plunging, swerving, out of control... To his shame, Kovet was utterly terrified.

No need, no need, no need, he told himself. Ships have crews, and crews are accustomed to riding out raging storms at sea. The *Nickelodeon* hit a knot of cross-currents. There was a cacophony of screaming from under the hatches – and from Kovet himself. He fell forwards and slid along the deck on hands and knees until he collided with the ladder to the wheelhouse. When the ship steadied, he hauled himself up the steps. At the top, the bridge-house door hit him in the face.

The sailor was not in uniform but in overalls. He appeared to be in a life-or-death struggle, his body twisting violently from side to side.

"Where's the Captain?" Kovet demanded, but got only a stare in reply. "Turn the ship around and go back to port."

"Don't just stand there – help, won't you!" was the only answer he got.

"I'm Sir Kovet, Senator for Home Affairs, and I am instructing you to... Look here, where's the Captain? I need to speak to the Captain."

The sailor laughed loudly, without a trace of mirth. "I'm it. I'm what you get. Captain and crew. Filthy rust bucket."

In the wildness of the moment, Kovet thought it must be the sailor's name.

"Grab hold, for pity's sake!" said Rust Bucket.

Kovet scurried along the bridge on hands and knees, before staggering to his feet face-to-face with the sailor and taking hold of the wheel. It was like grabbing the horns of a rampaging bull: two men's combined strength was barely enough to keep it from spinning. Standing nose-to-nose, Kovet saw an expression on the other man's face that chilled him to the marrow. Rust Bucket knew nothing of the plan to take the ship downriver.

"I'm sent to start the engine. 'Why?' I say. 'Why d'you want the engine? She's a floatin' hotel! She's going nowhere!' But there I am, down below, and I hear them letting go the chains! Run back on deck – there's everyone gone – done a bunk – jumped ship – Captain and all. And she's adrift. That was never on the cards! There's kids on board! What kind of fool sets a hulk full of kids adrift in *this*?"

"A terrible accident! The ship broke loose!" Kovet lied staunchly. "I saw it with my own eyes."

"Nah. She was let go – or why'd they want the engines to be running? If I ever get my hands on who—"

Petrified, Kovet tried to look as if an idea had just struck him. "Tell you what! You could always moor up at Eyot Island, couldn't you? Shelter in its lee. Ride out the storm, as it were. You *can* do it, can't you?"

Bucket whimpered; he actually whimpered. "If we make it that far, we can maybe run her aground. Somehow. Some place. An' if she don't fall apart... But there's nickel ore below! Flood came so sudden they never finished off-loading. Hold Three's half full of the muck."

"So? What does that have to—"

"That hatch had better be watertight, mate, or it's all up with us!" And Bucket actually bared his teeth at Kovet like a rabid dog. There was even foam in the corners of his mouth.

Daisy, after skidding to and fro, wedged herself between two deckhouses, like a book between bookends. She could hear the children screaming in the hold. She could feel the ship rise and fall, judder and slew – could hear the clatter of floating things pattering down the side of the hull. She could smell the same acrid stink of nickel ore she had smelled at Factory Five (Foundry). None of it made sense. She startled herself by being suddenly sick.

Generally speaking, Daisy bumbled about, loving people and (largely) being loved. Food fell into her mouth without much explanation. She made no decisions for herself. A cleverer dog would have raced around alerting people to the danger, calculating what would happen next, digging for a remedy where there was none. Wedged in the here and now, Daisy did not know how to form a plan. Even so...

She followed the noise of wailing to Hold One. Astonished to see so many children all in one place, and all crying, she leaned forward as if her tongue might somehow reach them. The ship rolled and she somersaulted into the cloth chute and slid down it on her back.

Fifty children burst out laughing. The rest stopped crying in surprise.

That afternoon, Daisy took the weight of numberless sorrows and fears on her beamy back. Her well of comfort never dried up. One small child – as white and still as wet salt – sat in the rust-red water that swilled around the hold.

The eyes were blank, the skin cold, the hands like shrivelled spiders. Daisy put a paw in the lap, leaned her face against the cheek, nudged the arm. Invisible distress was cascading down off the child. Daisy licked it up and swallowed it. Then she simply stood with her forehead pressed against the chest, until the two twiggy arms rose up and hugged and hugged and hugged her.

Be great in fur, soft of mouth and tireless in love, the DogMaster had said to the world's first golden retriever. And Daisy never swerved from her duty.

Kovet's thoughts returned to his sons. If they were not in the cabins, perhaps Myld had simply thrown them into one of the holds with all the other children. He went aft, calling their names. Searching for just two faces, his gaze was met by two hundred. The children, already ankle-deep in rainwater, stared mutely up at him. Kovet turned away and ran the length of the ship to Hold One, calling and calling – "*Shalto! Augusto!*" – but there were only the faces of other people's children...and a dog who recognized him and wagged her tail.

So! His sons *were* still safe on land. It had just been Myld's ruse to trap him aboard. Such a surge of relief went through him that he laughed out loud.

Then he squatted down and studied the faces below, this

time with the eyes of a father. All these children had fathers, too.

"We really must get you all out of there, mustn't we?" he said.

For two hours he hauled children out of fore and aft holds awash with rainwater, and stowed them in cabins, lockers, deckhouses and lifeboats. Every covered passageway was packed with bleak little faces. The noise of their chattering teeth followed him about the ship. He must feed them! Food would warm them up. He remembered ordering food supplies for the time the children and crew would spend on Eyot Island, but where had those been stowed? Why hadn't he paid more attention?

The golden retriever joined him on his search. Thrown off-balance by the ship's lurching, Kovet laid a hand on her back. It was warm – the only thing on the whole ship that was warm. "Good, dog. Food," he muttered, and Daisy teetered off across the tilting deck to a lifeboat, where she stuck her head in under the canvas. A gust of children's laughter came from inside. The tail wagged. Daisy withdrew her head and looked back at Kovet, who believed her despite himself. Opening up the canvas, he pulled out the snap-locked metal box Daisy had covered in drool. It contained chocolate, raisins and biscuits. Distributing a small amount to the children in the boat, he made more friends in a minute than he had made in his life. But two bars of chocolate and five packs of biscuits were not going to feed five hundred. He ate nothing himself; his stomach had closed up, like a salmon's when it swims upstream.

The dog led him next to Hold Three, the only one with its hatch closed. He looked from dog to hatch, from hatch to dog. "No, you're wrong, dog. Rusty Bucket said there was ore in here, not food..." And he sat down wearily on the metal hatch-cover. It crumbled under his weight, and a shower of rust tinkled down onto things below. When he had unplugged himself from the hole, daylight showed him tins and sacks of food, stashed on top of the nickel ore – food intended for maybe a week's stay on the island. He tried to lift the hatch but it was impossibly heavy. He reached in through the hole his bottom had made, but could not reach any of the sacks. But with his arm through the hole and his cheek pressed to the hatch-cover, he could see that the whole hatch-cover was lacy with rust.

"There's food in Hold Three," Kovet called up to the bridge. "How do I get it open?"

Bucket's voice was ragged from wrestling with the ship's wheel. "Try it and I'll beat your head in."

Kovet seemed to have slid down the social scale to a point

where a junior sailor outranked a Senator. He crawled up the metal steps, holding on so tightly that he cut his fingers. When his head was above the door sill, he asked, "Why?"

"*Told* you! Because there's poxy nickel ore in there, is why, dimwit!" He made his voice slow and sing-song, as if speaking to a child. "It never got unloaded. Never got its chance to be forks and spoons. Aaaaah. But if it's got wet, *we* will get liquefaction. *You want some of that?*"

Liquefaction. Kovet had no idea what it meant, but it sounded like one of those big words people use to exaggerate: Catastrophe! Cataclysm! Annihilation! It seemed a perfect description of what had happened to Afalia – a world turned to liquid. Kovet made a mental note to use it in a speech some time: *liquefaction.* "How long before we reach Eyot Island?" he asked.

"What? Must've passed it way back, idiot! Underwater. Gone. Nothing left to see."

Dismay swallowed Kovet whole. Up till now, he had at least known where he was heading – the *Nickelodeon* had been bound for Eyot Island. But his destination had sunk beneath the waves. It no longer existed! No going back and nowhere to go, except the distant sea.

He did not mention the hole he had put in the rusty hatch-cover, for fear Bucket would beat his head in.

Daisy, as she blundered her way around the ship, read her duty in every sorry little face. Her tail hung heavy, because, above all, she was looking for Gloria and could not find her. But until she did, there was this deep pool of salty sorrow to lick up. Daisy might never have mastered fetching a ball, but she had been born knowing how to retrieve smiles and fetch them back to their owners.

Way downstream, but far inland from the ocean, the waters of the Furca collided with salt water. The incoming sea-tide pushed back against the current. In the normal way of things, it slowed the river almost to a standstill. Now, with the Furca in full flood, the two bodies of water clashed like cavalry, throwing up masses of white, brown and black water, tossing flotsam, jetsam and dead things into the air. Watersmeet.

They reached it after dark. The moon was just rising. The sound of crashing water was thunderous. The moon watched from a safe distance. Both men needed every atom of their strength to keep *Nickelodeon* facing forward as the bow carved into breakers as tall as the ship. Water sluiced over the rails and poured along the companionways. There was a noise of children wakened from sleep by being doused in cold water. The gaping storage holds swallowed fresh and salt water. The ship's propeller, lifted clear of the water, threw up a fan of spray. Its shrill clamour drowned out even the noise of Rust Bucket screaming swearwords. Large litter in the water crashed against the hull as if giants were trying to kick their way in – *fee fie foe BOOM*. The ship bucked – bow down, bow up, bow down, bow up – a 15,000-tonne rocking horse. The moon covered its eyes with grey strands of cloud.

"She should never pitch like that!" yelled Bucket. "Tell me you never tried opening Hold Three!"

"No, no. But the lid's pretty rusty. It's probably awash in there."

Now, in place of swearwords, Bucket launched a kick at Kovet which, in missing, saw his rope-soled shoe fly out of the wheelhouse door and over the rails.

"*I* didn't make it rust!" retorted Kovet. "I don't know why you're—"

"You know nothing, you useless piece of… We're finished. We're dead. Listen, when nickel ore gets wet, it turns liquid. It slops around…" But his scientific explanation dissolved into prayers. He let go of the wheel and fled. Sliding down between the handrails of the steps, he set off to run along the deck – no object in mind, simply running, the streaming water breaking round his ankles. A glassy wave rose up ahead of the ship and the sharp bow shattered it into silver shards. When the spray fell, so did Rust Bucket, skidding on his back under the ship's rail and disappearing as though he had never been.

Down in Hold Three, three hundred tons of nickel ore finished its slow liquefaction into slurry. It had slopped fore

IN ATRAMENTO NON EST VERITAS

FIVE HUNDRED GO TO EYOT ISLAND

Sometimes when lives hang in the balance a Senate must take firm action

A MESSAGE FROM SENATOR SIR KOVET, VICE-SUPREMO

Yesterday, I took the radical step of removing five hundred children to Eyot Island for safety. The city walls are weakening by the hour. The children will be safer there. But to ensure they remain safe we MUST bomb Big Rock Dam. The river is flowing too fast for Noah's Ark to sail upstream again. Only when the dam is destroyed and the river is tamed will the children be able to return to Praesto.

But perhaps you WISH the factories to flood and the machines to be destroyed? Perhaps you want NO employment in the future? NO means of feeding your family? Perhaps you DO NOT CARE if the flood batters down the city walls?

The Suprema and I do care. We have a solemn duty not only to end to the flood, but to secure this city and the jobs of its people. That is why we shall NOT send planes to destroy Big Rock Dam until and if you RETURN TO THE PUMPS.

I repeat:

Only when you begin work again will bombers be sent to Big Rock.

Only when Big Rock Dam is destroyed can Noah's Ark sail home.

The children on Eyot Island await your answer with trembling hearts.

It is with great sadness that *The Voice* announces the death of our much-loved Editor, Professor Hecuba Lightfoot, after a short illness.

Her scholarly intelligence and devotion to the truth will be greatly missed by colleagues and readers alike.

1875 – 1928

CHAPTER THIRTY-TWO

Blackmail

PRAESTO CITY

Foremost Mansion was woken early by the familiar *thump, thump, thump* of the pumps, the soft susurrations of the hoses pushing water out over the city walls in dingy fountains. It was like the heart-flicker of a dead man being resuscitated. Over the next half-hour, the speed picked up, the drumming grew louder, as men and women laboured in all five factories to drive the floodwater out of swamped machine halls. The strike was well and truly over.

There was shouting in the street outside. One shift from each of the five factories had been released onto the streets by the factory owners, to "express their patriotic feelings". A mob was massing outside the Mansion. Faces were thrust between the iron railings. They looked like zoo animals baying to be fed. Their clothes were so ragged that they could have come from another century – and they were so weary that only desperation had given them the energy to climb Foremost Hill.

"*Bomb the dam! Bomb the dam!*" they yelled. "*We're pumping, listen! We're pumping! Fetch back the children!*"

Timor telephoned for the Civil Guard. The phone was dead.

A mounted rider in a long leather coat forged a path through the mob, the horse's hooves slipping on the steep tarmac. He seemed less alarmed than his horse by the noise and tidal surge of bodies.

"It's Myld!" Timor called up the stairs.

"Could you come and help me get my—" begged Gloria, struggling with her hat and her too-much hair.

Appis the chauffeur had crossed the road from his house and was already unlocking the gate for Myld to enter. Several people pushed their way into the front garden behind the horse.

Gloria did up the interminable buttons on her green satin jacket, kicked her maid's uniform under the Suprema's bed. The lipstick mouth drawn on the mirror mocked the sixteen-year-old in her fancy-dress disguise. She lowered the veil so as to blur the sight of herself.

When Gloria and Timor entered the Audience Chamber, Myld was already there. So was the fancy document, back on her desk: same gold deckle edging, same peacock feather pen, same curly handwriting ordering the bombing of Big Rock Dam.

"Where is Sir Kovet?" asked Gloria.

"Ah. He sends his apologies," Myld answered. "He is… unavailable. Scared to show himself, in the circumstances. He is holding their children to ransom, after all. Ruthless, yes, but he did what he felt he needed to do. As you see, some of the factory hands have been given time off to come here and tell you how strongly they feel."

Faces were pressed hard up against the windowpanes. The chandelier tinkled at the sound of the shouting outside: "*Bomb the dam!*"

"Well, Madame? Will you give the People what they want?"

Gloria picked up the pen. The feather exaggerated how much her hand was shaking, so she put it down again.

"No. I won't. I don't believe the people in Rose City are all mad and bad. And even if they are, it's wrong to drown people. Children. Babies." Shivers ran down her back, as a hand came to rest on the scruff of her neck.

"*Sign it,*" said Timor, pushing her head towards the document.

"What?"

"Sign it, you stupid woman. How many times do I have to tell you? *Sign it. For once in your silly, brainless little life, do as I tell you or by God you'll be sorry.*" It was shouted so loudly and so close to her ear that she cringed from the noise.

And it was as if the floor had slid away and dropped her into a dark cellar: Timor was not on her side.

Well, it made a sort of sense. He had already made her commit treason when he dressed her up as his wife. Now he was just making her do something a little bit worse – kill a lot of innocent people in Rose City.

"I won't," she told Myld. "Not unless you move everybody out of the way first – where they can be…not dead."

Myld spread his small, elegant hands and smiled broadly. "Agreed. Spoken like a true humanitarian. We shall leaflet Rose City from the air. And when it's empty, we shall bomb the dam."

"Promise?"

"I promise."

"On your honour?"

"On my honour."

Gloria grinned. So! Timor would not get the last word! It was true what Cook had said! Gloria *was* the Suprema now! Timor might make her suffer for it later, but right now she could achieve good things! It made her feel ferociously clever. "When I've got proof they are safe, *then* I'll sign," said Gloria, and threw the pen like a javelin across the desk.

Myld looked down at the ink stain on his leather coat. He adopted a slight frown. His nostrils widened. His long lashes drooped once, and then he sighed deeply.

"I don't need this."

He leaned across the desk as if he might slap her, but only turned the document round to face him and, at the bottom, drew a scratchy, seismic knot – a first-class likeness of the Suprema's signature. "Bits of paper like this are strictly for the historians," he said. "Sticking plasters to hide the blood. I've already sent two bombers up to Rose City in the last fortnight. Unfortunately, neither seems to have succeeded in blowing the dam. But we'll keep on sending more until they get the job done. Useful as you are to me, girl, I have no intention of letting a *housemaid* get in the way of what has to be done."

Timor punched the air and gave a vicious yell of delight. "*Finally!*" He appeared to collect himself. "Forgive me, Mr Myld. I was under orders from my wife to find a 'stand-in' for her till her return. I think she feared some usurper might seize power while she's gone. Pity me! You only had to tolerate this wretched girl at meetings. Picture having to pretend she's your wife!" And he gleefully tore off Gloria's hat, so that her hair spilled over her face.

Myld patted the air. "Oh please, Timmy, don't be hasty! Let us not unmask this one just yet. The public feel safer thinking the Suprema is actually here, *in* the city. I'm not surprised the workers were fooled, but it's a mystery to me why the Senate were. Simple souls. Even Kovet was taken in. I found it so amusing that I did not put him right. The secret remains between us three."

Timor growled, shrugged and smacked the hat against Gloria's head. "This bombing mission," he muttered. "I'll do it."

He moved smartly towards the hall stairs, calling over his shoulder, "I flew bombers in the war. I'm good. I'll get the job done for you." He ran up the stairs and across the ballroom to the French doors and the balcony that overlooked the street. The doors had not been opened for so long that he wrenched one handle off before they would let him out onto the balcony. A breathless silence fell over the crowds in the garden and beyond the fence.

"My wife the Suprema has just signed a decree ordering the bombing of Big Rock Dam in accordance with your wishes. As a pilot, and husband of Madame, I feel it my duty to do the job myself! Is that to your liking?"

The cheers were so loud that Myld's horse shied and fled to the orchard.

From the back of the ballroom, Gloria and Myld watched Timor's silhouette waving to the crowds from the balcony. "Where's Daisy?" Gloria asked quietly.

"With all the other hostages, of course," said Myld. He looked at his watch. "By now they'll be on Eyot Island having a thoroughly miserable time. Want your doggy back? It can be arranged. Likewise, the children. *After* the dam's destroyed, that is, and the pumps are running night and day. There are certain things, though, that I'll need you to do first. I have already arrested – correction! – *Kovet* has already arrested the Senate, factory owners, lawyers and bankers, for 'planning to desert the city aboard Noah's Ark'. You will declare a State of Emergency. That will allow 'Madame Suprema' to take *absolute control* of just about everything – well, she and her faithful Vice Supremo, First Senator Kovet."

"Kovet? Not you?"

"Of course not! In due course, the people will hound Kovet through the city, kick in his door and shred him into tiny pieces for kidnapping their children and holding them to ransom. They'll call him a tyrant and a bully and burn down his house. Someone has to take the blame when this is all over and the flood goes down. I suppose that's the reason the Real One chose to run away. Someone *always* has to take the blame. But it isn't going to be 'that nice man, Mr Myld'. Nor *La* Suprema, don't fret – you still have your uses. Oh no. It's going to be Kovet, the tiresome prig. Don't waste tears on *him*, will you? He went along with the child-kidnap plan when I suggested it. He just wasn't expecting to make the voyage himself... Oops, have I said too much? Yes, indeed, at this very moment Kovet is on Eyot Island – unwilling nursemaid to five hundred children and a dog." The sheer delight at his own cleverness put colour in Myld's cheeks.

"So, when he comes back and gets killed by the mob, then it will be 'Supremo Myld', right?" said Gloria.

"Who, me? Mr mild-mannered Myld? I'm no one, me. Invisible." Suddenly and violently, he thrust his hand up the back of her green silk jacket and grabbed a hank of her hair. "I am the puppeteer in the Punch and Judy show." He tugged her head right and left, forward and back. "No one sees me or gives me a second thought. But from now on, I'll be pulling *all* the strings."

He went down the stairs at a run and crossed the hall.

Hearing unfamiliar footsteps outside her prison, Lixi started up again with her cries for help, her offers of secret information. Myld called back up to Gloria, "Oh, I must remember to send a rat exterminator to see to the vermin in the cupboard. See how I look after you? But do remember, won't you? I am unique in my genius. Lookalike Supremas are ten-a-penny. They can always be replaced if they don't do *exactly* as they are told."

 The Voice

IN ATRAMENTO NON EST VERITAS

THE PEOPLE HAVE SPOKEN AND WE HAVE LISTENED

"Yesterday those same people who have poured blood, sweat and tears into keeping the heart of Praesto pumping, called with one voice for the destruction of Big Rock Dam and the 'dousing' of Rose City, which has proved itself our Enemy.

Now we turn, with gladness and thanks, to the Afalian Air Force. The Suprema's husband, Captain

Timor Philotapantasol, told a crowd of the cheering workers that he has volunteered to 'get the job done.' Let your prayers go with him on his dangerous mission."

Vice-Supremo Sir Kovet, Senate House

In yesterday's referendum, the people of Praesto City voted unanimously for the bombing of Big Rock Dam, halving the amount of water flowing down the Furca River. It is thought there will be a great rivalry among the officers of the AAF for the honour of flying the mission.

LETTER FROM ONE OF OUR READERS

Madam,

I did not fight in the last war only to see louts and hooligans behaving like savages. It makes my blood boil to think of them laughing at our suffering and waiting their chance to take over Afalia. Pour cold water on the brutes and let us see Law and Order triumph over Anarchy and Wickedness!

I remain your patriotic and faithful servant,

Sergeant Bunny Warren,

Trigger Lane.

CHAPTER THIRTY-THREE

Between Big Rock and a Hard Place

PRAESTO CITY

Gloria was resolved to jump off the city walls into the flood sooner than have to do what Myld told her – or speak to Timor ever again. He had used her. He had never been on her side.

But then a thought struck her: if she jumped off the city walls right away, no one would know where Daisy was. So now she stood in the doorway of Timor's office and threw the information at him like a dart. "Daisy was on the ship. She's on Eyot Island now, with the children."

"That's a blow," said Timor. "She's a lovely creature." He was putting on his wartime outfit: leather coat, short boots, roomy trousers...

"And Myld's sending someone round here to kill Lixi."

Timor's hands fumbled the laces of his boots. "Your problem's solved then."

"Oh, I'd never—" But no. She refused to argue with Timor.

He was not worth it. He had told her – *shouted* at her – to sign that murderous decree. He had been against her all along. He was a lying, two-faced—

Timor coughed. "Forgive my dreadful overacting earlier," he said quietly. "I needed the use of a plane. And I had to make Myld believe it wasn't *my* idea to pass you off as the Suprema – he had to think I'd been saddled with you against my will. And that we hate the sight of each other. If he thought we were in cahoots, he'd just have me killed, and then what good would I be to you? More importantly, if I hadn't offered to do the bombing, yet another pilot would have been sent to do it – and *he* might have obeyed orders."

Gloria stood bolt upright, like a March hare. "And you won't? Drop a bomb?"

"Good heavens, no."

"You were *lying?*" An unaccountable bolt of fear went through Gloria. "Say you didn't lie about being a pilot! You can *fly* a plane? You really *are* a pilot?"

Timor held up his leather helmet by way of proof. "I would still be one, but it was judged an 'unsuitable career' for the husband of the Head of State. The Suprema preferred me not to work at all. Don't worry. I can get you out of here."

"Out?"

"Out. Out of Praesto. Out of Myld's reach. I got you into this. Now it's too dangerous. So it's my job to get you out."

"Oh! But I can't *leave!*"

She tried to explain. The reasons crowded into her head, driving out-of-mind entirely her plan to throw herself off the city walls.

There was Lixi to hide somewhere: "Back in the factory, I thought – as if she never left. She'll go anywhere Myld can't find her."

There were the children to rescue from Eyot Island. "And Daisy! Oh, poor Daisy! She doesn't have her sleeping basket or her ball or anything, and I know she's only a dog, but…"

There was Myld, who ought to be fed to the jackals (if the jackals hadn't all been eaten at the banquet)…

And the Civil Guard, who ought to be shot for helping Myld kidnap all those children.

There were the Senators and factory owners and bankers to rescue from prison, if Myld had only put them there out of spite.

There needed to be a statue put up to Hecuba Lightfoot, and the newspaper had to be closed down before it could tell any more lies.

The carcases of those dead zoo animals hanging up in the cellars of the Banqueting Hall had to be shared out among the hungry – "Pies! I thought pies would be not so revolting. I'd rather bury them in proper graves – animals deserve graves, same as people! – but I have to be pragmatic."

And she had to invent a way to net lots of fish from the river, now all the food had run out. "Though I've seen a lot of dead ones floating past and you mustn't eat fish that are already dead – dead before you catch them, I mean...

"And if the worst comes to the worst, we can probably use the shelves in the library to build lifeboats!"

The more tasks she listed, the more Timor laughed. He laughed so hard he had to loosen his Afalian Air Force tie. He laughed so much he couldn't refold his flight map. He laughed till the anger he had been wearing for so long, like a suit of heavy armour, shook itself to pieces. Then he walked over and hugged her until she stopped crying. "You women. Is there no end to your ambition?"

"I can't leave," she whispered into his jacket.

"You can and you must. I'll have to come back here, but not you...not till things are back to normal. Alright?"

"But I'm supposed to be responsible for everyone!"

"No. Supremas are, yes. Supremas' husbands, probably. But housemaids, no. They aren't qualified. And a good housemaid is too valuable to risk losing to the likes of Myld. Besides, she who fights and runs away lives to make a nuisance of herself another day. Now, can we please get you somewhere safe?"

It was five o'clock in the morning, and day was nothing but a red-hot poker lying along the horizon. Take-off was scheduled for noon, and was supposed to involve Myld, a ten-piece

Afalian Air Force band and a press photographer. But Timor wanted to be gone long before then.

When the rain had threatened to turn the military airfield into a swamp, the whole Air Force fleet had been flown to higher ground and rehoused in a vast, arched, corrugated-iron shed on a hilltop. Now troop-carriers, bombers and spotter planes were lined up inside it, facing east across the flat concrete roofs of Factory Five (Foundry).

"Well, will you look at that," said Timor, pointing at the shed wall. "This used to be a paint warehouse; belonged to a chap called Noah Pinkney. That's been there for years." On the rusty iron, Noah Pinkney had long ago daubed the words NOAH'S ARCH. Timor suddenly knew what had been troubling him about the "Noah's Ark plot". "It never was a ship! When all those bigwigs at the banquet talked about it, they were just expecting to be flown out by the Air Force! My wife probably promised them a seat in return for a bribe. A scandal, yes – twenty or so rats planning to leave a sinking ship – but Myld decided to blow it up into this huge, fake conspiracy. He's using it to arrest just about everyone with any power... And then the master stroke: why not put the children on board some real live 'Noah's Ark' and hold them to ransom downriver, so that the workers will do exactly as they're told? He'd have the whole city in the palm of his hand."

Gloria gasped, and a shiver of revulsion ran down her spine as she thought of Myld's hand tugging her hair.

"He's such a liar, that man! You know what, I bet he hasn't really sent *anybody* to bomb Rose. That was just another lie. Those pilots 'delivering blankets' and stuff were just invented by the newspaper, weren't they? You went and checked, didn't you, and they weren't missing at all, were they? It was just the newspaper lying."

Timor leaned a hand against the metal building. He seemed unwilling to answer. Then he said: "I checked, yes. I just didn't choose to tell you what I found: families in mourning, front doors painted black, everything. They'd been told their sons died delivering help and comfort to folk upriver. I refrained from saying their sons had died on a bombing mission. But it looks as if they did. I checked with my friends in the Air Force: two bombers are missing."

So two planes really had flown out of Praesto City, laden with explosives. Neither had returned. Now two huge bombs nestled beneath the wings of AAF66.

Gloria tried not to see them as she climbed into the cockpit. Timor settled himself beside her, all leather and flight manuals, sweat on his top lip and speaking in the kind of measured sentences meant to show he was at his ease. "Are you all set? Did Lixi go quietly?"

"Oh yes. Since she heard Myld say about extermerating her, she hasn't said a word."

"Good, good. Now. We fly down to the sea, drop the bombs into deep water, then I set you down somewhere you'll be safe until the flood subsides."

"Set *me* down? Just me? What about you? You mustn't come back here! Myld would kill you!"

Timor simply tapped the fuel indicator. The arrow, hard up against *FULL*, did not so much as shiver. He put his fingertips to the rim and unscrewed the glass disc in front of it, just a fraction. The needle swung back to below halfway – the glass had been pinning the needle in place. "Enough fuel to get to the dam. Not enough to get back again. I'm starting to like Mr Myld less and less." Timor slid the cockpit hatch open again.

"Where are you going now?" asked Gloria in a panic.

"To top up the fuel tank, then spin the propeller. When I do, I'll need you to throttle up – I knew there had to be a reason I brought you."

"What if there isn't any more fuel? What if it's run out?"

"Aircraft fuel is no good for cars and generators. If it were, the Civil Guard would certainly have stolen it to sell on the black market... Oh. You can leave that loathsome hat. You won't be needing it again."

He tried to tug the veiled tricorn out of her hands, but her hands refused to let go. It was too strange to think of not wearing it any more; Gloria feared that, without it, she might prove to be nobody at all. She shut her eyes while

he was gone and tried not to think about leaving Praesto
for ever.

As they juddered across the forecourt, he added. "You deserve
to know all the facts. It's eleven years since I've flown. And I
was in spotter planes back then, not bombers."

"Thank you, sir. But if it's all the same, no more facts.
Where's the runway?"

"You're looking at it." The concrete forecourt in front of
the shelter overlooked the flat concrete roof of Factory Five.
"If you can gather enough speed across the forecourt, you can
hop across to the Foundry roof and use that for a runway.
With luck, you get airborne before running out of roof."

It did nothing to settle Gloria's mind.

The plane hopped down with a thud onto the roof of the
factory and sped up, noisy on the tarry surface. The set of
Timor's shoulders said he was willing the plane to lift. Gloria
could feel the weight of the bombs as if they were inside her
guts, heavy and painful. The vast Foundry roof suddenly
seemed as short as a diving board. They were pitching towards
the end... *Come on, come on, come on.*

They never lifted at all, simply shot off the end...but
without plummeting nose-first onto the derelict university
beyond. The statues of various learned men atop their pillars
seemed to duck as AAF66 finally lifted into flight. When they

had gained enough height, they turned back over the city. The sun's rim had risen above the horizon wearing a crest of crimson and Gloria had a perfect, eagle's-eye view of the town.

The Furca had turned Praesto City into an island in a vast sea. A string of telegraph poles was just then tumbling downstream, still laced together by their wires. They struck the city wall where a thousand other pieces of debris had struck, scraped, then been swept onwards. But the telegraph poles were one blow too many.

A large section of brickwork swelled inwards, like a boil, then burst to let in a geyser of water. A shed for storing market stalls was smashed by the downpour, and brightly striped canvases washed away down Railway Avenue. The six telegraph poles still tussled to climb through the gaping V in the top of the wall.

"Damnation!" said Timor. "It really is possible." He scooped the oxygen mask off his chest and breathed so hard from it that his throat was sucked into hollows. With the mask over his face, he looked doglike. It scared Gloria.

"What is?"

He let go of the mask, but he was only really talking to himself. "It's possible. It really could... Maybe it's begun. A thousand years couldn't break it down, so we thought, *It can't happen. It'll never happen.* Along comes Nature and, with a bit of help from us with our marvellous dam, we're done for. Praesto can fall! The whole city – nothing but grit and litter washing down to the sea!"

"It was just a *bit* of wall, wasn't it?" Gloria pleaded.

Timor wriggled upright in his bucket seat. "Absolutely. Quite right. Just a *bit* of wall." And they flew on in silence.

Gloria examined the Suprema's hat, still clutched in her hand. She would keep it for a souvenir (along with the gold-plated carving set given to her by Knives and her cuttings from *The Voice*).

"Why the veil always?" she asked.

She thought Timor was going to ignore her impertinence, but finally he spoke. "My wife says that behind the veil she can be 'all things to all people'. The young can't say she's too old to understand them; the old can imagine she's as old and wise as they are. She can be whatever age people *want* her to be."

"That's a good thought!" said Gloria, who had feared the Suprema was simply vain.

"Good, but untrue," said Timor. "There was a time – long ago – when she didn't wear it. Smiling is important for politicians. They need to smile at all and sundry: visitors, voters, admirers, babies, cameras, bad jokes... She was a hugely ambitious woman. God knows, she did whatever she had to, to *become* Suprema. But once she had succeeded – got the job – she resented smiling, couldn't *do* it, really. The mouth smiled, but never the eyes, and if the eyes don't smile, people notice. I made the mistake of saying this once. She never forgave me. But clearly she believed me. 'Took the veil' then and there. So that no one could see how her eyes never smile. Or how much she despises them all."

Gloria set about pulling the veil off the hat, stitch by stitch: *click click click*. The sun shone obligingly over her right shoulder and lit her efforts. So…they were still flying north… "Where are we going? I thought we were going out to sea to drop the bombs!"

Timor said nothing.

Like a mythical monster, the Furca squirmed below them, brown and green, its transparent belly showing everything it had eaten up. Villages. Clumps of trees. Roads. Train tracks.

Gloria knew, with sudden certainty, that they were heading for Big Rock and the dam.

"Sixteen thousand people, you said!"

"And forty thousand in Praesto. Five hundred more on Eyot Island. Do the maths, child. Did you do maths ever? At all? *The city walls are starting to give way!* The only way to calm the river is to split it in two at Big Rock and reduce the flow by half. Forget Myld. Forget Kovet. And me, I'm damned whatever I do. Tell me: what else can I do now but bomb the dam?"

CHAPTER THIRTY-FOUR

The Simple Life

ROSE CITY

Apart from the List of New Arrivals, there was another place Clem visited every day – a hammock occupied by a pilot with a broken knee. He had arrived, engine sputtering, gliding low over the dam, *almost* avoiding some tents before tipping the plane onto one wing.

Asked where he had been going, the pilot said he had been on his way home from delivering blankets and medicine to people washed out by the flood. The town thought that was wonderful, treated him as a hero and plied him with cactus gin. They even set about mending his plane, as a surprise for when he was fit again.

Clem had a passion for aeroplanes. Back home, he and his ma had run outside whenever one flew over. After this one had crash-landed, he and the other boys had raced to see, and taken turns to sit in the pilot's seat. Desperate to meet a real pilot, Clem and his dog had arrived at the hammock like pilgrims at a shrine. "This is Heinz," he had said, holding Heinz up like an offering.

Now Clem visited every day, and the pilot regaled him with stories, while Heinz sat on the man's chest, trembling.

Heinz thought he remembered once *not* being anxious and afraid, but perhaps he was remembering some other dog in the pack. There had been a pack, hadn't there? His tail had not always hidden between his back legs, had it? No matter. The water had not eaten Clem or swept him away. When he slept on Clem's chest he dreamed of a cabin, trees, starry nights and fishing rods. Books. On good nights, no wall of water dashed the dream to pieces or washed him downstream into a sea of nightmares.

Clem tried to take him for walks, but Heinz was having none of it. He would sit down after a few minutes and not budge, for fear they were heading back to the river, snakes, fires, hail, mud, slaughter, guns... He feared gobbling hyacinths, leaping rats. But there was Clem. He had Clem – or (as he thought of him now) Myboy. *Myboy.*

CHAPTER THIRTY-FIVE

Flight Turbulence

ON BOARD THE AAF66 BOMBER

"Now do you understand why my wife ran away?" said Timor as they flew. "Sometimes things are so impossible that nothing you do is going to be right. Everyone was going to blame her. She'd made plenty of plans to keep her wretched factories dry, to keep the workers working right through the flood, come what may…but it all depended on the rain stopping. So when she read that weather forecast, she knew it was all going to fall apart and she was going to get the blame. And she lost her nerve. Would have been nice if she'd let me know… Maybe she was saving explanations for the train journey…"

Gloria had turned away from him as far as her seat harness would let her and was staring petulantly out of the window; what other weapon does a sixteen-year-old housemaid have but to silently sulk? He was going to bomb the dam. She would never speak to him again. The trouble was, thoughts kept piling up in her head like rubbish in a blocked drain.

"*You could warn them!*" she blurted out. "You could land in Rose City and warn them what's coming!"

"We are carrying two large bombs. I can't land anywhere till they're shed. And just how would *you* react to someone landing in your backyard laden with high explosives and telling you they were about to destroy your city?"

Gloria looked sharply away again, out of the window. She was only *just* sixteen, so no, she didn't know what they ought to do, but surely adults were cleverer than she was.

Things from the air are extraordinarily beautiful. Angels, she thought, must get a very skewed impression of how well everything is going, down below. The submerged railway line looked like a neat row of silver sewing…

Beside her Timor snatched in a breath. "*No!*" He had just seen the wreckage of a train in the river. It had been broken in pieces, but was still easily recognizable below the moving water: the last train out of Praesto City.

"Oh! I'm so sorry!" she blurted. "Your wife!"

He gave the bitterest of laughs. "I wish to God I'd stayed aboard with her! I wouldn't be here now, doing this. I knew she was running away. But I let her, because she's such a… force of Nature. Anyway, my word was good for nothing… Look, Gloria, there's something you really need to know." And he did not look across at her, so Gloria knew it was going to be bad. "The idea was to ditch the bombs then fly you somewhere safe, right? Only now I have to bomb the…"

"Don't *have* to."

"…and, as you know, I'm not the first to try. There have been two other planes sent here before us and neither came back. We know they didn't succeed, because the level of the river down at Praesto didn't drop. Alright, maybe a hailstorm brought them down. Maybe they dropped their bombs but the dam didn't give way. Maybe their bombs didn't detonate. But the most likely reason is that the Rosies shot them down. So Rose City will be expecting another attack. Yes? There's a better-than-even chance they'll shoot us down too. I don't mind about me: but I brought *you* along. So, it won't be the flood that kills you, nor Myld, nor non-existent rabid dogs… It will be *ME* – *my* doing. I'd apologize, but I don't think 'sorry' quite covers it, do you?"

He said it so fiercely that she felt as if she was being told off. Timor was so loud and scary when he shouted.

"*Well? Are you going to say something?*" he blared.

Gloria wondered if, as a condemned prisoner, she was entitled to a last wish. "Could we…maybe…fly up to Sawmills first and see if it's not got flooded? That's where I live. Lived. Used to."

"I don't have enough fuel – for Sawmills, then back here."

"Oh. Of course. Alright."

The reflection of the bomber swam upstream below them like a gigantic salmon on its way to spawn.

"I could maybe check out the nearest of the refugee camps

on Kovet's map. See if it actually exists," Timor offered.

"I'd like that," said Gloria politely, as if she had just been invited to a game of croquet on the back lawn.

Instead of tents, and field-kitchens serving food to happy children, the supposed refugee camp at Hog Heights was nothing but a bare, muddy hill sunk in floodwater. There was no sign of life – not a soul to be seen. The refugee camp had been just another lie. The bombs beneath the wings made for a thrumming noise like someone drumming their fingers on a table.

"They never sent anyone even to look, did they. They never sent food or blankets or anything," said Gloria. "Just two bombers they never told us about. I'll never forgive them."

"Maybe they just behaved like children – shut their eyes, put their fingers in their ears and said la la la, hoping it would all go away. More likely, Kovet or someone *did* send planes and either the planes didn't come back or they *did* and reported a situation so bad it was beyond help. Easier to lie. Easier to control a city full of people who haven't lost hope…" He broke off impatiently. "Look. Are you not going to reproach me, Gloria? Rage at me?"

Gloria shrugged. "That would be like answering back. Madame told me never to answer back… Don't *do* that."

"Do what?"

"Gasp like that. *Ptah*. Like you're exasperated. Madame did it all the time. I'm not exasperating," and she folded her hands in her lap.

After at least a minute he said, "Are too."

"Am not."

"Are too."

"Am not."

Then they laughed that way you do when it's that or cry.

And then there, in the very far distance, was Big Rock Dam.

"Fly over the town first," said Gloria. "Just to see."

"See what? What can you tell about a place from up here?"

"God manages."

"I don't think it works like that. The God business. Not geographically, I mean. Him up there, like a cruising spotter plane… If the dam's guarded – if they're expecting us – I've got seconds to make the drop. If we get hit, I'll fly head-on into the dam and hope the bombs detonate. Understood?"

"Now you're just trying to scare me." He had succeeded, too. It was a minute before she could put another sentence together. "Arrive from a different direction. They won't expect that. Don't come in off the river. Fly in over the city."

"Obdurate little madam!"

But he dipped the wing and the plane swooped away from the river, over steep cliffs and then a lower landscape of green and gold. The desert, coloured by weeks of unaccustomed rain, was unbearably beautiful. They skirted the city, climbing all the time until they were dodging from cloud to cloud and too high (they hoped) to be seen. Timor put on his oxygen mask. Fright wrung at Gloria's insides like period pains. She wondered if it was possible to die of fear. Flecks of black swam across her vision. Big dark grey flecks.

And then they saw what lay below.

Refugees.

"Hades! The whole world's here!" breathed Timor. He leaned forward and wiped at the windscreen with a gloved hand, to see better. Then he banked away north and headed back towards the wide, bleak river that had devoured his wife.

Twenty minutes later, with reckless panache, Timor brought the plane in low and pulled one of the two bomb-releases between their seats. For a moment the plane tilted with the uneven weight, then Gloria cheered out loud:

"Direct hit!"

In a dirty patch of swamp, the bulrushes quivered at the shock. Black mud belched marsh gas up at them. She leaned over to his side and tugged the other bomb-release.

"We did it! … Where did that one go? Did you see? … We didn't kill anybody! *We didn't, didn't, didn't!*" She was euphoric.

Timor was less so. "What's solved? Nothing's solved!"

Even the plane felt heavy-hearted. He was having trouble keeping the wings level.

"Go back! Go back to Rose, sir! Find out where all those people came from!"

He frowned, wiped the windscreen again (stupid, because the dirt was *still* on the outside) – but did set course for Rose City. "This is a young man's game," he said. "I think my eyesight is going."

He went in low and slow, so that any machine-gunner or rocketeer or lookouts watching for a third AAF bomber targeting the dam would see his bomb grips empty of bombs. The dam was magnificently huge. The river, five times deeper than usual, reached almost to the top, and still the dam withstood its pounding.

It was also empty of machine-gunners, lookouts or rocketeers. Timor raised his goggles and rubbed his eyes, not in disbelief but the better to see.

Gloria rubbed her eyes, too. "Yes, what *is* that?" she asked. "I thought it was inside my head, but…"

"*Ash!*"

"Bless you."

"Volcanic ash! Remember the weather people's letter? *Volcanic activity…below the mountains.* Remember? Something's erupted. It's ash! Blowing down from the Lacha Mountains!"

The plane seemed to agree. The propellor made a flurry of the floating flecks of grey and black. The engine coughed once, as if clearing its throat. The air-intake swallowed still more of the pretty flakes. And choked.

The engine died.

Below loomed the canyon that had once carried a rose-red river down to the plain. It was a steep gulch now, empty of all but a trickle of rainwater, full of sharp rocks and tall pink weeds with nettly leaves. All this they saw before the downdraught behind the dam snatched the plane out of the air.

And there was not a machine-gunner, a lookout, a rocketeer or any single soul around to see them go down.

CHAPTER THIRTY-SIX

Bird Down

ROSE CITY

A week after crashing in Rose City, the AAF pilot with the broken knee heard an aero-engine high, high up – too high even to be seen. But he instantly knew the sound of an AAF bomber. When Clem arrived for his daily visit, he found the pilot struggling to get out of his hammock.

"Help me! I heard a plane. I gotta go." It is difficult to get out of a hammock at the best of times, but with a broken kneecap the pilot floundered like a beached octopus, all arms, legs and curses.

"Why didn't I hear it?" said Clem, aggrieved that he had missed seeing a plane.

"Just fetch me that horse, damn you, and help me get up!" The swaggering hero was gone. Instead, this angry, scared invalid cursed the hammock, his knee and Clem. "That horse! Fetch me that horse – and *get this damn dog off me*, will you?"

There was Danger, plain as day. Heinz could smell both the Danger and hammock-man's fear. His hackles bristled. He willed Clem to sense it.

"What should I tell people?" asked Clem.

"Not a thing! You never saw me go, nor which way."

"Where are you going?"

"None of your damn business!" The sound of a Mark 12 bomber meant Praesto City had sent another pilot to do what he had tried – and failed – to do: bomb the dam. It might be lining itself up, even now, to make its bombing run. If it succeeded in breaching the dam, several million gallons of water was about to cascade down on him, and he was in no fit state to run. None of this he said to Clem, of course. Every man for himself.

Clem fetched Horse, and the pilot dragged himself astride her. He slapped at her rump with the knotted rope. Horse ambled off, ears swivelling. Clem and Heinz watched them go, baffled. Then Clem looked longingly at the empty hammock. Currently he slept on the ground, on two gunny sacks and under someone's hearthrug. Just an hour would be splendid. Just an hour swinging gently in mid-air...

Heinz set off to run a short way, then looked back at him expectantly.

"Steal your horse-friend, did he?" Clem sympathized.

Heinz ran back and bit into the cuff of Clem's pullover, and hauled.

"Alright. I'll come, I'll come. Is it the horse you're…?"

But to Clem's astonishment, Heinz did not set off after Horse. He ran to and fro, sniffing the air and whining.

The tug on Heinz's brain was no longer the anxiety that had reduced him to a whimpering halfwit. It was the DogMaster waking him with Bad News and an urgent mission. Something had happened over by the dam that demanded his attention.

"A walk? You want a walk?" Clem asked.

But Heinz wanted to run.

AAF66 lay in the upper canyon, aslant on the steep rocks, tail higher than its nose, its arrival unnoticed by the city below. A snow of ash was falling on it: earth to earth, dust to dust. Rainwater trickling down the canyon's sides had created a sizeable stream that was now washing through the plane, filling up the footwell and soaking the leather boots of the pilot. In fact, Timor glistened all over with slivers of silver, but they were not water – they were shards of the shattered windscreen. Gloria was picking them off his face and throat one by one, repeating over and over, "Don't be dead. Don't be dead. You're not to be dead."

There was blood on Timor's shirt front, but she could not tell where it had come from. She eased off his helmet. A hissing noise came from his throat, but it was just the oxygen mask resting on his sternum. She put it over his mouth in the hope it would make him breathe.

She could remember nothing of hitting the ground. Every one of those last five minutes must have shattered on impact. She had a dim impression of pain, but it seemed to flit about her body like a crow deciding where to start in on a meal. Only her nose hurt all the time. Outside the cockpit canopy, on the pilot's side, a smooth, grey, swelling curve was visible, like a shark cruising the wreck.

"I'll learn Greek if you'll wake up. I'll learn Latin and Greek and long division. And I won't be a liability ever again."

But Timor was not open to bribery. There was blood in the hollows of his ears, too. "You have nice ears, sir. Madame was lucky to get you. She's quite ordinary looking, really. Looks like me, sort of. Looked, I mean. Sorry."

There was a strong smell of aircraft fuel. It was starting to make her head spin. Alright for Timor, him being so much taller and nearer the fresh air… Except that things did not seem very alright for Timor at all. "Shall we get out now, sir? We should. We really should get out now. Hadn't we better?" Another large clot of blood from her nose fell onto Timor's shirt. She apologized.

"*Mogda!*" said Timor on a sharp intake of breath.

It woke Gloria in the nick of time. She wriggled upwards above the fuel fumes, pushed her head out through the broken windscreen and breathed fresh air.

"Who's Mogda? You said it before when you punched the statue thing on the sideboard." She hoped the question might give her time to get over the shock that he was not dead. She wondered if the promise about learning long division was absolutely binding.

Timor opened his eyes. "She's my wife, of course. Did you really think she was called Madame Suprema from birth? Mogda Gumbo."

"How did I never know that?"

"Oh, banned words, dear. Never to be spoken. I sometimes think all her ambition to be Head of State sprang from wanting to be rid of 'Mogda Gumbo'. Do you have a cigarette?"

"Course not! Maids mustn't... It's a sacking thing, sir."

"Quite right. I don't smoke either."

She begged him to get out of the plane, now that he had come-to. He turned his head a little, as if to judge the clemency of the weather. "I don't think so. Something tells me all is not cheerful down below. I can't move my legs. I suspect my back is broken."

Gloria crammed both hands over her mouth until the shriek subsided inside her. "It's just that I think that grey hump outside your window is the bomb, sir. The second one. It couldn't have dropped off when I pulled the handle."

"Ah. I thought she was handling heavy." He turned his head away. "Off you trot, then. Cheerio."

But how could she go? If he could pretend not to be scared, so could she. "Hasn't exploded so far. I expect it's fine." And Gloria sat tight. "There are flares in the back, in a metal case thing."

"No substitute for a cigarette, I feel."

"I meant I could read the instructions and pull one – light one – whatever you do with flares. People might come and help."

The whites of his eyes showed. "No! No, please! I don't want my head on a pole in the marketplace. Please. I know – when you're dead, you're dead, but till then, I'm not quite up to being brutalized by the locals. A bomb doesn't exactly say *I come in peace, friends*, does it? Oh, also, if you light a flare – or a cigarette, come to think of it – we'd go up like a firework. Smell the fuel vapour? Just go, will you? No more good ideas, for the love of…."

She hated herself for scaring him – might have gone, as he

asked, except that he had unknowingly grabbed hold of her wrist. So, Gloria sat tight.

"Bifurcate. Meteorologist. *In atramento est veritas.* Anagrams. Prangmatic," she said, checking she still remembered everything Timor had taught her.

"Pragmatic," said Timor with a smile. "A 'prang' is when you crash a car. Or indeed an aeroplane."

Heinz still recognized the smells within the gorge, from when he had been carried down it to Rose City. Every smell had a rag of memory attached to it. Over the rim of that summit, Horse had stood despairingly on a ledge. A landscape with tall pillars of rock peppered by hail... An old man's hands. The memories knocked on his skull, wanting his attention, but Heinz had no time to let them in. His heart hurt with the exertion of climbing. Time must have seized him by the backbone and shaken his youth out of him. Remarkable. He was suddenly an old dog, and he had always been so impatient of old age...

"Heinz, slow down!" Clem was calling.

Hound Death came loping up alongside.

"No," said Heinz. "I am Heinz, dog-of-many-Virtues. I'm not finished yet."

"I know," said Hound Death. "It's not you I've come for," and it ran on ahead.

"What is it you *do*, Mr Timor, sir?" asked Gloria, because, surely, when someone is busy talking, they can't get around to dying. "You have an office. People *do* things in offices. What do you do?"

"I write. Plays. Stories. Just now I'm writing an opera about a city in the middle of a sea where the people get about riding ostriches – if the ostriches are in the mood, you know? The men are building a ladder to the moon. The women are weaving themselves fabric out of birdsong and using it to make fabulous gowns when it was only ever meant for bandaging the broken-hearted. Each one thinks her husband will reach the moon first and become King, so she wants a suitably queenly frock. The men are all trying to climb the ladder at once, squabbling, all wanting to reach the top first. They're planning to build factories up there and cut down the trees for fuel. And yes, there are trees on the moon."

Gloria was intrigued. "What do they eat, your people?"

"Manna. It grows like sugar crystals on the island's reefs, and you have to eat it with your hands."

"No spoons or knives?"

"Absolutely no cutlery."

"One day, will you let people see it? Your opera?"

"Don't talk rot. There's no opera house in Praesto."

"It needs a *house*? I don't know what an opera is. I never heard of one. I'm sure we didn't have them in Sawmills."

"Like a play with songs," he said, from the brink of unconsciousness.

"Where will you get ostriches who can sing?"

Timor sighed. "Details. Details. I'll advertise," and slid away into sleep. Or something like it.

He was deathly cold. She promised to go for help, but didn't go, because then he would be on his own and the thought was unbearable. She reached into the back and emptied out her travel bag. The golden cutlery presented to her by the factories clattered onto the floor – her souvenir of being the Suprema. She spread her gingham dress and her sister's nightdress and then her cuttings from *The Voice* over Timor to try and warm him.

The newspaper fluttered in the draught from the broken windscreen, like plumage on a dead gull.

…*In atramento est veritas*…*enemies of Praesto*…*country cousins all safe*…*rabid dogs*… The torn newsprint taunted her with lies. She had no sooner finished than it began to rain – big sharp cold drops through the shattered glass, soaking the papers. The layer of ash flakes on the cockpit roof was washed away.

And there above her was a dog, standing on top of the plane, looking down at her, tongue dripping and flecks of foam on its teeth.

When Heinz arrived, Hound Death was relieving itself against one wheel of the aircraft, marking ownership. It dug under the fuselage, its gigantic paws shovelling pebbles and earth down into the gorge. The plane slid downhill. The propeller snapped with a noise like a pistol shot.

"Stop," said Heinz.

Why? Are these people something to you?

"No. But enough's enough. You've taken enough."

Are you going to fight me for them?

"If I have to."

The Hound gave a sagging, breathy laugh full of underworld smells: earth, tap-roots and decay. *It's my job. I have no choice.*

Heinz tipped his head. "Leave these two to Fate, why not?" he suggested.

But I AM FATE! Overwhelmed by overwork, Hound Death circled three times, as if about to sit down, but did not. It was exhausted. The floods had kept it busy night and day, from the Lacha Mountains to the ocean – so many thousands of people and creatures… It loped away to consider the matter, away from the dizzying stench of aero-fuel. Heinz jumped back onto the fuselage of the aeroplane and stood proud.

He barked, to guide Clem towards the plane. When the barking made him cough, he sat down and howled instead. He was intrigued to hear how his howls bounced to and fro between the walls of the canyon. By the time Clem came into view, Heinz was singing experimentally to the girl in the plane. He would have liked to lie on her chest; he had come to enjoy the rise and fall of human chests as much as he had once enjoyed swimming. But the girl seemed unsure about him, and he knew better than to sit on strangers without an invitation. She was much gladder to see Clem – Heinz could tell, because she cried with relief. (He had been three years old before he worked out that people cried for different reasons.)

"We shouldn't move him if he's broken his back," said Clem, when Gloria explained. "There was a man in Forest Bend had a pile of doors fall on him and people wouldn't move him for hours in case his back was broke."

"Forest Bend? You know Sawmills?" said Gloria with an uprush of hope.

"Course. Next door almost."

"And you got washed out?"

"Near enough the whole of everywhere got washed out up there."

Gloria gave a wail, cut short when the plane shifted. They both yelped. A rock, dislodged by the tail fin, rolled down and hit the bomb with a clang. Clem scrambled away as fast and as far as he could, calling desperately to his dog. Gloria hunched down, rigid. When no explosion obliterated them all, Clem ventured back a way.

"Him in there – he come here to bomb us?" he called, picking up the rock.

"NO! We tried to ditch the bombs in a bog, but one didn't drop off when I pulled the lever and then something happened, but I can't remember what."

Clem took a step closer, gesturing to his dog to come to him, but still Heinz stayed put. "He your pa?"

"No. He's Timor. I don't know if that's his first or last name. He's just Timor and we have to get him out 'cos there can't not be Timor. There just can't." And she began, with her empty holdall, to bail out the water in the footwell.

Clem said, "I got family. We got split up – the boat turned over. But we were headed for Rose. So they're gonna be along soon. We got split up. *But they'll be along soon. Right?*"

Gloria recoiled from the savage way he said it, but suddenly understood the boy perfectly. They were allies. A shared dread had united them. Unsayable as it was, the flood might have orphaned them both.

"His feet're trapped under the rudder bar," said Clem, climbing down beside the plane and squinnying in through the side of the cockpit.

Gloria squeezed down under the controls, and the rill of water flowing down through the plane seemed to pass clean through her, icy cold. There plainly was a metal bar across Timor's boots. She hauled on one end with all her might, but all that happened was that the other end gouged deeper into the right-hand boot. A multitude of columns and gadgets penned her round, hampering and prodding her. She told herself it was no worse than the hall cupboard with its jabbing umbrellas and coat hangers and mud-slimy galoshes. She tugged at the laces of Timor's flying-boots, but could not see what she was doing. Perhaps with a flare she would be able… The fumes were making her dizzier and more befuddled with every breath. Matches! There were matches in the flares box; they might help her see. She reached through between the seats…and cut herself on something.

Heinz, racing hysterically to and fro, infected by panic and the dreadful sound of metal scraping over sandstone, caught sight out of the corner of his eyes of the huge shape of Hound Death standing on the cement rim of the dam. Watching.

Gloria's head and shoulders emerged from the smashed front of the cockpit as she stood up on her seat, brandishing a golden carving knife.

"Nice weapon," said Clem admiringly, and beckoned. "Now will you get out of there?"

"No! I cut his bootlaces and got his feet out! Come and help me!"

A scurry of wind set the pink nettly flowers wagging.

It caught one of the aircraft's broken wings, too. The wing flopped downwards with a massive jerk and hung suspended from the fuselage by wires and electric cables that looked like sinews and blood vessels. It shifted the plane. Heinz leaped the widening gap between aircraft and hillside. Rock-chippings skittered down the canyon walls.

"Leave him, for pity's sake! Anyone can see he's dead," yelled Clem.

Gloria roared back at him wordlessly. A hand gripped her ankle.

"Am not," said Timor softly. "I can feel my legs."

"Are too," said Gloria, "if you don't get out this minute."

CHAPTER THIRTY-SEVEN

Plea for the Defence

ROSE CITY

"Now stay hidden right here, sir. Whatever you do, don't get seen," said Gloria, though the man curled up behind the boulder looked so battered that nothing could have got him to his feet.

Gloria and Clem walked down the steep slope towards Rose City. Timor was hidden far too close to the unexploded bomb for safety, but she dared not fetch him further down for fear he'd be seen and (as he put it) "brutalized by the locals". She had to explain. She would explain. She could explain. She was Madame Suprema and would persuade someone, somehow, that she and Timor had meant to come in peace.

In the end, it did not matter.

She and Clem had barely reached level ground when, with a noise like a falling building, the plane lost its grip on the pink nettly flowers and loose scree and renewed its slide down the rock face. Leaving its unexploded bomb behind like a fat grey pupa, it came bellying down the canyon, its severed wings banging and flailing behind it, until sparks from metal-on-rocks ignited the fuel tank and a column of fire consumed it.

The Citizens' Council leaned out of the sash windows of the Town Hall and asked what the commotion was – why people were crowding through the streets so excitedly.

Some thought the explosion in the canyon must have been their heroic injured pilot testing out his mended aircraft and crashing it again. Others thought the plane must have simply fallen out of the sky. Men, women and children swarmed up the ravine, even while the wreckage was still burning.

But when a pilot stumbled down the hill towards them, waving his arms, shouting about a bomb, it became plain to them that he was an enemy – and, like a pack of dogs, they took him down.

Some time later, a posse of men dragged him downhill with ropes, followed by the loud protests of a girl, a boy and a dog.

"Why could you not just *hide*?" Gloria railed at him. "Why could you not just *lie low and hide*? I told you to stay hidden until I could explain! But no. You had to unhide in your socks

and your Air-Force sheepskin and wave your arms around...
Now look at you! Look what those people did to you!"

"*Now* you sound like my wife," said Timor. "You have
mastered the intonation perfectly. Just the right level of
screech." He looked at the unlit cigarette in his hand and
could not remember how it had come to be there. "I *unhid*,
as you put it, because there were children. Among the mob.
What else could I do? Children running around near an
unexploded bomb? Not ideal. So I *unhid* and warned them."

They were sitting in the dock of a locked courtroom. The
dock was not a cage like the one in Praesto City High Court.
"More like a playpen really, isn't it?" said Timor. The walls of
the courtroom were covered in murals – exquisite paintings
of mythological justice and law-givers: Nemesis, King
Solomon, Hammurabi... "Did you see on the way here?
Every house is painted with pictures! Red, like henna. They
must get the pigments from the sandstone. And all the roofs
have flagstaffs. A lot of very patriotic Afalian citizens, plainly.
Unlike anything we read in *The Voice*. I doubt any single word
about Rose was true – that paper was just churning out lies
like spoons from a spoon factory. This place must have been
beautiful before the dam. And the refugees, of course. Messy
lot, refugees."

"What's going to happen, sir?" asked Gloria.

"Don't fret. You're not military and you're under criminal
age. You'll be fine."

"Not me. You."

"Oh. Don't ask."

"I'm asking."

"Well…I'm assuming this is the condemned man's last cigarette. Do you think the condemned man gets a match at some stage? I'm just grateful that dog sprang to my defence. What a first-rate animal. Talk about man's best friend."

"His name's Heinz."

"Well, Heaven bless Heinz and all his puppies. Firing squads are preferable to angry mobs any day… Chin up, Gloria. Don't undermine a chap's resolve. It's not kind. Oh, and don't *be* there. That's the condemned man's last request. Understood? Don't *be* there."

There was an excitable scrabbling, and a thin stream of yellow came under the door.

"That'll be Heinz," said Gloria.

And then a knocking…

"And that'll be Clem," said Timor. "They're inseparable, those two. Like you and Dai— Sorry. Not thinking."

Remarkably, Clem stuck his head into the "locked" courtroom.

"How did you do that, boy?"

"There's a key on a hook beside the door," said Clem. "Gloria! I been to the Lists! The Name Lists on the walls? There's *Winnows* on there. They might be your people! Come and see!"

Her heart detonated like a bomb. The figures on the wall seemed to lurch towards her and repeat the words. *They might be yours!* But things in print were so…unreliable. It would be a lie, a trick, a tease, a mistake. She hadn't the courage to look. And besides… "I can't come just now, Clem."

"Of course you can," said Timor. "Door's open, look. Come on. Fingers crossed."

"No."

Clem was astounded. The Lists were everything. To find a name on a List was to find the key that switched off the nightmares. To find the name you were looking for was to find a happy ending.

"Timor's more important," she said. "I have to…keep his end up."

The Citizens' Council of Rose City chose that moment to arrive, in a dignified line, and file into court. Each stepped in the yellow puddle, each scowled at Clem and then at the dog racing maniacally around the room, and back at Clem, who called Heinz, picked him up and dumped him in Timor's arms. "For luck," he said. "Heinz is full of luck." And he left, holding the door open for more arrivals.

A newspaper reporter scurried in and sat down in a corner. A stenographer prepared to take notes in shorthand. There was no jury, to see that justice was done. There was no lynch mob either.

"The Court is in session," murmured the Chairman of the

Bench, a man with curling grey hair round the very perimeter of his head. He picked up the judge's crimson cap but put it back down again, as if he thought the gold embroidery would not suit him. "Will the prisoner please rise." Then he assessed the number of bloodstains on Timor's clothes and how hampered he was by pain and dog, and told him to sit down again. "Name?"

"Captain Timor Philotapantasol of Foremost Mansion, Praesto City."

The stenographer sighed. "Can the prisoner spell his name?"

"Yes, thank you," said Timor.

"Have you anything to say, Captain…Timor," asked the Chairman.

"I'd like to say that this is a beautiful room, sir."

The Chairman looked around him. "It is, isn't it? A pity it gets used so little. And you are an officer in the Afalian Air Force?"

"He is not," said Gloria scornfully. "He writes operas."

The Chairman looked over his glasses at her. "And your name, miss?"

Gloria had stood up. "I, sir, am Madame Suprema, Supreme Head of the State of All Afalia."

The Bench tittered. Then, fearing the crash had driven the child out of her wits, the Chairman's wife smothered her laughter and said, "I don't think you are, dear. Do sit somewhere more—"

315

"No, you're right," said the diminutive figure, stepping down from the dock. "But until yesterday I was." And Gloria turned her face from one councillor to the next with a slow deliberation made even more impressive by the size of her broken nose. "The real Suprema ran away when the city gates were shutting. So I took over being her, just until she got back after the flood – which she won't now, because she's very unfortunately dead.

"That's how I got to know things that ordinary people don't know, because they're in the factories and they only know what they read in the newspaper and that's just been lies mostly. Someone once told me: when disasters happen, it isn't anyone's fault. And that's right. What's important is what you *do* about the disaster. Down in Praesto, they didn't *do* anything they should've. The Senate, I mean. They just tried to pretend it wasn't too bad. They should have said: 'We don't know what to do, we don't know anything, how would we?' But they just told lies instead and, when that made it all worse, they told more lies. Then they came up with a really wicked plan…"

Timor had sunk his head in his hands, but the Bench did not seem impatient to silence Gloria's chatter, for all they were unsettled by what she was saying. They grew more and more restless, their faces more and more stern. They seemed half inclined to believe that she might, briefly, have impersonated a stateswoman three times her age.

Running out of the words she had prepared, Gloria plunged on. Her voice flew higher. Her story grew wilder and more improbable: an entire city hoodwinked by newspaper stories? A murdered woman? Rabid dogs? Slaughtered zoos? Kidnapped children? The Bench tried to interrupt several times with questions or perhaps just to stem the torrent of chatter. The reporter ran out of paper in his notebook and tiptoed over to steal a fresh one from the stenographer.

"I had to get to see you, to explain, so I asked Captain Timor to bring me."

Timor looked up abruptly at this sudden departure from the truth.

"I said that Timor should be the one to bomb the dam, which I said because if *he* didn't get sent, someone *else* would be sent and they really *would* drop the bombs, whereas Timor was in spotter planes in the war and never would, not where there were children – or anybody, in actual fact. And it was my fault we crashed with the bomb aboard, because I leaned over and pulled the toggle but I didn't pull it hard enough. We thought it had landed in the mud like the other one – *splat!* – but it was still there. So if you are going to shoot anyone it should be me, but only because I'm a liability, not because I hate you all. I don't. Not at all. You're very nice."

The stenographer's pencil broke. The reporter lobbed her one of his.

"And now we can't get back, and the walls are falling in on

317

Praesto City and there's five hundred children down on Eyot Island and Myld won't fetch them back till the flood ends. And why? Because the filthy factories *have* to keep going, don't they – because everything's all about money and machines and teaspoons and forks and nickel-plated everything, and Myld wants all the power for himself... And Timor isn't in the Air Force – he writes operas." (She said it again, in case they had forgotten since the first time.)

The Citizens' Council of the Rose City sat forward on their red leather chairs, elbows on the Bench. They did not look serenely wise, like the people painted on the walls. They looked muddled and angry, and as if they wished they'd gone to the dentist rather than listen to this child's testimony. Even the dog in the dock was whimpering, feeling the distress in the room and the tightness of the pilot's grip.

Gloria went on: "My mother told me when I left home: 'Try to stay on the side of the angels and you won't go wrong.' But it's not that easy. In Praesto you can't tell who the angels are. It's hard in big cities where there's politics and money, and some people who are much cleverer than other people, and people whose mothers didn't tell them the same thing about the angels. But at least with Timor I know he's clever and he's one of the angels. That's why I'm staying on his side."

Looking along the faces of the Bench of Judges, her heart sank. The Chairman had his bottom lip pushed out and was staring at the red judge's cap in his hands, turning it inside out, then right-side out – red/black, black/red. "We need a hole in the ground. A deep hole," he murmured.

In the dock, Timor blenched, picturing some quaint regional custom of burying a condemned man alive.

The Chairman's wife reached over and patted the Chairman's hand. "My husband is a little overcome, I'm afraid. When the flood grew so huge and went on so long, we did start to worry about Praesto City. We lost the telegraph very early on, so we had no idea how you were all managing. We sent a party of Adventure Scouts off to see if they could find out. But they simply couldn't get close enough. The city is completely cut off, isn't it? And we have no planes here, you see. My husband realized that the dam would be making matters worse for you all."

"We did start digging *under* the dam. We did, truly!" said the Chairman, recovering his voice. "Deep – right down under the foundations – to try to divert some of the water through here."

"But then the refugees started to arrive, you see," said the Deputy Chairman. "Tens, then hundreds every week!"

"It took up every minute of every day!" wailed a fourth Officer of Justice. "Sanitation, sickness, finding food... We never had a moment to spare for the digging after that!"

The fifth plunged in: "We will, though! We will! It's not as if we don't have the labour force now. We just cannot apologize enough that we didn't help earlier. The city walls are falling in, you say?"

"The north wall was starting to crumble as we took off, yes, ma'am," said Timor.

"What I don't understand…" (The Chairman consulted his notes.) "…is why the Senate and Mr…I can't read my writing…did not just *ask for our help*. *You* have planes, after all! One crashed here with engine failure, but the pilot simply said he had been delivering aid to people upriver. He said nothing about the pickle you people were in. So we thought you must be managing."

Other members of the Bench also murmured their bewilderment.

Timor pulled himself to his feet so that Heinz slithered to the floor. "Why didn't we ask for your help?" he exclaimed, loud now and agitated. "Because we built the damn dam, didn't we? Because we've cut you people off from water for seventy years and caused generations of Rosies to work in our factories rather than in the sweet outdoors! The papers cooked up the notion that Rose was some little huddle of work-shy foreign immigrants camping out in the ruins of an empty city. That pilot you mentioned wasn't delivering aid. He came here to *bomb the dam* – a blatant act of war! I'm guessing his plane got into difficulties, same as ours, and he ditched his bombs and landed, all smiles and innocence.

"And you ask why *we* didn't ask *you* for help? I'll tell you.

Because we couldn't imagine there were decent, gracious people like you left in the world! Because our papers invented a pack of lies that made you out to be subhuman, unnatural barbarians! Because our top people gave up on compassion years ago! Compassion doesn't keep the wheels of industry turning, does it? Generosity costs money. I couldn't imagine you would even *forgive* us, let along worry about us! I'm deeply ashamed that the thought never occurred to me! I am ashamed of my city…well not the ordinary people, obviously – they've been fed on lies and threats till they wouldn't know the truth if it… Tell you what!"

He clapped his hands so loudly that the stenographer squealed.

"If you can trust such a tainted man as me, I'll shift the bomb – *my* unexploded bomb – dump it in the hole you began under the dam. If I can direct the blast downwards – into the ground – I might just be able to blow a vent through the base of the dam rather than demolish the whole thing. Just me, mind. No one else. If you can lend me block-and-tackle, I reckon I might manage it. Or die trying. But…oh Hades, what am I talking about?" Timor broke off, his plans crumbling to pieces even as he formed them. "No! No, no, no! There's *no time!* It would take days – weeks even – and we don't have days!" He ran both hands through his hair.

From the walls of the courtroom, Nemesis, King Solomon and Hammurabi waited impassively to hear what new crime the prisoner was about to confess to. Timor turned towards the window, unable to face the wall paintings, let alone the five unhappy people trying him.

"Look – Praesto thinks I've come here to bomb the dam. By now, they're hoping the job's done. They're expecting that, within the day, the Furca will shrink to half its flow. When nothing happens – when the flood doesn't ease – they'll think I failed. So, they'll just send *another plane* – and another – and another, until the job's done. The next bomber could be on its way right now. There's no *time* to undermine the dam. So you *have* to get everyone in the city out of their homes and into the desert. All the refugees, too. Within the day. *You have to abandon Rose City.*"

There was a terrible, swarming silence that ate up his words, like a flock of locusts eating leaves. The Bench considered the prisoner's testimony. Hands trembled as they doodled sketches of falling bombs, doves of peace, block-and-tackle, aeroplanes… Notes were passed along the Bench to the Chairman, who barely looked at them.

"No, indeed, Captain," he said, the judge's cap screwed tight between both hands now. "Please don't worry about the bomb. It's much more important that you go back and tell the people in Praesto how things are up here, ask them please not to bomb us. And offer them our help, of course."

Timor gaped at him. "You still think, after all we said, that they'd *listen*? And there isn't time. Anyway, how can I, sir?

I don't have a plane! *Evacuate, for pity's sake! EVACUATE!* Please hear what I'm telling you: I don't have a plane and there isn't time!"

Clem put his head round the courtroom door. "That pilot had a plane. He ran off before you got here – don't know why. But his plane's all mended."

CHAPTER THIRTY-EIGHT

Nowhere

ROSE CITY

The people of Rose City had repaired the young pilot's pranged bomber with loving devotion. Like children preparing a present, they had wanted it to be a surprise. So "Hammock Man" had set off into the desert on horseback without ever realizing he could have flown home. The repaired plane, like everything else in Rose City, had been decorated with pictures – the Afalian flag, mermaids, suns and moons… There were even ribbons tied to the wing tips. Shining under a glaring sun, it looked like a fairground ride.

Remarkably, there was oil in plenty to fuel it.

"You have fuel here?"

The Citizens' Council looked ill at ease and unwilling to answer.

"We found a little pocket of oil," said the wife of the Chairman of the Bench, palpably lying. "Oil and agriculture do not mix, Captain. If you could possibly avoid mentioning the oil, we would be so grateful. I understand it is in great demand in big cities like Praesto."

"Madam! You mean to say you don't crave a hideous oil refinery at the heart of Rose City belching black, stinking smoke into the sky? You astound me!"

She kissed him on the cheek. "So glad you understand. We would *much* prefer an opera house."

"But you will evacuate the city. Please. NOW. I beg you. It's urgent."

"We'll see," said the Chairman's wife chirpily, and his heart sank. He was eager to leave before he punched someone for their perky, hope-for-the-best optimism – also, before Gloria came back from finding (or not finding) her family.

"Would someone brave please rotate my propeller?" he asked. "I for one don't want to be here if the dam gets blown. Oh, and keep everyone away from the bomb in the canyon. Put up a fence. Post guards. Whatever it takes. While I'm gone, *no one* goes anywhere near. Understood? I want no one dying on my account."

Clem had taken Gloria to see the Lists. He was so excited for her that he did not notice how reluctantly she followed him there. The entry read:

Winnow family, arrived 27/8. Grid ref 13/78.

"The whole camp's divided up into squares," Clem

explained. "See? So there's your people – the Winnows – and just along here, 'Clement Wollen (boy)'. So when my people come, *they'*ll know where to find *me*. You get sent to a particular square and that's your place – till you're found, see? Like treasure on a treasure map."

"I want to see, but it won't be them and even if it is, I can't talk to them," said Gloria.

Clem was bewildered. "They kick you out or something? You the bad girl in the family?"

"They're fine, wonderful people, and I love them, but I've got a plane to catch."

Clem grew angrier and angrier. "You any idea what I'd give to find my people this way?"

"You will. And if you don't, track down mine and say I sent you. They'll love you to pieces till kingdom come. They're like that." Gloria stopped dead. There, sitting under an Afalian flag held up with beanpoles, sat her mother, grandpa, sister and brother. Her knees turned to water.

Heinz leaped out of her arms and ran towards the knot of people shading themselves from the sun, scaring them into movement. Shielding their eyes with their hands, they looked in the direction the dog had come from. Mamma Winnow started to get to her feet. But Gloria had already turned her back.

"Time to go," said Gloria to Clem. "I can't stay. And you mustn't say I came, you hear? I've got to go back with Timor.

There's things not finished. We'll likely get shot the moment we land. But Timor needs me. We're a team."

"Nah. You just like being Madame Suprema more than you like your own people."

Gloria slapped him soundly, which brought the dog racing back, barking, barking.

Voices by the tent said, "It is. It could be... She'd be taller now..."

"There's plenty gingham dresses in the world, sweetheart..."

"Our Gloz wouldn't slap nobody."

Gloria hurried Clem away. "What's the point, Clem? What's the point in me saying, *Woohoo! Here I am!* – and then going off and getting killed? Wouldn't that make it worse? For them? They maybe think I'm safe in Praesto right now. It wouldn't be fair. Right now, all I want to do is to hug them and hug them and... But they'd never let me go. And I've got to go... Just you make them 'vacuate. *Promise me*. You must! And you get out, too. What's wrong with everyone? Haven't they seen enough bad things happen to know that, that...*bad things happen*? Myld'll try again with the bombing! He truly will!" And she set off to run at full tilt – even though she had to drag her heart behind her across five acres of desert. Clem ran after her.

Beside the plane, she hugged Clem with all the ferocity she had been saving up for her family. She shouted above the noise of the aircraft engine, "Thank you for finding them! At least now I've got a good reason not to get killed, haven't I! Where's Heinz gone? I wanted to say goodbye…"

"I didn't want you back," said Timor as the plane bumped over a strip of land raked smooth by the refugees and townspeople.

"Did too," said Gloria.

"No. No. Honestly. Hand on heart. I used to think I'd've liked children. Until I saddled myself with you."

They lifted off to the sound of cheering and kept climbing until the city and its moat of refugees was no more than a pattern below them. The ribbons on the wingtips were swiftly ripped off as the plane gathered speed. The empty bomb-grips made a noise like tearing cloth. Between them, Timor and Gloria had no idea what they would find or what they would do when they reached Praesto City, but they flew on in silence, half expecting at every moment to see an AAF bomber coming towards them with fresh bombs slung underneath it.

"Why didn't you then? Have children?" she said after an hour.

"Madame quickly made it quite clear that none were required… Anyway, I know nothing about them. I know more about typewriters than I do about children."

"You *were* one once."

"Oh? Maybe. Possibly. I don't recall. I remember great importance being put on *being a man*. 'Homesick, Timor? Be a man.' 'Nightmares, Timor? *Be a man*.' 'Scared of heights, Timor? *Be a...*' It's why I became a pilot, I suppose – I like to oblige. I'd still be one now, probably, but Mogda informed me, on our wedding day, that I was giving up the Air Force. We were perfectly matched, you see – I like to oblige and she likes to be obliged. Liked. She liked. Past tense."

"Mogda and Timor," said Gloria reflectively.

"Mmm. Moggy and Timmy. Sound like cat and mouse, don't we? Not a recipe for a quiet life... What about *your* family? Wouldn't you much rather be with them?"

"It wasn't them," said Gloria shortly. "Different Winnows. Can't we go any faster, sir?"

"No. The wind's gone round to the south. We're flying directly into it. Are you in such a hurry to get there?"

"Where will we land?"

"On the Foundry roof, I suppose. We have the benefit of surprise, at least. Myld may have worked out by now that I didn't blow the dam, but he'll still assume I ran out of fuel and crashed... Talking of surprises, please tell me you didn't rescue some other waif and stray from Rose City?" He nodded his head towards a noise in the rear of the plane.

"No. I thought *you* must've," said Gloria.

Both looked round into the dark interior for the source of

the unexplained noise. The eerie sound of singing stood their hair on end. A trick of the wind? A hole in the fuselage? Timor dropped the nose of the plane sharply, and a skidding, scraping noise was proof of loose live cargo sliding forward through the belly of the aircraft.

"Oh, a souvenir, no less!" Timor exclaimed irritably when the loose cargo joined them in the cockpit. "Thank you so much, Gloria."

"Wasn't me! He must've just climbed in when we weren't looking. Hello, Heinz!"

And though the dog really ought not to be there, Gloria was cheered, not just by the touch of warm fur, but by knowing that now they would absolutely have to survive to go back to Rose City. "We'll *have* to," she said earnestly. "Even if it was an accident, you can't go stealing another person's dog."

Heinz was reassured, for the rest of the flight, by sitting on Gloria's lap. The day had played him a cruel trick by terrifyingly snatching him into the sky and making his eardrums ache, but he had had to board the plane. It was his duty to stay close to the people in his charge. Why he, of all dogs, should have been chosen to look after these two was beyond him. But the DogMaster did not generally make mistakes. Heinz just hoped, when his duty was done, he would not have to walk all the way back to Rose City to find Clem again.

Pilot and passenger found themselves leaning forward in their seats long before they reached Praesto City. Would it still be there? Would the floodwaters have finally brought down the walls and swept death and ruin through the drowned streets?

When it did come into sight, the massive brick circle of the city walls had indeed begun to give way on the north side. A deep, V-shaped gap had been opened up by the relentless, hammering flood, and the water had rampaged through the streets, demolishing shop fronts, setting cars afloat, and leaving wreckage, rubbish and dead animals hanging from the lamp posts. The river had broken in and poured downhill to the low-lying districts. The city's industrial centre had been transformed into a maze of deep canals. The factories stood waist-deep in floodwater, and the pipes from the pumps were no longer twitching and pulsing but lay beneath the water like giant squid. The fall of the wall must have finally defeated every effort to save the machines. The factories' vast bulk rose now out of deep water – but at least they were still standing, their chimneys still reaching up to touch the sky.

"Myld sent me off with half a tankful. So he thinks I'm dead. Dead is the way he wants me, right? I wonder if my good friends in the Air Force will shoot me down if Myld tells them to. I do hope friendship is still good for something."

"He wouldn't shoot down the plane, though, would he?" said Gloria hopefully. "Not over the city! It might kill people on the ground!"

"So? Fewer mouths to feed."

"Buck up, sir! My ma used to say, 'Faint hearts, cold hands…' No… 'Faint hearts never…' Something about faint hearts."

"Faint hearts butter no parsnips?"

"'Faint heart never won fair lady' – that was it!"

"Fair ladies are not uppermost in my mind right now. *Just find me somewhere else to land!*"

For the roof of Factory Five (Foundry) was crammed with people.

They had clearly climbed out of the roof hatches onto the flat concrete roof. Every morsel of sooty concrete was taken up by workers sitting, standing, curled up trying to sleep or moving restlessly to and fro. Either the people had chosen to stop pumping, or the floodwater had finally swallowed the machinery and driven them skywards.

When they saw the plane bearing down on them, they began to scream and look around for an escape route. Like cattle scared by lightning, they were about to stampede towards the hangers or fling themselves over the edge of the roof.

Timor needed all his strength to pull the nose up. AAF64 laboured to regain height. Heinz stood up in Gloria's lap and whimpered with alarm or airsickness.

"The park! Use the park!" shouted Gloria over the shriek of the engine.

"Too wet!"

"Another factory?"

But every one of the factory roofs was crowned with crowds of workers trapped by the flooded streets all around.

"Eyot Island!" said Timor. "We used to do circuit-and-bump there when we were learning to fly. It's a hard sandbar. At least it was…"

No longer.

Half an hour later, they looked down and saw no hard sandbar where Eyot Island ought to be, no ugly bulk carrier lying at anchor alongside it. Gloria's heart sickened and staggered. "Where's the ship? Where are the children? Where's the *island*?"

Timor consulted the map yet again, but there was no mistaking: the flood had simply swallowed Eyot Island.

CHAPTER THIRTY-NINE
The Bell Tower

ROSE CITY

When Clem could not find his dog, he retraced his footsteps as far as square 13/78 on the grid map. Along the way, he asked everybody, "Have you seen my dog? Have you seen Heinz?" It seemed more urgent than shooing strangers into the desert. "Have you seen my dog? He's a three-colour mongrel." Most of the people he asked knew Heinz, but none had seen him within the last few hours.

Finding himself in front of Gloria's family, Clem could not think up a clever way of giving them Gloria's message – he was too busy fretting about his dog. "Gloria says you gotta 'vacuate into the desert 'cos they're coming to bomb the dam, and could you tell all the other people round about to move out too. Quick as you can."

It was a lot to take in. They boggled at him, this skinny boy spilling bad news over them and using their girl's name. "Gloria's here? You seen our Gloria?"

"Yep. She's gone now. She's a 'stonishing piece of work, that girl. I think she broke her nose when the aeroplane crashed, so you'd maybe not recognize her. She's been pretending to be the Suprema, did you know? Anyhow, she said I had to tell you to clear out fast and spread the word. So I'm telling you." Then he went back to looking for his dog.

He was startled when Gloria's mother came after him, pushed him over and pinioned him to the ground – "*Where's my daughter!*" – thumping him with questions, as with a rolling pin. Gloria had been right about upsetting her family – they were beside themselves when he finally escaped. And precious time had been wasted that Clem could have used searching for Heinz.

He tried the pilot's hammock, but it was occupied now by someone old and asleep. He went to the waste dumps where the rats gathered, in case Heinz was ratting. He went to the Lists of Arrivals, because it was somewhere he had gone every day with Heinz. When he found himself looking under the Hs for *Heinz*, he realized he was a little bit mad.

If he, too, could have gone up in Gloria's plane, he would have been able to spot Heinz from the air easily. He took himself off instead to the highest point he could reach in the city – a pink carillon tower in the central market square.

Its bells were being rung – on and on and on – a sound so clamorous, the notes so overlapping and loud, that it emptied his head of all thought. Halfway up the tower's steps he came to a standstill.

He seemed to be watching himself from outside: the boy on the spiral staircase who might have been blown to atoms by that bomb, drowned by that deer's carcase, swept away when the river burst its banks, eaten by river crocodiles, sucked under by black mud, or found face down half-eaten by eels… The pictures in his head left him no idea of time passing or what was happening outside.

He might have stood there, blankly, on the stairs, for minutes.

Or hours.

Or days.

CHAPTER FORTY

Appis

PRAESTO CITY

Appis the chauffeur sat in bomber AAF67, outside the aircraft hanger, and sulked. He resented being sent to bomb Big Rock Dam. He had been in the Intelligence Services for ten years – if he had wanted to fly planes, he would have joined the Air Force instead. True, he was the only man in Praesto who could be relied on absolutely to get the job done: *Give Appis the job and he'll get it done.*

Take-off was scary. Appis felt better. He enjoyed the hot surge of adrenalin he got at the crown of his stomach from extreme danger or violence. Praesto City grew smaller and smaller with distance, until it seemed no more than a damaged toy castle. His whole life had been dedicated to that small, walled city and the people who ran it.

"Fetch the car, Appis."

"Kill the weather people, Appis."

"Slaughter the zoo animals, Appis."

"Kill the newspaper woman, Appis."

"Blow the dam…"

Appis flew north, head filled with pictures of explosions, a collapsing dam, water thundering down onto a pink city. Pink like flesh. One propeller feathered for a moment – or perhaps it was an optical illusion.

He looked down and saw below him the wreckage of AAF33 – the first bomber to be sent – its wing hanging from a tree. Hail, lightning or engine failure must have brought it down. Adrenalin warmed him again: fear keeps a man on his mettle. Appis liked fear.

Still, if he was shot down – as Timor surely had been – would it be because he had volunteered? No.

No. He was just obeying orders. All his life he had been doing other people's dirty work. Suppose, just for once, he chose *not* to obey?

Then he saw it: Big Rock Dam – a sight fit to pump adrenalin stronger than neat brandy through a man! The propeller missed another revolution. Appis frowned. He checked the fuel indicator. Its needle was still on FULL. He punched the dial. The needle spun backwards to EMPTY. The plane had been only half-filled with fuel.

Enough to do the job. Not enough to get home.

Then the adrenalin kicked in. It streamed through Appis like a river in flood. It kicked his heart into the air. It made his vision rainbow bright, swelled his lungs, thrilled his guts, spilled through the palms of his hands. He had moments to make a decision, and his reflexes were lightning fast. Silly. There was no decision to make. All his life he had obeyed orders – what else did he know? What else was there? Nothing. Nothing. Nothing.

The engine cut out altogether, but Appis could still get the job done! That's what he prided himself on: *Give Appis a job and he'll get it done.* That was his motto. Adrenalin fountained through his heart and up into his brain, like erupting volcanic lava. He selected a particular slab in the dam wall, between rim and waterline, and flew directly at it, bawling the Afalian National Anthem as he went.

CHAPTER FORTY-ONE

Liquidation

ROSE CITY

Clem, standing on the stairs of the bell tower, realized the bells had stopped ringing. He looked around him. Every brick of the staircase walls was stippled with delicate red patterns, as if he was inside the gut of some giant, and being digested. The boy on the staircase was still utterly alone: no family, no belongings, no dog. Even Heinz had abandoned him. He pressed on up the stairs, feeling a raging envy of everyone in the world: Gloria, Timor, the horse… At the top of the tower there was a stiff breeze rocking the bells. Also, the drone of a distant aeroplane…

Looking towards the dam, he barely saw the explosion. A pillar of black smoke rose up, and through it came the tailplane of a bomber, somersaulting clear over the dam's rim and down into the canyon. Then there was a second explosion. The tailplane must have struck the bomb left behind by Timor's burned-out plane below, the bomb Clem had stood on as he helped Timor to climb out.

The impact of Appis's plane (and the twin bombs lashed beneath it) was probably enough to get the job done. But it was after the second explosion – when Timor's bomb was detonated – that a black pattern in the shape of forked lightning drew itself on the decorated stonework. The whole dam appeared to take a step towards the city, lose its footing and stumble forward, pitching slowly, slowly onto its face. From behind it came a brown monster, slick wet, all sinews and boils, foaming at the mouth. The remains of both aeroplanes were tiny in its grasp.

When Big Rock Dam came down, the Furca River split like a man torn in two by wild horses. One half spilled down the ravine towards Rose City. It clothed itself in a thousand Afalian flags. It pillaged hand carts, flower tubs, tents. It squeezed through the streets, ripping windows from their frames. Pillars were broken off at the ankles, towers toppled, maypoles uprooted. Walls dissolved like pink icing sugar.

The figures on the fresco of the courtroom watched as waves flung the wooden benches and tables about, then sank the murals up to their exquisite eyebrows in meltwater all the way from the Lacha Mountains.

Not a street of the dusty city escaped the inundation. A million tonnes of water and then a million more laid waste to carefully tended gardens, vineyards, the tin barns and ploughed fields of once fertile farms. The water smashed and savaged its way on and beyond the Rose City, carving out a trench three times wider than the old riverbed. It was laden with spoils stolen from the halls and houses.

CHAPTER FORTY-TWO

On the Beach

After Eyot, Timor and Gloria flew on southwards, scouring the river for the *Nickelodeon*. Just because Eyot Island had disappeared, the ship need not have.

It was exhausting. The sun was bright on the river and the dazzle sparked piercing headaches. What had become of the ship and its cargo of five hundred children? Once, Gloria thought she saw the water breaking against some large, sunken object, but Timor said it was just the river colliding with the incoming sea-tide. The sea was visible now in the distance, and still there was no sign of the "floating hotel" and its cargo of children. Timor checked the fuel gauge. "If we go any further, I won't make it back to Praesto." And yet he could not bring himself to stop searching.

And then they saw it.

From the air, it looked like some little upturned schooner. But as they came closer, they could see the true scale of the ore carrier lying almost upside down. There was no sign of life.

In silence, Timor and Gloria flew on, looking for survivors. Or bodies.

The main, central channel of the Furca thundered on as far as the sea, deep enough for big cargo ships to come and go. But to either side, shallower fronds of water reached out like the roots of a great tree and dunes of yellow sand stretched to west and east. Along the golden shoreline, hundreds of children were running races, digging, scavenging, fighting…waving.

The letters H-E-L-P were gouged in the sand, almost lost among countless names – JON, LEM, MARI, DIZZ… There was a big white dog, too, running from group to group, game to game, generally making a nuisance of herself.

They landed the plane among sea pinks and thrift.

Gloria did not recognize Kovet at first. The familiar features of his puffy face had sunk, haggard, into the bones of his skull. He looked thirty years older. His smart city suit was water-stained and caked with sand. His tie was holding up his trousers. Nor did *he* recognize *them*, though to his eyes they were Salvation.

His hands jerked and fluttered as he pointed out where the children slept among the dunes, where the girls washed, and where the boys did. He pointed out the sports gala he had organized, and the children he had appointed referees. He showed them the ocean-ash bushes, whose twigs made excellent fishing rods – also the scrub collected into heaps by day and lit at night for the cooking of fish and to keep them warm. He was like a child proud of the play-den he had built in the garden, tugging them by the wrist along the shore, now and then breaking off to try and call some passing child by their name: "Blane? Morri? Rasheal?" As often as not, he was wrong, but the children only laughed hilariously and those nearby shouted at him to guess their names, too.

"Excellent children – truly exceptional! They know *cooking*, some of them. And knots and fishing and all sorts. Of course, I couldn't have managed without Daisy. She's a wonder. Nurse, sheepdog, mother… Could find food on Mars, I swear it! Absolute nose for food! I held it steady after Bucket went over the side – I truly did! It was only when we touched a sandbar – just brushed it, you know? – over we went. Five seconds and it was gone. *She*. She was gone. Ships are female, did you know? Rusty Bucket, yes. Must find out his real name."

Children must have been lost. Their bodies must be lying under liquefied nickel ore on the bottom of the estuary. But Kovet did not refer to them, and Timor did not ask – as if there was an unspoken need to banish Unthinkable Things from life on the beach. Later, later, perhaps…

No children had died since the capsizing, though, since the Senator for Home Affairs had walked them, through waist-deep water, down the estuary to Outfall Beach. Now they were playing and fishing and practising their letters by writing them in the sand, learning wartime songs from Kovet and teaching him campfire songs in return. Each morning they sang the Afalian National Anthem. Mercifully, the weather had grown kinder, and they were all quite brown (though that might just have been dirt).

A portion of Kovet's brain was given over to inventing terrible torments to inflict on his assistant, Myld: "When we get back...when we get back... *And* that madwoman Suprema!" (Gloria opened her mouth to protest, but remembered in time that she no longer was.) "They were in this together, I swear! Two vipers in the nest! I'll have 'em shot! D'you know," he said suddenly, "you look uncommonly like whatshisname. The Suprema's poodle. The Husband. Who are you?"

"Oh, just Air Force, sir," Timor said. "Out looking for you, sir." And Timor steered the man's attention back to the children. "Do any of them know Morse?"

A girl in a Scouting uniform was instantly standing toe-to-toe with him, banging proudly on her chest. "I do!"

"SOS?"

"Simple!"

"Using a signalling mirror?"

"If you show how," claimed the girl, with only a moment's flicker of doubt.

Timor fetched the plane's emergency kit and set about demonstrating the use of the mirror. His class grew from three to eighty-three as more and more children crowded round. Gloria watched fondly, wondering how she had ever resented Timor's relentless lessons, his insistence on perfection. It seemed a lifetime since Timor had tamed her vowel sounds and handwriting.

"I have to go back and tell your parents where you are," Timor told the children. "But whenever a ship appears on the horizon, you must signal to it. No ship will refuse to answer an SOS. Fishing boats. Mail boats. Yes? You'll need four or five of them to take you all home…or to somewhere more comfortable anyway. Senator Kovet, if the flood eases, and ships can sail upriver again, promise the skippers good money if they'll sail to Praesto…"

Gloria crept away in search of her dog.

Daisy did not immediately recognize the girl in the gingham dress. The dog was accustomed to children lunging at her, wanting to hug her and tell her things in too-shrill voices, and never one at a time. So having been hugged by Gloria, she extricated herself and trotted further down the beach. Only then did a kind of cloud part in her head and a ray of sunlight stream painfully through heart, lungs and liver to stiffen her tail. She turned and looked. She returned and sniffed. Her big liquid eyes asked, *Where have you been?* Then she rolled over in the sand and stretched her legs to fore and aft.

Heinz broke off from a game of fetch-the-pine-cone, raced back to Timor and Gloria, and lay down on his back alongside Daisy. Daisy raised her head and looked at this new arrival but, when he did not seem intent on ripping out her windpipe, rested the top of her head back on the sand and half closed her eyes.

The world, too, seemed to roll over onto its back and wait blissfully for its belly to be rubbed.

Later, Daisy led Heinz on a tour through a gritty, yellow territory he had never seen before. In the sand dunes, there were partridge hiding in the marram grass. A pair flew up from under their noses and Daisy found her jaws had somehow collided with one of them. She was taken aback. Heinz waited for her to roll on it, but she just trotted along with it in her soft mouth. He caught the other partridge himself and she watched him fold it under his body and roll it dead. She tried to imitate him but ended up just lying on top of it like a chicken on a clutch of eggs. When she stood up, the partridge flew off, none the worse. Even the partridge looked at Daisy as if to say, *Idiot.*

Then Daisy introduced Heinz to the sea: a thing half landscape, half lunging beast. Despite the folds of cold hurling themselves at her, Daisy walked straight in and stood, doing nothing in particular, as fresh waves broke over her. Heinz tried to follow suit, but found it too alarming, and scurried back up the beach. When the retriever shook herself dry, he thought he had never seen a sight so awe-inspiring since Clem had pinned a Catherine wheel to the porch and lit it.

The light would be failing soon. Timor was in a hurry to take off from the beach. But it took some time to find the dogs. When they did, Gloria was desperate to take Daisy back with her in the plane.

But Senator Kovet was horrified. "No! Don't give her back to that wretched woman!" Confused and stricken, he said, "You can't! I need her here! She's such a help! Without Daisy, it would just be...me."

The phrase shivered through Gloria. She attached the lead (Kovet's trouser belt) to Daisy's collar and put it into Kovet's hand. "Please look after her. And be sure and bring her back with you when the boats come. I hope it's soon."

Twenty small children seemed to have taken possession of Heinz as well.

At the door of the plane, Kovet grabbed Gloria by the

wrist. His hair stood almost straight up from his head. It gave the impression he had just stepped on an electric cable.

"There was nothing else we could do! You do understand?" he pleaded. "It was all too big, you see! I mean, what should we have said? 'What the hell's going on? We're all going to die!' No! We kept herding the people along the way they needed to go. Keep 'em busy, we thought. Keep 'em pumping! I mean, we were all thinking the same, weren't we? 'Get me out of here. Don't let me starve! Don't let the water get me!' But what good's that? So we carried on keeping things normal. Stayed on top of things. Pretended. I mean, we had to keep the factories open, didn't we? What would we be without the factories? Do *you* know? Does *anyone*? Cutlery for the World, that's us! Bringing in the money. *She* said… the Suprema said, 'Everything's about money in the end.' Thing is, we never thought the river would…and then it did. D'you see?"

Timor had to prise the man's fingers off Gloria's arm. Somehow, he managed to make it look as if he simply wanted to shake Kovet's hand before leaving. "You fetch in those ships, old chap. And keep up the good work. See you back in Praesto."

"Do we have enough fuel to get back?" Gloria asked, climbing into the plane.

"If we don't," said Timor, "I promise you I'll get out and push."

Heinz broke free of the children who had adopted him and made an extraordinary leap onto the plane's wing, wriggling into the cockpit like a terrier into a burrow and defeating all efforts to throw him out again. Sea pinks and thrift snagged at the wheels. The hard-ridged sand bounced them in their seats, but the plane was lighter now, being low on fuel – it managed to lift off before the sun's lower rim touched the horizon.

After take-off, Timor said, "That was a good thing you did back there, Gloria. Leaving Daisy with Kovet."

"Well, she's not mine, is she?" she said flatly.

"Yes. Yes, she is. If we ever reach final curtain in this absurd melodrama, she's yours entirely. I promise."

From the air, it was immediately plain that the river had changed. Salt seawater was pushing further upstream, because the river's flow was weaker. Though the landscape was still underwater, the Furca's current had clearly slowed. After months of watching it pass faster than the eye could take in, it seemed to be travelling in slow motion.

"Has the flood stopped then?" Gloria asked, though she knew the true reason. Big Rock Dam had fallen, and the river had split itself between Furca and Rose. "Have they all died? All those lovely people?"

Timor did not answer, except to say, "Pray the fuel holds out as far as Praesto. Then find me somewhere to land. I can only think in one direction at a time."

"They will have 'vacuated, though?" said Gloria pleadingly. "The Rosies and the refugees – they will have. Won't they? They will. You told them. Clem was going around telling them. So, they won't be drowned! They'll have run away, Ma and Grandpa and... They will. They *were* there, and I didn't speak to them! I was saving them up! *Promise my people won't be dead.*"

Timor made a detailed check of the instrument panel, pressed finger and thumb into his eye sockets, as if to dispel weariness. "I promise," he said inaudibly.

"What?"

"I promise," he said. "Absolutely."

Gloria slumped back in her seat overwhelmed with relief. Both her nose and her heart gradually stopped throbbing.

SUPREMA'S HUSBAND FEARED KILLED IN VALIANT ATTACK ON "BIG ROCK"

Madame Suprema's husband, Captain Timor Philotapantasol, is thought to have been shot down by Rose City rebels during an attempt to divert water from the flooded Furca River and end the suffering of citizens throughout Southern Afalia.

The handsome and devoted couple were married for 15 years. Of Greek extraction, Captain Philotapantasol (40) moved to Praesto while still a child. He won the Afalian Cross during the War, for conspicuous valour, flying reconnaissance missions over enemy territory.

Our thoughts and hearts go out to Madame Suprema at this saddest of times.

EMERGENCY POWERS ACT PASSED

Following the arrest and imprisonment of 37 members of the Senate and several heads of industry, for corruption, profiteering and treason, the Emergency Powers Act has been invoked. This will allow sensible and helpful decisions to be made without delay or argument, by the Suprema and Vice-Supremo Sir Kovet.

CHAPTER FORTY-THREE

The Necessary Lie

PRAESTO CITY

Just as daylight faded into dusk, they sighted Praesto City. Three dark hills loomed up: Foremost Hill, the one topped by the AAF's aircraft hanger, and one sporting the Federal Bank's exclusive golf course. The factory roofs were all still crowded with people, so it was the golf course or nowhere. The fairway was narrow, but plush and well drained. It made an excellent landing strip…but for the bunker on hole eight, which broke the wheel struts as they fell into it.

The fuel needle rested on zero.

They struggled out of the wreck and into the city, armed only with Gloria's gold-plated cutlery, Timor's wartime pistol and a tri-colour dog.

There was a sound of gunfire – distant and not directed at them. A yellow Civil Guard van drove by at top speed, mounting the pavement as it rounded a street corner, but it was not hunting them.

"You shouldn't have come here, Heinz," said Gloria to the dog.

"He thought we were taking him back to Rose…as we are. Like you said, one cannot go stealing someone else's dog… We make directly for the Air Force hanger, alright? Pick up a smaller plane – with fuel but without bombs, this time – and fly on to Rose. We are not here, understand? Myld wants me dead and I don't intend to oblige him. Now the dam's down, the situation here will sort itself out. And there's no point in delivering an offer of help from Rose City when Myld has probably just annihilated it."

"Don't say that! Please!"

"Right now, I just want to get back there and find out."

"But you told the children from the ship! 'We'll tell your parents,' you said. We *must* tell people what happened to their children!"

"No. That's the last thing we must do…" He broke off as the lit windows of *The Voice* offices came into view. The sight brought him to a halt. Here was Myld's lair. It had to be, if he had used *The Voice* to work so much of his mischief.

"I don't understand! Why can't we tell them? That's not fair! I want to go to Spoons and tell the people there, at least!"

But Timor was not listening. "He's there. I can almost smell him," he said, and unfastened his holster.

Strangely, the doors of the newspaper offices were unguarded. Perhaps Myld felt safe, with all his rivals either dead or confined to prison. As they crossed the unmanned reception area and pushed through double doors, the sound of voices led them to the Editor's Office.

"Look after the dog, Gloria, and stay right here." Timor approached the room, sliding his back along the corridor wall so as not to be glimpsed through the office door's frosted-glass panel.

Inside the office, Myld seemed to be auditioning girls for a play. It was plain from the costumes that the role in question was "Madame Suprema". The girls were all the same height and colouring as the real thing. Their mouths had all been painted bright red with a lipstick that lay on the desk. A girl, wearing the desk lampshade on her head, was walking up and down as elegantly as she knew how, mouthing her words as if chewing gum. When Timor entered, she hesitated, not knowing whether to carry on or stop.

Myld's face showed nothing at all. He waved a hand to dismiss the girl in the lampshade. "These ladies are all eager to perform in a patriotic play about Afalia and everyone's favourite Suprema. Isn't that right, ladies? Wait outside, if you will." But the girls were staring at the newcomer in the torn and bloodstained leather coat, and did not hear. "*Wait outside, I said.*" Then the girls (who had never heard Myld raise his voice beyond a purr) fled for the door and bundled each other into the corridor.

"If it isn't old Timmy! Quite thought you were dead, old thing. In fact, my paper gave you a splendid obituary. Have you read it? If you don't mind me saying, you do look as if someone threw you down several flights of stairs."

Timor ignored him. "All for nothing then, was it, Myld? The plotting. The invented news. The murder. The kidnap. All to keep the machines dry. And all for nothing. The machines are underwater."

Myld threw back his head and laughed. "You are such a child, Timmy. All for nothing?" He counted off his achievements on his fingers. "I have established a state of emergency, dismantled the legal system by gaoling the lawyers and judges, confiscated all the banks' assets and gaoled the bankers. I've got everyone to vote for a bombing raid on their fellow citizens in time of peace, and by doing so very probably saved the city. Put in terms a simpleton like you can grasp, I have:

– taken control of everything and everyone,

– taken the Law and rewritten it,

– pocketed all the money, and

– come out of it with clean hands.

"The whole of Praesto is mine – the whole jolly nation, in fact! Of course, Mogda rather let me down. She really should have held her nerve. After a month of rain, when the city looked like closing its gates, we worked it all out between us

– our Survival Plan: How to Profit from Disaster. But then Mogda lost her nerve and ran away, didn't she? So I had to do it all myself. And we were so *close*, your wife and I. Night and day. So *deliciously* close."

As a torturer might stop and sharpen his blades, he paused to assess what pain he had managed to inflict on Timor, but was met only with an implacable stare. Myld shrugged. "As for the machines, machines can be mended. I shall have the factories up and running again, all in good time. *Mend the machines or you and your family starve*: there's a slogan to inspire *any* engineer, don't you think? So I have weathered the storm, Timmy! And when I choose to fetch back Kovet, *he's* the one who'll get the blame. He's my scapegoat. *He's* the one who gets lynched by an angry mob. *I'll* be the one who rescued the brats from Eyot Island. *I'll* be the one who soaks up the love and admiration of a grateful city. And you say it was all for nothing?"

Timor rolled his head, easing the stiffness in his shoulders. "You haven't heard then?"

"Heard?"

"There is no Eyot Island. The flood swamped it."

"What?"

"The ship was swept on downriver, where it turned over and sank with Kovet and all those little children on board. I've seen the wreck."

The complacent smugness of the assistant fell away.

He fumbled as he unlocked a drawer in the desk.

Timor went on: "Your bombing of the dam was a mistake, too. There were forty thousand country cousins camping out around Rose City – refugees from the north. You really should have sent a plane to have a look, you know. That's a *lot* of people to drown, Myld – not to mention the Rosies themselves."

But Myld was recovering himself. "Not me, Timmy! Kovet and the People, they're the ones who wanted it. *They* voted for the bombing. Naturally, I *begged* Kovet not to, but would he listen? My hands are clean... Dead, is he, the old duffer? Won't be saying much to question my version of the truth then, will he? Or defend himself. The dead don't make good witnesses in court. I assure you, Timmy, I am untouchable."

"If it wasn't for Hecuba's anagrams!" called Gloria from outside the door. To Timor's exasperation, she stepped grandly into the room, slammed the door behind her and declared, "*My lad did lilt!*"

Her taped, broken nose undermined the moment. Myld blinked blankly while he took in who she was and the fact that she was still in the city. "Ah! *You*. When I couldn't find you, I guessed you'd gone with Timmy. Did I say you could go? I'm afraid you're fired, Miss Winnow. As you've seen, I'm auditioning for a more...*compliant* actress. Still got all those ghastly clothes? I'll be needing them."

"*My lad did lilt!*" she said again.

"Did he indeed?" From behind his hand, he hissed exaggeratedly at Timor, "Rabies probably. Kinder to put the bitch down." And he drew a pistol out of his desk drawer and rested it on the blotter. With a show of extravagant boredom, Myld put his feet up on the desk, ankles crossed.

Gloria adopted a triumphant stance. "Hecuba put anagrams in the newspaper before you killed her, and her anagrams were *codes*!"

"Before *who* killed her?" Myld showed exaggerated surprise. "No, no. The Suprema's own chauffeur killed Professor Hecuba – on the evening of the State Banquet, as I recall. Of course, one day the papers will say it was done on the orders of the Suprema. She ordered it in a fit of jealousy because of a love affair between her husband and Professor Lightfoot. Ooh, yes, the public do like a juicy scandal. But all in good time, when I see fit – when the time comes for me to *discard* Madame. I shall enjoy repainting her as the perfect pantomime villain." And he mimed lavish brushstrokes in the air with one long, pale finger.

"Too late!" said Gloria, hiccupping slightly in her excitement. "It was an anagram, you see. In the newspaper. And everyone's already read it! And *that's* how people got wise to you, Myld, and they know it was you all along!" She snatched up the lipstick from the desk and wrote on the wall:

MY LAD DID LILT

Underneath it she wrote:

MYLD DID IT AL—

before the lipstick fell out of its tube onto the floor. "They *know*. They all solved the anagram. Soon as the water's gone down, they're planning to come after you. They want your head on a pole in the marketplace! Not Kovet's, not mine. Because Mr Myld did it all!"

Myld's eyes quivered in their sockets. His very hair trembled. He reached for the gun, but in folding his long legs out of the way, he knocked it off the desk – by which time, Timor had already drawn his own and fired. The girls outside in the corridor screamed at the sound. Gloria tried to flee, but turned the door handle the wrong way, and precious seconds ticked by before it would open. Myld, finding himself unhurt, leaned down to pick up his gun...

A parcel of colours – black, white and brown – collided with his head, dislodged him from his swivel chair and landed him on his knees before he could even make sense of what had rammed him. His palm came to rest on the butt of his gun...except that it was not a gun butt at all.

Heinz withdrew his paw – bony, sleek and clawed – from Myld's grasp and bared his teeth a breath away from Myld's face. There was another shot from Timor's gun.

Seconds later, Timor joined Gloria in the corridor outside, carrying both pistols and in the very act of tripping over

Heinz, who was fleeing between his ankles. Timor locked the office door from the outside.

"Is he dead?"

"I shot over his head."

"Why? Can't you shoot straight?"

"*Why?* Because I don't do killing people! And I thought I told you to stay out of it and mind the dog. Give me a hand."

Together they heaved a heavy metal cupboard in front of the office door to pen Myld in his office, arguing as they did so, half expecting Myld to crash his way through the barricade and join them in the corridor.

"How can you be in the Air Force *and* be a pacifist?"

"By being a hypocrite. What's your excuse? *You* wanted to save the workers and kill Cook's daughter."

"*You* shouldn't have said anybody drowned in Rose City, because they mustn't have…"

Timor came to a standstill. "Where are the girls?"

"What?"

"Where are the audition girls?"

The corridor was empty.

"They were here when I came in to help," said Gloria. "The gunshots must have scared them."

"Any chance they could have heard?"

"The gunshots?"

"No! What I said about the ship going down!"

"I was listening through the wall, so I did, but…I don't

know. It's possible. They did all start crying, and that was before the gunshots."

Timor gave such a roar that Gloria jumped backwards and Heinz froze, tail between his legs. "Damn! I've got to put them right! They can't take that home to…" He gave another yelp of frustration. "And I don't know which factory! They could have gone in five different directions!"

"Spoons. They all came from Spoons. I asked."

"Damnation, Gloria! You have your wish."

"Wish, sir?"

"We go to Spoons – and we get there before those girls do. There'll be hell to pay if they deliver that piece of news!"

They ran at full tilt through streets, silent but for the echo of their own footsteps. Then the road surfaces became silver and slippery with water, then splashy shallows as they approached the lowest part of the city. It was plain to Gloria that a plane crash and a kicking by an enraged mob had left Timor in no fit state to run anywhere, but she still struggled to keep up with him.

"No rush, sir! We can tell them the good news as soon as we get there!"

"No. We'll tell them nothing." And he tried to explain, though he could not really spare the breath, nor she the will to listen.

"Right now, everyone's staying put in the factories…"

"…because of the water, yes."

"No."

"Because of the shooting?"

"No."

"Because they might get eaten by invented lions and tigers!"

"No. Because their children...held hostage...Eyot Island. What'll they do if..." He pulled up, unable to catch his breath. "Secret... Important... A necessary lie."

Gloria absent-mindedly rested a hand on his back and patted him as she would have a winded horse. Heinz leaped up and down beside them, yapping, which made thinking even harder.

"Gloria...few days...that's all I'm... Secret. Vital."

Gloria took off and ran, leaving Timor to draw breath.

The five girls had run as far as they could on foot. They had reached the brink of the floodwater that had now turned the centre of the city into a vast lake, the factories standing within it like five castles in a shared moat. The dam might have been blown, but not before the crumbling city wall had sent a wealth more water cascading into the heart of Praesto.

The rowing boat that had fetched the girls over to dry land, and would carry them back to Factory One, had been dragged far enough uphill not to float away. Here they stood, pooling their sorrow, sobbing distractedly and hugging one another.

Gloria told them sharply, "Stop that noise, if you want to hear the good news. Who rowed you here? Did you row yourselves?"

One of the girls gave over crying for long enough to answer. "No. Gatekeeper. He took us to the newspaper office. Went off to see if there was food anywhere in those offices. S'pose when he can't find us, he'll come back to here. We're waiting for him."

The distant noise of gunfire came from the warehouse district. "We heard that noise earlier on. What's that about?" asked Gloria. "Should I be scared?"

A second girl blew her nose and engaged her brain. "Nah, that's just the Civil Guard. They're having a war with each other. Some of the Guards have children and some Guards don't. So now they're fighting, because the ones *without* children put the *other* ones' children on the ship, and snaffled them off to some island so they can't be got back."

"And now...and now all the children are..." The girls began sobbing again. Gloria glanced back down the road, hoping to see Timor coming, knowing he would find the right words. There was no sign of him – she would have to say something. "Thing is, we lied to the man back there at the newspaper office. His name is Myld and it was his idea to kidnap the littlies and hold them hostage. We wanted him to think his cunning plot had gone wrong, so we said the children were all dead." Another sorry wail went up from the covey of girls. "*But it wasn't true.* They're all alive and not prisoners, and living on the beach at the seaside having a jolly time."

As she went on talking, Gloria felt some sliver of her soul break off and float clear of her body to watch her telling lies. A necessary lie. A kind lie. A lie she liked so much more than the truth that she kept right on believing it. No children lay on the riverbed smothered in nickel ore. No mother need mourn them. No brother or sister need miss them. A necessary lie. A lie necessary to Gloria if she was ever to sleep sound again at night. When she had finished explaining, that sliver of soul re-entered her body like a glass knife; it hurt so much that she needed to cry. But the girls were overjoyed.

Timor appeared at the end of the street, limping and holding his ribs. He looked relieved to see the bevy of girls. Gloria ran to tell him what she had said.

The look he shot her said *Liability!* all over again. "Oh, Gloria. Why couldn't you just have said *we didn't know*? That we never flew south? That Eyot Island is just where it was, for all we know?"

Once again, that little shoot of pride growing up inside Gloria withered and died. "I wanted to make them happy, sir."

He looked at her sadly and took her chin in his hand. "I know you did, little person. I know."

CHAPTER FORTY-FOUR

Good People

Timor beckoned the girls together. Being so much taller, he crouched down conspiratorially to whisper. "The children on the beach really wanted to sail up the river and surprise everyone. I know it's silly, but they're only little and these things are important. You must remember from when you were young – how important secrets can feel? We promised them, didn't we, Gloria? So do you think you could possibly keep it a secret? Just till the children actually get here?"

The girls nodded obediently and said nothing.

Timor glanced over at Gloria. "Do they believe me?" he called.

Gloria shook her head. The girls scowled at her. "They're not eight, they're sixteen or something. Think Lixi. Would Lixi keep anything secret as a kindness?" She went and hauled Timor out of the way. "Listen up, girls. When he's not being a pilot, Captain Timor is a journalist. He wants to break the news first – big headline: *Good News! The Children Are Home!* If you keep quiet, he'll give you each a hundred afal, swear to goodness. He writes plays, too – don't you, sir?"

"I do."

"He's going to write a play about the flood. If you keep quiet till after the little ones are home, he'll give you all parts in it."

The girls looked at one another, each trying to see what her friend was thinking. "Swear to goodness?" one asked.

"Swear to goodness," said Gloria, adding, "Oh, and if you *do* split, he might just shoot you."

They shook hands on the deal.

One girl remained surly. "Why did he have to go and shoot the man doing the auditions?"

"Would you rather he had shot me?" asked Timor tartly. "And I didn't, I shot over his head."

The girl looked mutinous. "I really wanted to play Suprema."

"No, you didn't," said Gloria. "Trust me, you really didn't."

A boat ride away, across a vast moat of deep, dirty, moonlit water, Spoons rose up, frighteningly massive.

Timor wrote the girls' names on the back of his Air Force map, as a reminder to pay if they kept their side of the bargain. "Do you row?" he asked each one. To his dismay, not one of them did. "I shall have to row them back over to the factory," he told Gloria. "Their parents will be anxious for them. And quite rightly. There are warring Civil Guards stalking our streets tonight – and that's no newspaper story. They're driving round like drunken charioteers. And the manners taught me since birth say you don't leave sixteen-or-somethings alone at midnight."

"S'alright, sir. You're done in. I'll row," said Gloria.

"*Can* you row?"

"Can I row? Can I not! Better than you can, right now. But the girls have to make themselves useful and shift the boat into the water – you're not fit, and I have to preserve my energy."

"Conserve," he said. "You conserve energy."

"Don't be silly. That's jam."

It was a long push to get the boat into deep enough water to float it, but a much longer row to reach Spoons. Beneath the boat drifted countless rubber pipes like fat, white serpents. In fact, the water proved *so* deep that, even with seven people crammed into it, the rowing boat floated right over the high factory fence without so much as grating against its wrought-iron spikes. A fire escape let them enter Spoons on the second floor. From there, they climbed iron stairs to the metal grille of the topmost floor and called for the roof ladder to be lowered.

Frightened faces peered down. "We're not on strike!" was the first thing they said. "The water came up too high. We're not on strike! Honest we're not!"

From the foot of the ladder, Timor explained that he had simply brought home the girls from the auditions, and turned to go. "I'll leave the boat where we found it. For the Gatekeeper, you know?"

Gloria tugged at his coat. "Let me just say hello to my friend," she pleaded.

"Hello, Higgy," said Gloria, hoping she had not mistaken some other scarecrow for her friend. He was harder than ever to recognize by moonlight. His eyes were sunk deep in his skull and he could not remember how to smile.

Or that they were friends.

"What you doing here? I thought you were off queening it. Being Suprema."

She put her fingers against his lips. "Shshsh. Did Lixi tell you that? She swore she wouldn't." (So of course she had.)

Higgy shrugged. "Guess being Suprema beats breaking your back ten hours a day at the pumps."

Gloria flinched. Of course, nothing that had happened to her was as bad as what Higgy had endured. "I missed you, Hig. When I brought Lixi back here, I gave her a note to give you. About the newspaper telling lies?"

"Yeah: *Don't believe any of it. S'all made up.* Makes sense. I spread that around. Even semaphored it from the roof to the other four factories."

"Semaphore? You're so clever! I didn't know you could do semaphore! And?"

"And nothing. No use knowing we're being lied to – they've still got us by the short and curlies. Everyone just wants their children back, don't they? If we don't pump, they don't get them back. Right now, everyone's scared stupid, 'cos the water's up so high we can't pump. And the machines are swamped so there's no point pumping anyway. But maybe they think it's our fault, 'cos we went on strike or shirked. So maybe we don't get the children back after all." He turned away and looked out across the water. "How's Daisy? I've missed *her*," he said sourly.

Gloria was desperate to make things right – give Higgy something nice, take the bitter sneer out of his voice. She reached her hand into his and drew him aside to whisper: "You mustn't, mustn't, *mustn't* tell a soul, but if you promise to keep it to yourself…they're fine."

"What are?"

"The children. They're not on Eyot Island because that isn't there any more. They're down by the sea. Quite happy. Timor and I flew down there. He showed them how to signal passing ships. Now the river's dropping, they can sail home as soon as a ship sees the SOS."

Higgy seemed to be reading every fragment of her face – the dirt on her jaw, the tape across her nose, the broken filaments of hair around her hairline. She beamed at him, nodding to affirm the good news.

All he said was, "Good."

Timor, meanwhile, thanks to his Air Force coat, was being bombarded with questions. Was the dam blown? Was the river dropping? Though their voices were excitable, their faces were rigid with fatigue, as if the hinges of their jaws had rusted in the damp. Timor seemed to recoil from their questions. Finally he said, "Ask me about Rose City, why don't you? All the people up there."

But Higgy's new, man-sized voice interrupted: "This girl here says the children are safe. Escaped. Down at the mouth of the river. Says she's been there and seen them."

"Higgy!"

"Might not be true. She's a born liar. Her maid Lixi told me she's been playing 'Suprema', 'cos the real one's dead or gone or something. Dressing up. Pretending. Living in the Big House. Plenty to eat. Getting in with all the right people. Visiting us like Lady Muck. Fooling us…"

"Higgy, stop!"

"So *is* she, *Mister* Timor? Is she lying about the nippers?" Higgy sneered.

Timor waited for the hubbub to subside before he answered. "She is not. The children are safe."

"Ahhh! You schmuck, Higson!" lamented one of the audition girls. "We're down a hundred afal, thanks to you!"

Then the faces woke, the eyes focussed. They herded towards Gloria so eagerly that she thought she would be trampled underfoot.

"Why didn't you say straight off?"

"Is it true?"

"Is she lying?"

And Gloria said, "Honest – hope to die – they're alright."

They called out particular names. Had she seen Tomasz? Had she seen Galia? It was as if their children, stolen away by the Pied Piper, had just been sighted on the road home, skipping, singing and kicking tin cans. Why ever had Timor wanted to keep them from being this happy?

Beside her, Higgy said, in a matter-of-fact voice: "So now we get even."

Several of the older men nodded thoughtfully. Their hands came out of their jacket pockets, calloused fingers flexing. "Yeah. Make 'em pay."

Higgy took hold of Gloria's upper arm in a painfully tight grip. "*She's* not in prison, look. *She's* still out and about. So *they* still think she's Suprema. And we've got her now. We've got ourselves a hostage."

"Higgy, they know I'm n—"

He shook her into silence – put his face close to her ear and hissed, "You could've got me outta this hellhole with one snap of your fingers! But you didn't. You got Lixi out, but not me."

Timor had inched sideways – little by little, twisting from toes to heel – till he was standing on the rim of the open roof hatch. His eyes never once left Gloria. The first time he caught her gaze, she closed her lids by way of reply.

"Know what we should do?" Higgy told the crowds. "We should hold her to ransom for all the money we're owed in wages…"

A roar of agreement rose into the night sky.

"…and till they've given us everything we want – new clothes, compensation, shares…"

"That's mad!" roared Gloria and pointed randomly through the crowd. "Ask *her*. That woman there… She'll tell you! She knows! Tell them, Mogda!"

As the mob turned to look behind them, Gloria broke free of Higgy and leaped after Timor through the open roof hatch and onto the ladder. When he reached the bottom – "*Jump!*" – he caught her as she dropped. They hurled themselves down the metal stairs a flight at a time and headed back to the fire escape door. Clanging came from the floor above them – feet setting off in pursuit. But however fast she ran, Gloria could not outrun Higgy's words; they buzzed around her head like wasps. Their sting brought tears to her eyes – whether of rage or sorrow, she couldn't tell. Footsteps thudded on the plank floor behind them.

Timor's and Gloria's leap into the rowing boat propelled it away from the factory wall and out across the "moat". Shapeless shouts came from the gaunt faces at the hatchway and second-floor windows. Like dogs disturbing a flurry of birds, the mob barely knew what they were chasing or why.

Shoulder to shoulder, they sat, each plying an oar.

"Just a few days more not knowing, that's all I asked!" Timor groaned. "With the children home, they'd be cheerful – taken up with playing happy families…" He broke off to cough with the exertion of running and rowing. "The children would have made them…mellower. Gentler. Kinder. *Busier.* Not a mob."

"I'm sorry! I'm so sorry!"

"Picture it, Gloria! You've had nothing to do for days except think how much you hate whoever stole your children – wanting to get even, but not daring to. Suddenly the threat's gone! Your children aren't held hostage and they're on their way home. There's nothing to hold you back! The water's going down – you're free to make mayhem. Back there is a big mess of anger and fright, packed tight in one place. Like a barrel bomb, you know? When those explode, a *lot* of people get hurt. And we just lit the fuse."

"I did it! I lit it! I'm so, so sorry!"

With a jolt, their boat collided with the wrought-iron

spikes of the factory gate – taller than the fence – and wedged there. The water level was dropping with every passing hour. Both stood up, each with an oar, to try and prise it loose. The boat rocked violently. The people at the windows began to bay like hounds.

"Damn. I prayed for months for the flood to end, and now I just want it deeper, to keep them shut up for a few more days."

"Like you said. Good People. Two words that don't go together," said Gloria. Splinters broke from her paddle, sharp as spite.

"Don't you dare go blaming them!" he snapped. She took his oar so that he could lean over the side and push the boat free of the spikes. It left him with barely enough breath to shout at her. "Lied to, locked in, worked night-and-day, fed on dog meat and weeds… They have every right to get even. But who'll be the losers in the end? They will." Hand over hand, he moved the boat sideways to where the fence was lower. "Praesto's their home, Gloria! You don't burn down your home without regretting it afterwards. But as soon as this lot can wade to dry land, they'll be going after everybody they blame – and anyone they don't like. A small handful of villains caused all this…but it'll be more than a handful who get hurt."

As the boat floated over the factory fence, the factory hands began breaking the windows and hurling the broken shards of glass – like skimming stones – at the people who had brought them the good news: it was time for Riot, Destruction and Revenge.

Amazingly, unbelievably, Heinz was waiting patiently for Timor and Gloria at the edge of the floodwater. At the sight of their boat coming, he dashed in and out of the water, barking. Once ashore, Timor scooped him up in his arms like a consolation prize. "This animal," he said, "is like a good deed in a naughty world."

But for Gloria there was no consolation. As her fright eased, she felt hollowed out, guilty and wretched. To Timor, she was a liability. To Higgy, she was one of the despicable Enemy. And she had just lit the fuse that might burn Praesto to the ground.

CHAPTER FORTY-FIVE

Myld

PRAESTO CITY

Myld had a thousand-and-one reasons to escape the barricaded Editor's Office:

He needed to have Timor and Gloria killed.

Kovet had to be blamed for the shipwreck and all those dead children.

The remaining senators, judges and bankers must be executed – and quickly – while Kovet could still take the blame for that, too.

The successful demolition of the dam meant that the city would soon open its gates again, and that would set him a host of new challenges.

He surveyed the room for a means of escape.

His eyes lit on the compositor's desk with all its shelves and pull-out trays of metal letters, numbers and symbols. Some were missing – he had already started compiling a front page for the next day's *Voice*, declaring:

FLOOD OVER – TIME TO DRY OUR TEARS
OUR ORDEAL IS OVER. THE WATERS HAVE PARTED. WE CAN SEE ALL THE WAY TO HOPE!

Since Hecuba's death, Myld had become quite a dab hand at typesetting, trusting no one else to set the articles he wrote. In a way, that tall desk was his war chariot. It even had wheels, look, as befits a chariot! And though it generally needed four men to move it, Myld considered himself quite the equal of four lesser men. Had he not crammed himself full to the very scalp with power?

He put his shoulder to the desk and pushed with all his might. His feet slid out of the back of his shoes. He put his back to it, but felt his knee ligaments crackle. So he took a run and hurled himself against the side. Success! The big steel castors rolled. The shelves shook, trays of print-slugs rattled, and the desk trundled towards the glass-panelled door. It struck the doorpost with a cacophony of crunching wood and breaking glass, felling the metal cupboard Timor had used to barricade the door.

He was out! At the impact, all the desk's trays slid out like tongues, making the whole thing sway. Myld made to push them back in…

So he was in front of the desk when it rocked forwards a second time and toppled, showering metal slugs in his face. Faster and faster they fell – each sharply embossed with a letter, number, symbol, punctuation mark… All those special fonts, all those special logos – *In atramento non est veritas**…

When the rioters found him, his mouth and eye-sockets, hands and hollows of his throat were full of unintelligible metal words. A flagon of printing ink stored in the base of the desk had rolled out and spilled, surrounding his body with a lake of blackness. Even his blond hair was now the colour of night.

*There is no truth in the ink

CHAPTER FORTY-SIX

Rose in Ruins

Keeping to the shadows, skirting round skirmishes between Civil Guards, Gloria and Timor hurried uphill towards the AAF hanger. By the time they reached it and looked back at the city, Spoons was already alight.

"Well, look at that. No mean feat to torch a factory up to its waist in water," said Timor. "The ingenuity of mankind, eh? Trouble with rioters is, they never break the right windows... The wrong people always get hurt."

The workers in the Five Factories were indeed ingenious that night. Instead of waiting for the floodwater to drain away, they ripped up the floorboards, built rafts and pontoons to escape the moated factories, then rampaged through the streets. They went in search of Senators and factory owners and anyone they might blame for their months of hunger and toil. But fortunately they did not think to look in the prison, where Myld had shut up anyone who stood in his way to absolute power. So the rioters missed their chance for slaughter. (The prisoners themselves begged the warders not to unlock any gate or door until the mob had exhausted itself and tempers had cooled.)

Senate buildings were set alight, as well as the barracks that had screened from sight the kidnap of their children. They broke into shops in search of food that was not there and threw bricks through the windows of the newspaper offices Hecuba had so cherished. The river, shrinking by the hour, was soon tamer than the rioters.

The Afalian Air Force had received orders (from Myld) to "obey only the express commands of the Senate". The Air Marshal had been imprisoned for refusing to authorize the bombing raids. Leaderless, the men sat chafing and appalled but awaiting orders, while the city descended into chaos.

So they were glad enough when the Suprema's husband arrived at the hilltop aerodrome.

"You're near enough 'Senate', aren't you?" they said. "Tell us what to do."

Besides, Captain Timor Philotapantasol was a man ablaze with energy, issuing a torrent of commands and giving off sparks of extreme bad temper.

"Within days, God willing, boats will be coming upriver full of children. Be there to meet them. Senator Kovet will be aboard. Make good use of him. He's fairly deranged, but the children like him and they'll do as he tells them… Oh, and there will also be a large white dog. She's Mascot of the Workers and important to national security. Return her to Foremost Mansion and see that someone feeds her. In the meantime, arm yourselves. Turn out the Fire Brigade, if we still have one. Disarm the two factions of the Civil Guard and clap them up in different cages at the zoo… *Well, of course they're empty, man*: the animals have all been eaten. Locked in one of the offices of *The Voice* you'll find Kovet's assistant, Myld. Lock him up. A small oubliette in the basement of Hell for choice, but anywhere will do, just so long as he can't get loose… How are we doing for aero-fuel? Fuel me up a spotter plane… Yes, *now*, sergeant. Miss Winnow and I have to fly north. I shall return shortly. Any questions?"

Timor cut such an intimidating figure, wearing his torn leather coat and aura of urgency, that the airmen shook their heads: no questions.

Gloria, too, was intimidated. "Are you hurting, sir?" she whispered.

"Please be silent, Gloria."

"Sorry, sir."

Only when Heinz came and pushed his face between

Timor's thighs, scared by the smell of fire, did Timor lug the dog into his arms, turn away and confide to him alone, "Let's get back there, eh, boy? Not knowing is killing me."

Gloria overheard.

They took off as soon as there was enough daylight to see by. By then, they could see all of the Great Five Factories burning, along with the hospital and art gallery and the wheel-less buses in the terminus.

There was another unfamiliar sight on the river – a vision no one had seen for several months. A trawler – no, two trawlers – were ploughing upriver, making for the city port, whose dock walls were once again showing above water. Their decks were crowded with tiny figures, and there were flags at both mastheads – white with a red saltire, signalling *I require assistance.*

Timor banked into a turn and flew in a tight circle over the boats. The figures on the decks shielded their eyes against the sun and waved. He rocked the wings, in an answering salute. The first of the kidnapped children were making it home.

"Thank God. The great thing about children," he said, "is that they bring adults to their senses."

"Everything will be alright now," said Gloria. But she could not manage to believe it.

After a minute or two Timor said, "Complicated, isn't it? This living business."

Although Gloria was becoming quite accustomed to flying and had not felt airsick once, the further they flew upriver, the more queasiness churned inside her. It grew into a pain, a ghastly, griping nausea. She had to put Heinz down on the floor for fear of being sick on him.

"What's wrong?" asked Timor.

"Nothing. Tickety-boo, sir." But she was lying.

Everything came down to lying, didn't it? Timor had told Myld the children and Kovet had all gone down with the ship. It had sounded so convincing. She had promised the people on the factory roof – "*honest, hope to die*" – that their children were all safe, because she had not dared say that some… weren't. Timor had promised her that everybody in Rose City would have evacuated before the dam burst, and she had believed him because she needed to. Now the bile in her mouth told her his promise was worthless. He could not possibly know.

Gloria had seen a wedding cake once made for the Archduchess of Moldavia when she visited Afalia and dined at Foremost Mansion. Pink sugar icing, in three tiers, with fondant curlicues and spires of spun sugar. *After* the grand dinner, the cake had been reduced to a heap of crumbs, lumps of fondant like bird droppings and sharp shards of snapped-off sugar.

That was Rose City now. The water had feasted on its rosy arcades and painted houses. Now, one day later, a swollen river was lapping around its foundations, but the torrent that had burst through the dam had been ravenous for the soft red sandstone and had clawed into it. The refugee camps had been entirely sluiced away, and all that remained were the ruins of a dusty city washed clean of life and litter and loveliness.

Neither spoke a word. Gloria fixed her eyes on the plane's shadow racing over the ground and thought of nothing, nothing but that little scurrying shape, until they were directly over the ruins and the plane's shadow was jumping and nosing and wriggling its way through the rubble.

Then suddenly they began to see people – now two, now a dozen, then too many to count, picking their way through the ruins, salvaging anything left whole.

Beyond the city, wherever the invading river had left dry land, clutches of people were making their way back to the city, like bees regrouping round a smashed hive. And, beyond them, tens of thousands more followed on.

"*Thank you. Thank you,*" Timor kept saying under his breath. "*Thank you, thank you, thank you.*"

A million tonnes of water and a million more. But the withered trees and dried-up soil had drunk it, the aquifers had guzzled it down. The fields had swallowed it, the cactuses marvelled at it. As the water settled, 25,000 people had been left on opposite banks of a river reborn. They waved to each other, appalled, thankful, terrified, dumb with shock, mesmerized by the swift pink water flowing past their feet. The refugees among them slumped down, clutching their children and baggage. As the shallowest water soaked into the hard ground, dozens and dozens of fish were left jumping and twitching, stranded. Supper!

But the locals instantly set off back the way they had come, needing to know what remained of their city, their homes.

Far, far to the north, the Lacha Mountains stopped grumbling and seething, as if to listen to the news the south wind brought them. The Furca River had split in two, and the Rose Desert was crackling with life.

"Have you been thinking that the whole time? That they were all dead?" asked Gloria. "You should've said."

"Why? So that we could both be miserable?"

"Well, yes! If, say, twelve people are miserable, it stands to reason there's less 'miserable' to go around. But if you try to carry it all yourself, you get squashed down flat. You have to share it, you really do."

Timor considered this. "That is the least logical piece of

reasoning I ever heard. Promise me you will never attempt to study Logic."

"Promise."

"I suppose, miss, *you* knew all along they'd be alive."

"Course I did! Some lying pilot promised me, so it had to be true."

"Your city! Your beautiful city…" Gloria kept saying when they met up again with the Citizens' Council of the Rose City – the same five people who had tried Timor in court. The Chairman nodded, stunned into silence by the destruction. His wife took off her hat, with its hatband of roses and herbs, and put it on his head, which had been starting to burn in the hot sun. "My husband is a little overcome. But it's funny, isn't it? This city has stood here for six centuries. Men and women live such a little time. So you would expect the city to matter much more than the people. Are we silly to mind so much more about the people?"

Timor took off his flying helmet and put it on the head of a passing child. "Not at all. If need be, I'll rebuild the city brick by brick myself; but if people had been lost…well, there's no replacing them, is there? And Rosies are a particularly rare and wonderful species, well worth preserving."

"And preserve us you have, Captain! You told us to evacuate, so evacuate we did!"

Heinz was intrigued by this place the plane had brought him to. He knew it, and yet it was as if all its scents had been tossed into the air and had landed in different places. The stench of rotting litter was all but gone. The dry smells were plumped out with water. The water smelled of brick dust. Dregs of fear were still falling out of the air.

"Find Clem, Heinz!" urged Gloria.

Clem, yes… But Heinz had not yet recovered his land legs after the flight. He kept walking diagonally. Clem, yes. He should find Clem. Gloria seemed to be looking for Clem, too – she was certainly searching for *someone* amid the tide of people:

"Have you seen…? Do you know…?"

Heinz trotted after her, gradually getting mastery of his paws.

Gloria found her "someone"…but it was not Clem. She flung herself so fiercely at the woman that Heinz bounced and pounced up against the two, barking. But Gloria had no arms free to gather him up, as two, then three, then four more people joined in the embrace. Gloria was crying – everyone was crying – the happy kind. *Ma! Grandpa! Sis!* Words and shouts burst skywards like those partridge he and Daisy had scared out of the dunes. The thought made Heinz miss Daisy. He appeared to have left some part of himself on the beach, fluttering in Daisy's soft mouth.

He wondered if his task of looking after the flying man and girl was finished. The man Timor, for all he was battered, bruised and agitated, had grown taller lately, in that way people can but dogs can't. Perhaps he had won some fight or fathered puppies or won best of breed in a competition. Whatever it was, Timor had definitely risen in prestige within his pack. People did just as he told them. They looked towards him for orders, just as once Heinz had looked towards Clem.

Clem, yes. Heinz ought to find Clem. Everything else had been a distraction, and Heinz had let slip his duty to look after Clem.

But when, after an hour, he had still not found his boy, Heinz joined those scouring the ruins of the town for loved ones.

Too frail, stubborn or disbelieving, some Rosies had stayed behind when the bell tower had clamoured out the alarm and the others had fled. Heinz helped to sniff out their bodies – under rubble or floating in flooded cellars. And still the red dust settled out of the air and the scents whirled about him in a hopeless, unreadable tangle. The only smell Heinz could identify for sure was the scent of Hound Death, so he began to follow that, zigzagging between lumps of fallen masonry, the litter of tablecloths, buckets, doors, shoes…

Hound Death's paw prints were damp, as if he had ridden the torrent of invading water. The trail led Heinz to the ruins of the bell tower, now no more than the height of a tree –

a tree whose bark had been torn away. The tower's huge bells lay around the base, like the golden helmets of ancient giants, the bell-ropes snaking away from them. Heinz trotted up steps worn shallow over the centuries by the feet of bell-ringers.

And there, at last, he found Clem. There was river reed in his hair, though his clothes had dried in the sun.

Heinz licked the boy's face, plucked at his shirt with a paw, then lay on his chest. There was no rise-and-fall, but it was a familiar shape, with memories in every crease.

Hound Death lay on the topmost step of the staircase – a dark mirage pinned beneath a ray of sunlight.

"Fight you for him," said Heinz.

War's over, said Hound Death. *He was the last. I am tired now. Dog-tired.*

"You had a choice. You got it wrong! You chose wrong!"

Choice? said Hound Death. *I have no choice. Only my duty. As we all have. You* think *life's hard? You should try my job.* And tears welled from bloodshot eyes and rolled down a greying snout.

The mirage evaporated. Heinz sat up and howled. The howl climbed the exact same spiral as the staircase had once done and rose high above the ruined city.

CHAPTER FORTY-SEVEN

So Much To Do

The Senate and captains of industry were strewn about the sofas and floor of the living room in Foremost Mansion, sharing chairs and footstools. Journalists, newly out of hiding, stood in three corners, like standard lamps. The men were unshaven and had been wearing their suits night and day. The women, too, fingered their greasy hair and rubbed at stains on their clothing. Until the early morning they had all been packed in prison cells behind the Courts of Justice, fearing for their lives.

Robbed of their sofas, Daisy and Heinz were bumbling about the room, treading on the visitors, excited by the strong smell of sweaty, unwashed bodies. When honey buns were brought in, the whole room yearned towards them.

"Wherever did you get them?" the Senator for Finance asked the maid.

"The kind people up in Rose City," said Gloria, bobbing

a curtsey. "They baked them in clay ovens. And fish dried on sticks. Corn cobs baked in hot ashes. They're very resourceful. And cheery, all things considered. They can do wonders with an avocado. They made up a big food parcel for Captain Philotapantasol before he came back."

"Who?"

Gloria left, taking Daisy with her, at which point Heinz climbed into Timor's lap.

The visitors had never much appreciated the Suprema draping herself in dogs, but this nervy, dishevelled mongrel somehow added to the man's feral energy. Prison had left them no energy of their own.

"The priority will be shipbuilding – shallow-draught, medium-sized boats that can reach all the settlements between the sea and the mountains. Most of the carpenters and joiners are refugees in Rose City now. We need to get them back up to the timberlands as soon as possible to begin reconstruction of the houses the flood demolished. I've hired the three trawlers that brought the children back upriver… The crews have agreed to fish for us for three months – that should keep starvation at bay till we can build or buy trawlers of our own… We need to plant wheat for bread, make a thousand hives for honey and pollination. A telegraph link between here and the larger towns would speed up everything… May I have volunteers from the Senate to fly abroad and beg help from our neighbours: food, doctors, architects, engineers…?

We need to clear the river of dead animals or the water will find new ways of killing us – typhus, cholera... There's a danger of cholera among the refugees in Rose, too..."

The senators, lawyers and industrialists, muzzy with hunger and lack of sleep, boggled at Timor and counted the pages of *Matters for Discussion* they had been handed when they arrived. There were seventeen close-printed pages covering:

- Assessment of damage
- Costing of damage
- Recruitment of new Civil Guard
- Replanting of trees
- Netting of river for fish
- Importation of food/medicine
- Restoration of communications
- Restoration and compensation for Rose City
- Fostering/rehoming of orphaned children
- Restocking of cattle farms
- Replanting of arable farms
- Legal proceedings against Afalia Insurance Company for failure to pay out
- Election of Suprema/Supremo

"Why are we talking to The Husband?" the Senator for Health asked the maid when she brought round shots of cactus gin on a tray. "Where's the Suprema?"

"Drowned, I'm afraid, sir," whispered Gloria.

The Senator downed his gin in one.

Three hours later, when the seventeen sheets of paper were covered in scribbles, ticks and question marks, news of the Suprema's death had reached everyone in the room by way of whispers.

"May we express our sorrow, Captain, at the death of your poor dear lady wife," said the Senator for Family Affairs, pinching together the rips in her skirt. "And may I propose a motion for the election of yourself to the post of Supremo." The room moo'd its approval. This was clearly the man for the job. They, personally, wanted nothing but to get back home to their children and their own beds.

Gloria, by now, was listening from outside in the corridor, having her hands licked clean of honey and mixed spices. She was no longer forty but sixteen again and, on the whole, it felt good. She thought she was delighted at the idea of Timor being Supremo…but found her heart trailed behind her in rejoicing. Why? Did she really want to be maid to some new Supremo she didn't know? No. If Timor ruled in Praesto, at least she would see him every day and know what he was doing and if he was eating enough and if the opera was finished. (Probably it wouldn't be.) But not only was she sixteen again, she was a maid again. And maids bob curtseys. They speak when spoken to. They keep their opinions to themselves and never enter a room where people are arguing/

dozing/kissing/talking-Senate-business. Life would never be the same as when the two of them were quarrelling or finding dead people or flying through volcanic ash or exasperating each other.

The meeting would be ending soon. She must fetch coats – except that the visitors with coats had clung onto them, because in prison they had needed them for security blankets or bedding. Daisy looked at her with blue-brown eyes as wise as Time – you would have sworn she knew all the secrets of the world, including what the future held for Gloria.

There was a knock at the garden window. Security had lapsed since Appis had disappeared. Absolutely anybody could stroll through the gate of Foremost Mansion and wander about the garden with their children, enjoying the view, free at last of the factories. But this was Higgy. He was holding a bouquet of cow parsley. At the sight of him, a big, cold sadness pushed past Gloria, like a wet dog.

As an alternative to looking each other in the eye, the two took in the view over the city.

"Back to normal then," said Higgy.

"Hardly."

The burned-out buildings were still smoking. The factory chimneys were not. Long queues of people could be seen leading up to the aircraft hangar on the hill next-door – there were rumours of AAF planes bringing in food from over the border. There was no newspaper to tell them if the rumours were true or not.

All in a rush, Gloria said: "I should have got you out. You're right. I meant to, the day I took Lixi home. And you would've been much less trouble than Lixi. But Timor said no more…and I hadn't shut *your* mother in the hall cupboard. And I owed it to Cook. And what if Appis had vetted you? What would I have said you *were*?"

Sooner than wrestle with this bewildering outburst, Higgy said, "I'm not going back to Spoons."

"No? Well. I can see why… Also, it's not really there to go back to, is it?" Their eyes turned towards the roofless ruins of Factory One. It could have been mistaken for some tumbledown mediaeval castle, *sans* roof, *sans* floors, *sans* worth, *sans* anything.

"Did you see the black smoke that come off that rubber piping when it burned?" said Higgy with a flash of excitement. "Hell, it was lethal!"

"I heard. It near killed Lixi, what with her asthma… So. You joining the Clean-Up Corps then?"

"Nope." She noticed that his hands were shaking so much that the white bits fell off the cow parsley. Like volcanic ash. "Going back upcountry. Sawmills or somewhere. Get myself a craft. Paying work." He glanced at her to see if she was impressed. (She felt the glance.) "Are you busy cosying up to The Husband, now he's all set to be Supremo?"

She shot him a look so fierce that he swiftly changed tack.

"I know Morse as well as semaphore. Genius me, see? Get a job anywhere with my skills." Then he waved the bouquet in the direction of Daisy. "That dog's in pup," he said.

"You always say that. She's just a bit fat," said Gloria.

"Lucky her."

Forgetting to give her the flowers, Higgy turned and scuffed his way back round the house. Nothing was mended. It would take a bomb to demolish the wall that had sprung up between her and Higgy. Or slow erosion by Time.

A chant had begun in the living room – a schoolboyish display in favour of Timor's election as Supremo. Even Heinz was barking along – though he had probably just been woken by the noise. It died away abruptly. Gloria went to eavesdrop.

"Much as I appreciate the vote of confidence," Timor was saying, "I have different ambitions from those of my wife. Kovet would do a better job than I would." There was a roar of angry dissent. "No? I know he hasn't exactly covered himself in glory. But since the *Nickelodeon* disaster, he's much fonder of children. And I don't just mean his own. He minds much more what becomes of the whole breed. Understands evil, too, which I don't think I ever did or ever will, quite. No? Not Kovet? Maybe not. But let's not sink to revenge and kill the man, eh? Myld was the one pulling his strings. Myld and my w…his cronies."

Closing the front door behind the last of the delegates, Gloria went back into the living room to plump cushions and move the furniture. Daisy followed her in. Daring herself to speak (as once she had dared to drop a crumpled letter beside Timor's breakfast plate) Gloria said, "I suppose you plan to run *The Voice*, sir. To please Hecuba. So it tells the truth again."

Timor had ousted Heinz and started picking burrs out of Daisy's coat and tail, collecting them on a crumpled copy of *Matters for Discussion*. "No. I need to be in Rose City. Building. I helped knock it down. I have to put it back together."

"*But what about your opera!*" She had not realized she was going to say it or that it would come out so loud.

For the first time since the beach, Timor laughed. "Priorities, dear. Priorities. First things first… What about you?"

"Me? Well, back to the usual, I suppose."

"What? You want to stay and serve breakfast to the next Suprema – Supremo – whoever? Give it a few years, get in some schooling, and you could BE Suprema – the one-after-next, maybe. The job's simple enough. All you have to do, basically, is surround yourself with clever experts and shoot them if they start plotting… Oh, while I remember, I owe you back wages now that money has some value again." And he counted out a large number of paper notes onto the coffee table. There you go: two thousand afal."

She giggled. "I only earn ten a month, sir."

"Yes, but – this may surprise you, Gloria – Supremas earn a *little* bit more than maids… And look, there's a five-thousand bonus for saving my life – though it's hard to put a price on such things and I dare say I'm underpaying you. Got any plans for it? Tell me, what *is* Gloria Winnow's ambition in life?"

She recoiled shyly, laughing at the absurd pictures that came to mind – things she had never confided to anyone but Daisy on their walks in the park. The money in her hands smelled of daydreams. "I always wanted to make yoghurt from water buffalo."

Timor feigned disgust. "Urgh. You must have to mince them up really small to get them in the pots."

"No! Not yoghurt with buffalo *in*, silly! Yoghurt from their *milk!* It's supposed to be the most delicious in the entire world!" And though it made her nose bleed yet again, once she had started laughing, she could not stop; could not keep from crying, either, because with seven thousand afal she could perfectly well buy water buffalo and a field to put them in and a shelter for them in bad weather and a house for her family… But she couldn't keep it. She offered back the money. "I just want Daisy, really."

He pushed her hands back towards her. "She's yours already. I told you."

"Yes, but people lie. All the time. Especially about important things, like dogs."

"Let's make it a rule then." He added it to the end of *Matters for Discussion*. "A law. No more lies. Not in Praesto. Not in all Afalia. On pain of de—"

He was stopped from saying the word by Daisy turning her head and licking his face. It was as if the dog had eaten it off his lips, and though Timor wiped his mouth with his sleeve, he could not regret the lick. *Death* was not a word he wanted any more to do with.

"But then *I'll* have Ma and Grandpa and Daisy and my brother and sister and a herd of water buffalo and…what will *you* have, sir?" She winced at her own impertinence.

"I don't know. Work. Music. Words. Guilt. New friends, maybe."

"But not children."

He flinched visibly but recovered himself. "Ooof, no. Not since I found out how exasperating they can be."

"But I was thinking…you could always write *plays* about children. And then they'd be sort of real. And you would have 'created' them."

He asked wryly: "Who'd go and see a child dressed up in costume, pretending to be someone different? Too far-fetched."

Gloria bit her lip. "Well, in that case, I could sort of… since I'll be far enough away not to be annoying…and if I didn't send letters spelled wrong…and if I learned Latin, I could maybe sort of be your—"

"Deal," said Timor, standing up so abruptly that both dogs were unsettled. "*Filia cara et amica semper.*"*

"Is that Greek?"

"No, it's not bloody Greek! It's Latin! Your turn to teach me something I don't know. How does one set about buying a water buffalo?"

Beloved daughter and friend always.

CHAPTER FORTY-EIGHT
Happy and Gloria's

SWEETWATER RIVER, UPCOUNTRY

Much as they hated dogs, the water buffalo put up with Daisy. Dogs can be very wolfish and worrying. But having seen Daisy try to get through a paling fence while holding a branch in her mouth, they had decided she lacked the wits to be a wolf.

Even so, today she was behaving oddly and it made them nervous. Now and then a bark would startle them and her blue-brown eyes asked them questions – questions they could not answer. Three times she tried to squeeze through the fence, but she was far too fat. At last a loose slat let her into the field, and she trotted, head up, towards the big byre in the corner.

She was intrigued by the prickling of the deep straw inside, and why exactly she felt the need to hide in it. If she had done wrong, she would surely remember what? If there was Danger, she would surely smell it? Danger has a smell to it – one she had smelled more often than she cared to remember. Here, beside the little Sweetwater River, where the big oaks stood sentry-duty around the farmhouse, why should Danger threaten? She wanted God's help, in the shape of Gloria, but instinct had decreed Daisy hide herself in the cattle shed instead. Pain like an invisible pitchfork stabbed her in the belly.

One of the water buffalo was scratching itself noisily against the shed wall. The rattling truck passed by. Twice a day, it collected the milk churns and drove them down the lane to the dairy buildings. Though Daisy was not allowed inside the dairies, she usually rode the truck there and back, because she liked the wind in her ears. Not today. Something was coming; something too important and dangerous to ignore. Like brown trout in a river, mysterious feelings were swimming through Daisy's bloodstream – feelings she could neither account for nor ignore.

The puppies came as a big surprise. They slipped out of her like peaches out of their skins. Licking them clean was delicious – well, a feeling like delicious, anyway. Instead of panic, age-old wisdoms inherited from her mother came to her aid, and she somehow knew what to do. Serenity came a little later, too – a thing like vagueness, but fluffier and more joyful and grown-up.

When Gloria found her there, an hour later, she did not seem angry. "This is where you chose, is it? You really spooked

IN ATRAMENTO EST VERITAS

PRAESTO MARKS
TEN-YEAR MILESTONE

We have travelled a steep and difficult road to reach this tenth anniversary since the reopening of Praesto City's gates. No one can doubt the suffering and hardship caused by the catastrophic flood. No one can doubt the effort it took to rebuild a country devastated by disaster. Though the memories are still raw, and the loss of loved ones can never be laid aside, still, there is reason to celebrate the sheer courage and perseverance of the Afalian people and to hail the heroes who brought us through to today.

TELEGRAPH/TELEPHONE GRID
COMPLETED ON TIME

The nationwide telegraph and telephone network is finished. It stretches from Lacha in the north to Oceanville in the south; from Rose City in the west to Petar in the east, crossing some of the most difficult terrain ever tackled. Operation Chief, Higson "Higgy" Flym said, "Instead of mending the old network, we started afresh with new kit. This system should

last well into the twenty-first century. I would like to congratulate everyone on their hard work. It was tough. Ten years ago, I was dredging poles out of the river. Now new poles stand proud on every horizon."

UNIVERSITY ATTRACTS WORLD EXPERT

Praesto University has tempted yet another famous scholar to join their staff. Professor Atacama of Litniof is said to be the world's leading name in Natural Sciences. She will take up her post in September. Dr Ned Herge, Chancellor of the University said, "Our reputation for excellence is growing with each passing year. To think we were closed ten years ago, with no one expecting to study past the age of fourteen! Now the sky is the limit for any bright student, rich or poor, from the city or the smallest village.

ROSE OPERA HOUSE OPENS

The Clem Wollen Opera House in Rose City opened its doors to audiences last week with the glittering gala premiere of a new opera. Until now,  the Rose Dance & Music Co. has had to perform in open-air venues. Now it will occupy beautiful premises on the banks of the Rose River. The first production to be performed will be *The Honey Tree* by our own beloved son of Praesto, Sir Timor. Following his acclaimed production of *The Treacle Ladder*, tickets for the premiere were sold out before the building was even completed.

A NEW ERA BEGINS HERE

OPEN DAYS ANNOUNCED
THROUGHOUT THE CITY

Each of the "Five Great Workshops", the Old Civil Guard Barracks and Newspaper House will throw open their doors on the following days to exhibit and celebrate YOUR hard work!

———

WORKSHOP ONE
APRIL 1st
FISH, FRUIT & VEGETABLES

———

WORKSHOP TWO
APRIL 2nd
TOOLS & FARM MACHINERY

———

WORKSHOP THREE
APRIL 3rd
CLOTHING & FOOTWEAR

———

WORKSHOP FOUR
APRIL 4th
DAIRY & GRAIN

———

WORKSHOP FIVE
APRIL 5th
FURNITURE & OTHER TIMBER PRODUCTS

THE OLD BARRACKS
APRIL 6th
HONEY, HERBS & HEALING PRODUCTS

NEWSPAPER HOUSE
APRIL 8th
PAPER & BOOKS

OPEN DAYS SPONSORED BY

daisy

Y O G H U R T

"THE FINEST IN AFALIA"

TODAY'S ANAGRAM: A IGNORANT LOCUST

A NOTE FROM GERALDINE

I've never invented a country before. I can thoroughly recommend the fun of it. Of course, things weren't so much fun for my characters because I invariably give my protagonists such a hard time – but that's adventure stories for you.

In America in 1928 there really was a flood far worse than this one, and the politicians of the time behaved despicably. In fact, it brought out the worst in a great many people who could have helped and didn't. That was the spark that lit this story, though once it was lit, I left it up to my characters – good and bad alike – to decide the course it would take.

Afalia could be any country where bad stuff happens and people have to decide what to do to get through it. The book wants to ask: what would you do in the same circumstances? The book also wants to say, be careful what you believe – on the internet, in the papers, in advertising and so on. News reporters and politicians are not generally liars, but they really do want you to think as they think and believe what they tell you. Whereas you might just want to decide for yourself.

MY THANKS ARE DUE TO...

EVERYONE at Usborne Publishing, but above all to my editor Anne Finnis who coaxed me into changing what needed changing, shortening what needed shortening and who kept track of who was where – and when – and what they knew and what they were wearing... She rode the bucking bronco of the plot and never once fell off and checked the text more times than anybody should reasonably have to. All in the middle of Covid 'lockdown'. Rebecca and the rest, too, dipped in and out of the process. I wanted newspaper pages – which was a lot to ask, and then the artwork began to arrive, redolent with atmosphere. Thank you to Keith Robinson for capturing the 'look' of the 1920s and to Leo Nickolls for the delicious cover.

Thank you to my naval husband who taught me about things like liquefaction, ships' bridges and engine rooms, and to my daughter Ailsa who is always my very first reader and a kind, constructive critic. Also to Zachary and Ella for 'test driving' the story before it was published.

Most importantly, thank you for being here, at the end of the book which (I hope) means that you read it all the way through. (Although, of course, you may just have opened the book at the wrong end.)

GERALDINE McCAUGHREAN WRITES EXTRAORDINARY BOOKS!

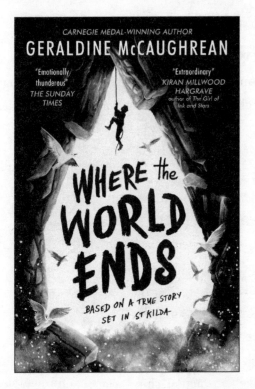

WINNER OF THE CILIP CARNEGIE MEDAL 2018

"A haunting, immersive and unforgettable reading experience." The CILIP Carnegie Children's Book Awards

"The best book I've read this year. Extraordinary."
Kiran Millwood Hargrave

"Harshly beautiful, and stark with near-despair…"
The Guardian

"This novel about courage, love and tolerance sings with McCaughrean's glorious, new-minted phrase-making."
The Sunday Times

"Full of phrases, images and ideas that pull you up short, and is a brilliant adventure too."
Books for Keeps

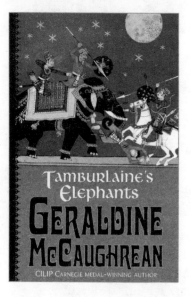

"…An awe-inspiring writer with a miraculous talent for bringing to life past times and faraway lands."
The Sunday Telegraph

For more information please visit
usborne.com/fiction